The
Crossing

ALSO BY MATT BROLLY

Zero

Lynch and Rose series:

The Controller

DCI Lambert series:

Dead Water
Dead Eyed
Dead Lucky
Dead Embers
Dead Time

The Crossing

MATT BROLLY

THOMAS & MERCER

Text copyright © 2020 by Matthew Brolly
All rights reserved.

Published by Thomas & Mercer, Seattle

www.apub.com

Amazon, the Amazon logo, and Thomas & Mercer are trademarks of Amazon.com, Inc., or its affiliates.

ISBN-13: 9781542006156
ISBN-10: 1542006155

Cover design by Tom Sanderson

Printed in the United States of America

For Alison

Prologue

Fortune had led them to the deserted farm on the outskirts of Bridgwater, where they had arrived late at night more out of desperation than hope. They'd been trailing Max Walton for over a year, DI Louise Blackwell and her colleague DI Finch a pivotal part of the investigative team.

The smell of the place would never leave Louise. The farm was divided into a series of metallic barns and as they entered the outer shed she was hit by an unimaginable stench, the decay and waste of decades of animals. The ground appeared to move as she shone her torch over the various swarming mounds lining the barn floor, and she had to turn away and retch.

'Louise,' said Finch, his voice low and unnerved.

Louise battled her nausea and returned to the matter in hand. Finch was in one corner of the barn, his torch shining on the corpses of the missing mother and daughter.

Louise called the station.

The correct move was to stay where they were and wait for backup, but Finch wasn't about to let the opportunity go to waste. 'You go round the back,' he whispered.

Louise didn't want to wait either. They'd been chasing this sick bastard for over a year and if he was still here then she was damned if she was going to let him escape due to her inactivity.

She rushed back outside, the cold night air doing little to mask the smell of decay clinging to her clothes and skin. She felt as if it had crawled through her nostrils and mouth and taken root within her. She aimed the torch in front of her and followed the uneven path to the back of the barn. It was then that she saw a flicker of light in the remains of the farmhouse. It flashed off as she turned the corner, lighting the space behind the cracked windows.

'Someone's here,' she said, radioing Finch before pulling out her gun. After Walton's latest killing, a gruesome shooting by the docks in Bristol, they'd been allocated firearms. Louise was fully trained, but being armed still didn't feel natural.

'I'm coming through the back of the barn now,' said Finch.

Louise's pulse spiked as the doors opened, the light from Finch's torch slicing the darkness before his shadow emerged. 'Where?' he whispered, his own gun in his right hand.

Louise nodded to the main farmhouse. 'Front or back?' she said.

In hindsight, that had been her biggest mistake. They shouldn't have split up at that stage, whatever the risk of the killer absconding.

'You take the back,' said Finch.

'We should tell them we've located him.'

Finch began moving towards the house. 'No time,' he said, under his breath.

Louise hesitated.

'Come on.'

She shook her head, calling in her position and situation to the station before proceeding behind the farmhouse. She slipped as she rounded the corner, the ground slick and wet. She kept her torch low. The field at the rear of the farmhouse was a graveyard of farming machinery, the centrepiece a rusted combine harvester. Vines and weeds poked through the vast structure as if holding it in place, or sucking it into the ground. Beyond the field was a woodland area, and Louise shivered at the thought of how many bodies they might find in that wasteland.

The back door of the farmhouse creaked and Louise swivelled on the spot, her gun held out in front of her as she'd been trained to do, but no one was there. She didn't want to call Finch on the radio in case it revealed his position, so reluctantly she made her way towards the door alone.

The smell inside was reminiscent of the decay in the barn. Her stomach was more accustomed to it now. There was a chance Finch was in danger so she edged along the walls, her ears primed for the faintest sound. She secured the ground floor as well as she was able, the torch revealing more mounds of unidentifiable matter.

'Finch,' she muttered under her breath at the sound of breaking glass from upstairs. She wasted no time, sprinting up the wooden staircase and almost breaking her ankle as her right foot lodged itself in a hole in one of the stairs before she shook it free.

'The end room on your right,' came Finch's voice. 'I think he's carrying,' he added.

Now on her knees, she crawled along the landing of the hall-way to meet Finch, who was instructing Walton to come out. The man didn't answer.

'I'm going in,' Finch told her.

'He's not going anywhere, Tim. Let's wait it out. Backup will be here soon,' said Louise, but she had already sensed it was too late at that point. Finch wouldn't want to wait for police backup. His sights were set higher than merely apprehending the killer. He wanted the glory, and she knew at that moment that he wanted it all for himself.

'Cover me,' he said, stepping over the threshold.

It all happened so fast, Finch tripping as he edged through the doorway, Louise ducking as the figure in the corner threw something at her, and finally Finch's words: 'He's holding!'

EIGHTEEN MONTHS LATER

.

Chapter One

Geoff Simmons secured the boat and stumbled up the hill, tripping over his feet in his haste. He'd come close to missing the tide, but he was here now. He stopped at the top of the incline, his breath returning, secure in his isolation. The gentle ache he'd experienced was still with him and he wondered how long it would remain. He understood his other pains – the bruising on his shoulder, the heaviness in his legs – but the nagging tug at the centre of his stomach could not so easily be explained.

His makeshift home was calling, but would have to wait. Instead, he battled across the barren plateau of the small island until the silhouette of the mainland revealed itself in the murk of the early-morning light. Taking out his high-powered binoculars from his rucksack, he stopped and slumped on to the damp ground. His palms itched, and he took off his leather gloves to scratch his scarred flesh as the sound of the waves battering the rocks beneath him filled his ears.

From where he sat, the mainland was little more than a shadow – a blotch of gloom lit by the occasional streetlight. He'd lived in Weston-super-Mare all his life, yet he felt more affinity with the small lump of rock where he lay now. The peacefulness he experienced on the island was absent on the mainland. There were rarely any people – at this time of the year, the island was deserted – unlike in Weston, where they crawled the town like ants. Even now, through the mist, he could make out the shape of a sea fisherman walking from the shoreline towards the retreating sea. Geoff adjusted the scope on his binoculars, sharpening the outline of the man. It was a peculiar time to go fishing – the tide would soon be so low the fisherman would be unable to cast far enough to wet his bait – but Geoff wasn't all that surprised. There was more to sea fishing than catching fish and he presumed the fisherman sought the same kind of peace he was currently experiencing on the island.

Either way, the man would soon serve his purpose.

Geoff clutched his binoculars as the fisherman stopped dead and dropped his equipment. For a second, he thought the fisherman was going to turn his back and run from the sight only metres away from him and he heard himself willing him onwards.

Time stalled as the man glanced in all directions before inching forwards. Geoff kept his focus solely on the figure, as if losing sight of him would make him vanish. He realised he'd been holding his breath as the man dropped to his knees, and then the air left Geoff's lungs in a rush of noise he half-feared would reach the mainland.

Only then did he move the binoculars to focus for a split second on what the fisherman had discovered.

Was it relief he felt? If anything, the ache in his stomach became tighter as he made his way through the wild-peony bushes – Steep Holm, along with its sister island, Flat Holm, being the only place in the UK where the plant grew – to the crawl space carved into the limestone rock. Dad had shown him the place when he was only six years old. It had been their secret, one he hadn't shared with anyone until the last couple of days. They'd spent many nights over the years camping close to the nook, neither of them quite willing to use the shelter within the rock. Nothing had changed on that front. He would never sleep in the cave, and still used his one-man tent when camping, but someone was living there now.

His torch found the bound figure, blinking at the light as if caught in an unspeakable act. Loosening the gag, Geoff dropped water into the offered mouth like Communion wine.

'You don't have to do this,' said the figure.

He'd found it easier than he'd imagined to ignore the sounds the man made. His words dissolved into the noises of the chattering seagulls and the gentle hum of the sea. Geoff allowed him a few more swigs of water before replacing the gag, the man's eyes wide with confusion and fear.

Before rolling him back into the opening, Geoff showed his prisoner an offering that he stuffed into the soiled pocket of the man's trousers.

A thick, rusted nail steeped in blood.

Chapter Two

Her niece's eyes were already full of tears by the time Louise Blackwell dropped to her haunches to say goodbye. 'I'll see you next weekend,' said Louise, but her niece, Emily, was inconsolable.

'You could stay?' said the girl, who'd turned five just three weeks ago.

Louise bit her lip, trying to control the emotion in her voice. There was a spare room at her brother's place but staying would only make things worse. 'I've really enjoyed today but I've got to get back to work.'

'Catching the bad guys?'

Louise kissed her niece on the cheek and pulled her close. 'Catching the bad guys.'

She stuck her head into the living room before leaving. 'I'm off now, Paul,' she said to her brother.

'Yep.' Paul didn't glance her way, his focus on the football match on the screen. He was nursing a glass of red wine, the bottle on the sideboard now empty.

'Do you want me to stay?' said Louise, regretting the question as soon as the words left her mouth.

Paul drank more wine before answering, the drink staining his lips. 'You think I can't look after my own daughter?' he said, a refrain Louise had heard too many times over the last two years.

She knew it was pointless to argue with him. 'Well, you know where I am.'

Paul grunted and returned to his football match.

Emily held on to her coat as she opened the front door, her grip so tight that Louise wanted to pick her niece up and take her home. 'You'll be okay,' she said, gently prising the girl's fingers away. 'Go and get ready for bed and I'm sure Daddy will read to you when the football has finished.'

Emily pursed her lips before sighing, the gesture so heartbreaking and beyond her years that Louise cursed her brother for putting her in this situation, despite everything that had befallen him. Two years ago, his wife Dianne had died within two weeks of receiving a diagnosis of skin cancer – a whirlwind of a terminal disease which had ultimately ripped both Dianne and her brother from Louise.

She kissed her niece once more before closing the door behind her.

In her car, she sat and waited for the heater to warm the chill of the October air from her bones, and fought the urge to return to her brother's flat. Instead she sent a text to her mother, who lived only ten minutes away, and suggested that she pay Paul a quick visit before the night was out.

The journey along the M5 to Louise's new home in Weston-super-Mare was always difficult, and not only because she was leaving Emily behind. Each time she was on the road going south, moving away from the city she loved, she felt a deep sense of loss for her old job in the Major Investigation Team. Although officially based out of the Avon and Somerset headquarters in Portishead, the majority of her work in MIT had been conducted in Bristol.

The Avonmouth Bridge signalled her departure from the city, heralding another world. Beneath the concrete crossing, a vast tanker sat in the channel of water and Louise imagined the depths that were keeping the vessel afloat and her mood darkened. She could have chosen to stay in Bristol and make the daily commute, but living in Weston was easier than having to travel there and back on a daily basis.

Forty minutes later she pulled off the motorway and made the short journey to her new residence in Worle, on the outskirts of Weston. She'd rented the property, a two-bedroom semi-detached bungalow, on an impulse, when she'd received the news of her transfer from MIT. The home had once belonged to an elderly lady who'd recently passed away and her family were desperate to offload it for a cheap monthly fee. It wasn't where she'd imagined herself to be at thirty-eight. From what she'd seen of her fellow residents she was the youngest person in the area by a good thirty years.

Her next-door neighbour, an elderly man she knew only as Mr Thornton, was filling his rubbish bin as she walked up the stone path to her house. The man eyed her suspiciously and offered her only a curt nod in response to her 'good evening'.

The smell of damp, and something indefinable – a musky, sour odour – greeted her as she opened the door to the bungalow. In Bristol she'd lived in a smart studio apartment in Clifton, and the memory made her wince as she passed the faded floral wallpaper in the small corridor that led to her living room.

It was a self-inflicted penance. The studio flat in Clifton was still within her means, but she'd convinced herself she needed to live in the town where she was working, that Bristol had to be placed in the past. Her phone pinged and she was pleased to see her parents were planning on stopping by at Paul's later that evening. She could now at least rest before she was due back at work the following morning.

Dinner was chicken curry from the freezer in front of the television. As she channel-flicked through Sunday night's predictable television offerings she tried not to dwell on her situation.

She considered calling DS Thomas Ireland, one of her team in Weston, the only person she'd really connected with in the last year and a half, but that was impossible for numerous reasons, not least the fact that he was married and would be at home with his family. Instead, she showered, and was in bed reading when another text arrived.

She'd expected it, but the words *no caller ID* on her phone always made her heart race. The text was less than original. She'd received something similar nearly every evening since she had left Bristol eighteen months ago.

I hope you sleep well, Louise x

Cursing the slight tremor in her hand, DI Louise Blackwell did what she always did. She took out her notebook and made a note of the message – the date and time – before putting the notebook away and turning the phone to silent.

Chapter Three

Louise woke with a jolt at 6 a.m., reaching for her mobile phone in case he'd texted her again. She was almost disappointed to see the screen was blank.

Thirty minutes later, she left for work. From her bungalow, she took the old toll road along the coast towards Kewstoke, entering Weston's seafront from the north of the town. As a child, she'd sat in the back of the car with Paul, her parents up front, as they'd driven along the same stretch of road. She recalled the sense of anticipation as her dad steered through the narrow bends, the nervous excitement laced with fear as she'd gaped at the sheer drop of the cliff edge. It was her parents who'd really felt her departure from Bristol. Her father still hadn't come to terms with the injustice of it all, and every time she saw him he would suggest suing the police department. She shared his frustration but had to bide her time. She hadn't forgotten what had happened to her, or forgiven those responsible. Their time would come, but for now she had to get on with her life and what was left of her career.

The sun was rising behind the black clouds that rolled towards the horizon. Passing the antiquated facades of the hotels and the dilapidated crazy-golf course on the front, she registered the dirty brown of the beach. She could count the times she'd noticed the sea at high tide on the fingers of one hand. It always appeared to be somewhere in the distance – beyond the layers of sand and mud and the garish Grand Pier dominating the seafront – a murky stretch of water in permanent retreat from the town.

Following the one-way system, she drove briefly inland, away from the amusement arcades, cafés and bars, dark and deserted, as if long ago abandoned, before returning to the seafront. She pulled up opposite the Kalimera – a Greek restaurant she visited almost every day, the only place open at this time of the morning. The same woman, the owner of the restaurant, served her every time. A striking woman in her forties, dark hair pulled tightly away from her face, she never entered into conversation with Louise. As always, she took her order – Louise only ever drank black coffee – and placed it on the counter without a word.

Louise took the coffee and sat by the window and gazed across the road towards the seafront, a habit she'd acquired since her first day working in Weston. It was still an hour before her shift was due to start and this was the only time she would have to herself during the day. The little restaurant was a haven of peace. She was usually the only person there and the solitude gave her space to plan her day before facing the numerous distractions of the office. The majority of her work since arriving in Weston had been leading the drugs teams. North Somerset was one of the country's worst areas for drug abuse and a large percentage of her time was spent on the small clusters of gangs that had infiltrated the seaside town. Recently her work had focused on the influx of a new designer drug responsible for the deaths of three citizens in the small town in the last two months. Weston-super-Mare contained over a tenth of all the drug rehabilitation centres in the country, a fact that still amazed Louise. And with recovering addicts came both demand and supply chains.

'Thank you,' Louise said, placing the correct money on the counter. She received no response as she left the restaurant. Five minutes later she was at work.

The station building was a white-grey structure next to the town hall, a short walk from the seafront. Next year the building was to be closed and the majority of the staff moved to a new purpose-built police 'centre' close to Louise's bungalow in Worle. Louise packed up and exchanged nods with some of the personnel as she made her way to the CID department. Despite being eighteen months in the role, most people at the station were still wary of her and her past. The nuances were subtle – conversations stalling when she entered a room, the odd glance and exchange she wasn't included in – but she was aware enough to notice them. Louise didn't let it bother her, was in no rush to be accepted, but what she did miss about her last job was the pace. She was used to being in a bustling office, lots of officers working on numerous cases, but here things moved that tiny bit slower, sometimes so much so that the difference in atmosphere as she entered her department that morning was tangible. The place was much busier than normal, the officers and support staff alert and focused.

Simone, the office manager, stopped her before she'd even had time to reach her desk. 'I've been calling you. DCI Robertson would like to see you immediately,' said the woman, who had a permanent look of distaste etched on to her face.

Louise checked her phone – the screen displaying five missed calls in the last twenty minutes – and cursed herself for forgetting to switch it off silent mode. She dumped her bag on her desk and made the walk of shame to DCI Robertson's office, a number of her colleagues stopping what they were doing to glance at her.

'Sir,' she said, deciding formality was her best option, in the circumstances.

DCI Robertson looked up from his screen and stared at her. A native Glaswegian, he'd been in Weston for twenty years. 'Late night, was it?' he said, his thick accent unaffected by his years in the West Country.

'Phone on silent.'

Robertson raised his eyebrows. 'Sit,' he said.

'What's going on, Iain?' said Louise, relieved he hadn't reprimanded her for missing the calls.

'A body's been found on the beach. First responder got there at five thirty this morning, not long before we began calling you.'

Louise glanced at the clock on the wall: seven fifteen.

'A body?' she asked, ignoring his unsubtle dig.

'Female, aged sixty-eight, found by a sea fisherman. Looks like you've finally got yourself a murder.'

It wasn't, technically, her first murder case since arriving in Weston. She'd been the SIO – the senior investigating officer – in a domestic case where a husband had killed his wife following an argument over her suspected adultery. The man had confessed at the scene, and the case had been over before it started. This was potentially something different, closer to her work in Bristol, and she couldn't help feeling the familiar rush of excitement as she walked towards the seafront.

On the south side of the pier, the white tent erected by the SOCOs – the scene of crime officers – billowed in the crosswinds of the beach. It was pitched about two hundred metres from the promenade, the sea at least another two hundred metres in the distance.

The air was tinged with the smell of sulphur and rotting seaweed. The wind carried grains of sand that stung her face as she moved across the powdery surface to the damp, mud-like substance where the tent was pitched. Behind the tent in the far distance, a mound of land, the island of Steep Holm, jutted out from the sea – a piece of forgotten rock she'd never visited, despite living in the south-west all her life.

She greeted the uniformed officer standing guard and moved inside the tent, catching a glimpse of the victim at the far end as she entered. A wave of familiarity hit her as she pulled on her white SOCO protective overall. The smells and sounds of a murder scene, the twitch of anticipation in her bones and the adrenalin forcing her onwards, protecting her in part from the realisation that she was about to deal with a dead body, something she was glad to acknowledge she'd never yet fully come to terms with.

She was moving towards the corpse when a sense of dizziness overcame her. The heat of her suit and the cloying atmosphere of the cramped interior surprised her and she paused on the spot, fighting the wave of nausea rising in her throat as she was taken back to her last murder case.

The Max Walton case had been her obsession for two years and was the reason she had been stationed in Weston. It was as if she could smell the abandoned pig farm, standing in the tent. The scent coated her skin and filled her nostrils even now, and threatened to force her out of the tent.

Her fellow officers stared at her and she sensed that they would be thinking the same thing: this was her first proper murder scene since that night, since she'd taken the action she'd thought necessary. She felt their lack of trust in her as she willed herself forward to the victim, stability returning to her legs.

She knew some of the people but introduced herself anyway. 'DI Louise Blackwell, SIO. What have we got?' she said, pleased to hear her voice was strong and steady.

It was the county pathologist, Stephen Dempsey, who spoke first. 'Ah, DI Blackwell, you heading up this one?'

She nodded with a formal smile. He sounded in command, aloof, in front of his colleagues, but Louise knew better. His bravado was a show. The real Stephen Dempsey was insecure and awkward, unable to hold on to the act of being someone else for very long. Her face felt hot as she recalled how she'd discovered this about him.

The victim, Veronica Lloyd, lay on her back, her skin as white as the tent surrounding her, apart from the black-purple discolouration on various parts of her body. The pathologist pointed to the remains of the woman's right hand. 'Quite a mess,' he said, needlessly. 'The poor woman is littered with injuries, all recently inflicted. Her legs have been smashed in numerous places and she has severe abrasions to her shoulders. It would appear she was bound,' he added, pointing to the deep grooves on the woman's ankles and wrists, where it looked like rope or wire had been pulled tight, tearing at the skin and biting into the flesh.

Despite the incisions, there wasn't much blood at the scene and, though it could have seeped into the damp sand beneath her, this suggested something to Louise. 'She's been moved?'

'Very good, DI Blackwell. The signs of post-mortem lividity on her front suggest she has been tampered with posthumously.' Dempsey hovered his hand over the woman's right wrist. 'The killer sliced her radial artery just here. There would have been a lot of blood. We'll need to take samples of the surrounding sand when she's moved. He really did some job on her palm,' he added, lifting the victim's hand, the bottom part of which was a ragged mess. 'I believe he pierced her here, in a downward movement which pushed into her wrist. Obviously, we'll know more later.'

The dizziness returned as Louise moved to the corner of the tent and pretended to check her phone. The image of Max Walton just before she shot him to death flashed in her mind and it took all her control to remain in the tent for a few more minutes. She fought the claustrophobic atmosphere, confused by her reaction to being there, and watched as the SOCOs took pictures and videos of the scene. She kept her eyes focused on the body, forcing herself to survey every millimetre of the poor woman's troubled flesh until she could take no more. She eased towards the exit, making eye contact with one of the SOCOs, and pushed through the thick coating of the tent's door, welcoming the rush of the cold wind outside.

She peeled off her suit, when all she wanted to do was tear it from her flesh. With it removed, the dizziness subsided and the sense of rotting flesh and pig excrement faded. 'We need to expand this cordon,' she said to one of the uniformed officers. At present the police tape stretched only fifty metres from the tent.

'How far?' asked the officer, a towering man she knew only as Hughes. The question was asked with a hint of impatience and Louise stared hard at him, making her displeasure visible.

Towards the horizon, the sea had all but disappeared, leaving a seemingly endless blanket of mud in its place. Despite the commotion on the beach, the area was deserted. Louise glanced around the vast expanse of damp sand and wondered why the killer had chosen to leave the body there.

'I want the whole beach vacated,' she said.

'The whole beach?' said Hughes, the surprised look on his face almost comical.

'Yes, the whole beach. And I mean the whole of the beach. That too much trouble for you, Constable Hughes?'

Hughes frowned, glancing at one of his colleagues standing guard outside the tent. 'No ma'am,' he said, his eyes darting towards the sand.

'Good, get it done.'

Louise turned three hundred and sixty degrees and, aside from police officers, counted four other people on the sand, as far as she could see. She knew she may have gone too far by suggesting the whole beach be vacated, but the dismissive look in Hughes's eyes had aggravated her. When she'd been finding her feet in the town, still weighed down with her Bristol history, she'd probably been more tolerant of incompetence than she would have been while in the MIT. She'd been reeling from the events that had conspired to send her to Weston, the aftermath of the Walton case, and only recently had come to accept how much her departure had affected her. That had to change now, and forcing a belligerent career cop to do some extra work was merely a small step. It was not as if it was the height of summer.

As Hughes passed on her instructions to his colleagues, Louise quickly moved away from the tent, pleased to get some distance from the turmoil within. She walked along the expanse of sand to the area where cars were allowed to park. This had always been a quirk of Weston she remembered from childhood, and she'd been surprised to discover they still let cars on to the beach. As a child, her father had joked that he was going to drive into the sea. Later, Louise and Paul had taken turns sitting on his lap in the driver's seat and had been allowed to hold the steering wheel as the car moved along the sand, while their mother fretted in the passenger seat.

A sunny backdrop always accompanied her recollections of her time in Weston, as if the seaside retreat of her childhood had been some Caribbean paradise. She guessed her parents always chose the sunny days for their day trips, but the dank, grey, windswept environment she battled through now was so different to her memories that it was difficult to align the two.

She stopped at the foot of a bank of sand dunes. She'd struggled up the same steep inclines with Paul, the sun beating down on their heads as they staggered up and over. Now the dunes had lost their power. They appeared to be little more than small lumps in the land and she wondered if, over time, the tide had worn them down.

But she was avoiding confronting what was really bothering her.

She'd seen much worse in her time than the body of Veronica Lloyd. She'd seen things that would never leave her, and although the wounds inflicted on the poor woman were horrendous, she had become accustomed to such scenes. Or so she had thought. It was, after all, eighteen months since she'd left the MIT, and it was possible she'd softened in that time. Part of her welcomed the idea. The day the sight of a murder victim didn't bother her would be the day she would have to leave the job. But still, her reaction disappointed her. In particular, it highlighted that she'd yet to fully recover from the Max Walton incident and her relationship with the officer she'd been with at the time.

She scaled the sand dune, annoyed that the short climb had left her breathless, and glanced out at the sweeping panorama of the beach. She pictured the wounds on Veronica Lloyd, the severe incisions on her wrists, the bruising of the skin on her shoulders, the mangled bones of her legs. Pushing herself through the vines and brambles at the back of the dunes, she gazed down on the greens of the golf course behind the beach. A lone golfer lined his ball up on the tee, going through a number of practice swings, before making contact with the ball, which landed hard on the green and careered off into a bunker.

She turned away, reflecting on the thought she was trying to avoid.

DCI Finch.

However hard she fought it, pretended it didn't matter, it was the thought of Finch that had triggered her reaction at the tent. Timothy Finch, such an unassuming name. They'd started in Bristol at roughly the same time and had worked in the MIT for the last five years together, both colleagues, both detective inspectors, occasional lovers. Everything came back to Finch. She saw it so clearly now, had done so the split second after the Walton case was resolved. The way he'd manipulated her, led her down pathways she would never have chosen alone.

Louise would never know if Finch really thought Walton had been holding a gun that night, or if he'd even been cunning enough to think about setting her up. She hadn't hesitated. She'd seen the bodies in the barn, Walton had used a gun before, and Finch had told her the man was holding. She had aimed her own pistol into the shadowy figure and let out three shots, the figure slumping to the ground instantly.

She'd been suspended on pay while they investigated the killing. Walton's DNA was everywhere. He was linked conclusively to all the victims and four more bodies that were found in the woodland behind the farmhouse. To some, she was a hero. She'd killed a cold-blooded murderer. But to others, she'd killed an unarmed man. She'd pleaded with Finch to tell the truth. The man was a great actor, if nothing else. Even when they were alone he kept up the pretence.

'I'm sorry, Louise, at no point did I say he was holding a gun,' he had said, so convincingly that she came close to believing it herself.

And then, in her absence, he was promoted to DCI and things started to make sense. There was no way he could have planned it all, and had he not tripped, it could have been him who'd fired at the unarmed man. But he'd seen an opportunity and grabbed it. They'd both joked that they'd been pitted against each other in the race for the promotion, but Louise had never dreamt he would ever be that ruthless.

The tribunal concluded she'd been negligent but, considering the circumstances, and despite Finch's conflicting account, they decided that the shooting was lawful. Unfortunately, the chief constable, and in particular his assistant, Morley, were not of the same mind. They were tired of the negative media attention the case received, and offered her a take-it-or-leave-it move to Weston.

She would have accepted all that, would have conceded her role in the events that ended with Walton's death at the farmhouse, if only Finch had left her alone. But eighteen months later, he was still on her case. After the promotion, he cut her off immediately, and had been instrumental in her leaving for Weston. Yet that wasn't enough. Finch was the one texting her every night. She had no proof, of course, he was too careful for that, but it couldn't be anyone else.

And now this. She hadn't seen him in almost a year and a half, but still he was having this effect on her. It was the way he worked, the tiny manipulations and displays of strength. She should have seen it at the time – friends had warned her – but she'd chosen to doubt herself.

She hadn't reacted that way in the tent because of what she'd seen or even what had happened at Max Walton's farmhouse. She'd reacted that way because of Finch, the things he'd made her do and the hold he still had over her.

Well, fuck that, she thought, as she watched the golfer shank his approach shot. It was time she got on with her life and time for Finch to get what was coming to him.

Chapter Four

Eileen Boswell loved her weekly pilgrimage, the early-morning walk to her one and only job. She could have taken the bus, and would concede that luxury when the winter fully took hold of the town, but she hadn't reached the age of eighty-one by taking the easy way. She always followed the same route, down the stairs at the train station car park and along the pathway next to the sea.

She'd lived in the Cornish seaside town of St Ives all her life. The place had changed beyond recognition in that time, but alone here, the sea lapping against the harbour wall, she could almost imagine she was a little girl again. What she wouldn't give to have the energy and resilience to do what she would have done all those years ago: to dive from the wall into the beautiful, clear water. She stooped and chuckled to herself. Maybe one of these days she would do just that. Let the water have its final way with her.

But not today. Today she had to get to Mr Lanegan's house. Although the man was a good ten years her junior, he was in no position to look after himself. He gave her a few quid each week, and in turn she gave the house a good clean. The money wasn't important. Cleaning gave her a reason to get out of the house, and when he was on form Mr Lanegan was quite the conversationalist.

Eileen left the seafront and took the short slope towards the cinema, which was mercifully free of tourists. She walked along the cobbled avenue, tutting to herself as she passed the surf shops and new fish restaurants, paused outside the cinema, squinting at the garish posters, and waited for her breath to return. The hill seemed to get steeper every week and she glanced at the bus pulling up at the stop ahead of her before setting off again.

No one warned you about getting old – especially the old themselves. Her mother and grandmother had both lived into their nineties, and not once had she heard them complain. Had they suffered as she did? Her creaking bones were audible to her as she crept up the hill, what was left of her muscles aching as she forced her limbs onwards.

She thought about Terrence as she battled the icy wind. It had been six months since he'd last called, and then the conversation had lasted less than five minutes. She couldn't blame him. He had his own family now, lived in a different country. Children were meant to grow up, move out, weren't they? She'd given him his independence, so she should be pleased that he'd moved on.

Still. She'd only met her grandchildren once, and even after that meeting they'd never had any time for her. The flights from Australia were too expensive, Terrence had protested, and that one time she'd plucked up the courage to visit the travel agent she'd discovered he was right. She'd been saving ever since, but the pension didn't stretch the way it did before, even with her cleaning job, and she was still a few hundred pounds shy of a return journey.

She stopped again at the fire station before turning left and heading up another hill to Mr Lanegan's house, and was surprised to find there was no answer when she rang the doorbell. Mr Lanegan liked his home comforts. He usually had one of those fancy coffee pots on the go and would pour her a cup when she arrived. He would always ask her how she was, how her week had gone, and he would be smiling. *Oh, that smile of his*, she thought, as she fumbled in her carrier bag for her keys.

It had been so long since she'd had to open the door herself that she couldn't remember which of the many keys on her key ring – she collected keys like years – belonged to Mr Lanegan. She tried each in turn, the cold aggravating her arthritis as her shaking hands sought the keyhole. Eventually she found the right one, her skin cracking from the cold as she prised open the lock.

'Hello,' she called in the hall, taking off her coat and hanging it on the hook by the door. Her voice echoed within the walls, and she felt a chill, as if Mr Lanegan hadn't been using his heater. 'Hello,' she called again, hesitating before moving into the kitchen where Mr Lanegan spent most of his time. She frowned at the empty space, disappointed to see the coffee machine sitting on the sideboard clean and empty.

He must have forgotten to tell me he was out for the day, she thought as she took her cleaning materials from beneath the kitchen sink. It was odd, though. In the last ten years, she couldn't recall a time when Mr Lanegan hadn't been in when she'd called. She scrubbed the sink, noticing it was cleaner than usual, before starting on the floor with less gusto than usual.

As she cleaned the living room, doing her best to ignore the leering figure of Jesus Christ on the giant crucifix that dominated the room, she tried to work out what was bothering her. Obviously, she missed her morning cup of coffee but, deep down, she knew it was more than that. She didn't want to admit it, refused to make it an issue, but she considered Mr Lanegan to be her only friend. She looked forward to this day every week, endured the long walk up the hill because it was part of the process. The few hours she got to spend with Mr Lanegan were so very precious, and now she would have to wait another week before seeing him again, another week without a friendly conversation.

The house didn't take as long as normal to clean. There was less of Mr Lanegan's usual clutter and the job was done with at least half an hour to spare. She pulled on her coat and wrote a note for Mr Lanegan, saying she would see him next week and not to worry about not having left money for her.

She took a quick look at the thermostat, thinking she should do something about the cold, but was confused by the digital display so left it alone. She locked up and moved away from the house, whispering softly, 'See you next week.'

Chapter Five

By the time Louise returned to the tent, the cordon had widened and a crowd had gathered on the promenade. She entered the tent without hesitation, glad to have identified what was bothering her. Louise reminded herself she was the most experienced officer in the place, and watched with professional detachment as Veronica Lloyd's body was carried away, Dempsey having finished with his analysis for the time being.

'Stephen, a word,' she said to the pathologist, who was packing away his equipment.

Dempsey smiled, and Louise felt a pang of guilt at the off-hand way she'd treated him after their night together. There was an innocence to him which, at another time, she might have found endearing.

'Louise, you left us in a hurry. Everything okay?'

'Everything is fine, Stephen. I need the autopsy completed as a matter of urgency.'

'Where have I heard that before?'

Louise offered him a smile. 'Go outside, you'll see the crowd. Unfortunately, I suspect this is going to be big news. Speed will benefit both of us.'

Dempsey smiled again, went to say something, and hesitated. 'I'll do my best for you,' he said, leaving the tent.

An incident room was set up at the station, and Louise spent the rest of the morning organising the roles and duties of her team as a picture of the victim began to emerge. Veronica Lloyd was a retired schoolteacher. She'd never married but had an active social life centred around the local tennis club and her local church, St Bernadette's. She had no living relatives and, as far as they could deduce, hadn't been in an active relationship.

Louise's years in the MIT meant she knew the procedure of a homicide investigation by heart. The methods and routines had been tried and tested over thousands of cases and she was content that everything was in place. Her role as SIO was primarily managerial, but unlike many officers in her position she insisted on being involved from the ground up. She trusted her officers, but she had the most murder experience in the team and wasn't about to waste it.

Restless, she took a drive to Veronica's housing estate. Her house was on the fringes of Oldmixon, near the hospital, at the end of a terraced row of identical post-war homes, each with a dour exterior of pebble-dashed grey.

Thomas greeted her as she entered Veronica's house. 'Ma'am,' he said, using the formal greeting in front of the uniformed officer guarding the door.

Ten years her junior, it wouldn't be long before he'd make the rank of inspector. Weston born and bred, Thomas Ireland had an easy charm, an affable way about him that made him popular with both his superiors and subordinates. She smiled to herself, thinking how close she'd come to calling him the night before.

'Thomas. What have you got for me?' asked Louise, walking into the living room.

'Not much, I'm afraid. Nothing suggests there was a break-in. Everything appears to be in place, and if there was a struggle, there's no sign of it.'

She looked around the place. The living room was well ordered and uncluttered, save for an overflowing bookcase above the fireplace. A single armchair, adorned by a flower-patterned throw, sat facing a small television. Next to it was a double-seated faux-leather sofa, still wrapped in protective plastic.

A pattern emerged as Louise made her way through the house. It was neat and well organised, possibly to an obsessive extent. Nothing in the home was out of place, everything scrubbed and polished to perfection, the only anomaly the unordered way books lined shelves in every room. The majority were paperback thrillers, but among these were a number of classics – Orwell, Greene, Austen, Woolf – as well as some children's books and non-fiction titles. Louise thought about the lack of books at her bungalow and wondered how sad her home life would appear should she one day suffer the same fate as Veronica.

The sight of a lone single bed in the bedroom filled Louise with an unexpected melancholy, and she reminded herself to think practically, not emotionally. Veronica had never married, and the single bed was indicative of a person who'd lived her life alone, either by choice or necessity. Louise was about to leave when she caught sight of an old jewellery box on top of a bookshelf. It was similar to one her mother had owned – an old wooden box that would play music when opened.

Louise stretched to the top of the shelf and retrieved it, noticing that the music box had recently been polished. She smiled when she opened the lid as an old tune she couldn't quite place was produced by the revolving cylinder inside. A yellow sticker indicated her officers had already searched the box, but she examined the contents anyway. The box opened out into three layers, each lined with cheap-looking, mainly silver-plated jewellery. She was about to seal it back up when she noticed a latch to the rear of the box. Squinting, she unclipped it to reveal a spring-loaded secret compartment. It contained a small cloth bag sealed with a thin thread.

She put on a pair of latex gloves before untying the bag, shaking her head as she accessed the contents of the plastic case within the bag. She'd seen similar cases many times before. This case contained four items – shoelace, spoon, syringe and paper wrap. She undid the wrap, revealing an off-white crumbly powder which, from Louise's experience, would shortly prove to be heroin.

DCI Robertson summoned her to his office after the afternoon briefing. As Louise took a seat, he placed a copy of the *Bristol Post* on his desk. She scanned the lead article: the discovery of Veronica's body on the beach.

'This is already gaining some interest,' he said.

'It's not every day we get a brutal murder on our beach, Iain.'

'I don't mean this,' said Robertson, flipping over the newspaper. 'HQ have been asking for regular updates. There's a lot of interest from the brass, and the head of your old team, especially.'

Louise closed her eyes and fought her rising anger at this revelation.

Finch.

She went to speak, ready to defend her position, to insist it was her case and that HQ shouldn't be getting involved, before deciding she'd be best served holding her tongue.

Robertson rubbed his right eye before returning his attention to her. 'Look, I don't care what happened to you there. I've no complaints about your work since you've moved here, but you've got to appreciate they'll be keeping a close eye on you.'

'I understand that, Iain.' Her snap reaction was to assume that was why he'd appointed her SIO on the Veronica Lloyd case – to avoid ultimate responsibility himself – but Robertson had always been fair. If anything, making her SIO was a compliment, an acknowledgement of his trust in her. There was nothing more she could have done on the opening day. He'd read her updates and would have understood that.

He sighed, clearly struggling with something internal. 'You need to be prepared. Because of . . .' He glanced away, rubbing his eye again, and Louise suppressed a laugh. 'Look, you're going to be under close scrutiny. More so than before. It always goes that way when we get something high profile here, and with your . . . history . . .'

'I understand, Iain,' Louise repeated. 'Everything will be meticulous and transparent.'

Robertson wasn't finished. She appreciated the careful way he was choosing his words, but it would have been easier on both of them if he'd just come out with what he had to say.

'Remember, I'm here for you twenty-four-seven.'

'I appreciate that, Iain.'

'So if it comes to it, you come to me. You don't engage in a confrontation.'

Her mind drifted to the text message she'd received from Finch last night, adrenalin flooding her system.

'Understood?' said Robertson, his accent guttural.

Louise held her superior's gaze for a number of seconds before replying. 'Understood.'

She reached home at 10 p.m. and prepared a bowl of cereal in the silence of her living room. On the wall, stretching the length of the room, she created a murder board and pinned numerous pictures of Veronica Lloyd, including those of her at the beach. 'Why would someone want to do this to you?' she asked the pictures, the cereal all but untouched.

She then wasted little time before going to bed as she wanted to be back at the office before 6 a.m. the next day.

Her phone pinged the second she switched off the bedroom light. She laughed, unsurprised by the timing. Stretching towards the bedside table, she grabbed the phone, squinting at the light as she read the message:

> *You've landed yourself an interesting case, Louise. I hope nothing goes wrong x*

Chapter Six

Sleep didn't come easy, and Louise's body ached the next morning as she crawled out of bed. Despite herself, Finch's latest text message had got to her. It was one thing when the texts were general – timed to coincide with her sleeping, or first thing in the morning – but this text was something different. It suggested he'd been monitoring her, probably had been all this time.

When they worked together, Louise had been blind to it, but in retrospect that side of Finch had always been present. There had been grievances with other members of the team, little grudges he would refuse to forget. Then there was his constant battle for control, the way he manipulated situations and results in his favour. A young member of their team in Portishead, Will Manning, had requested a transfer a couple of years after Louise started with the MIT. At the time, most of the team had thought he simply couldn't hack it in the MIT, but after the Walton case Louise had spoken to Manning, who'd told her about Finch's covert bullying. The way he'd constantly undermined him, had taken credit when Manning had done all the work. He'd decided not to speak out against Finch, fearing it would hinder his career. Louise had pleaded with him to help her in her own case against Finch, but he'd refused, as if he were scared of retribution.

She wondered now if Finch was monitoring Manning in the same way that he was monitoring her. So far, he'd been so careful that it was impossible to prove anything. The messages were untraceable, sent with encrypted software, and he chose his words with perfect economy: obvious enough that Louise knew they were from him but too subtle to be linked back to him.

Louise fought her growing rage by focusing all her attention on the case.

She called Thomas and arranged to meet him at the Kalimera before work, regretting it the moment she hung up. If she'd learnt one thing since arriving in Weston, it was that it was close to impossible to keep a secret. Her mistaken night with Dempsey when she'd first arrived in Weston – the result of her self-enforced loneliness and too many red wines – was testimony to that. It was no secret – there were no secrets in the small town – and although no one had dared mention it to her since, she saw it in their faces: the narrowing of the eyes, the hints of a smirk every time she spoke to the pathologist. And although her meeting with Thomas was a professional one, it wouldn't stop the innuendo-laced gossip spreading through the station if anyone found out.

She hesitated, wanting to call him again to cancel, before deciding she wouldn't have her actions determined by the threat of disapproval from people who already disapproved of her.

She took the central route through Worle towards the town centre. She'd hated it when her father had driven this way on their day trips to Weston – delaying the sight of the sea by further excruciating minutes – but it was quicker and she was restless. They were already twenty-four hours into the case and had nothing beyond a tentative link to Veronica's drug habit.

In a certain light, Weston could be beautiful. Today was not one of those days. A constant drizzle accompanied her car journey, a greyness enveloping the whole town, as if she were watching a black-and-white version of it through her windscreen. She was pleased when she reached the seafront. The sea was retreating, but at least she caught sight of it as she parked up and crossed over to the restaurant.

Thomas was already inside and had ordered her a coffee. The dark-haired owner gave her an impenetrable look as Louise took a seat opposite her colleague.

'So this is where you go every morning,' said Thomas, as Louise pulled her hair, still damp from her morning shower, over her shoulder. 'I'm honoured.'

'You tell anyone about this place and you're a dead man,' said Louise, deadpan.

Thomas leaned towards her and whispered, 'We already know about it, that's why no one else is ever here.'

Louise laughed. 'Good, keep it that way.'

'So why the early meeting, boss?'

Again, Louise worried that the conversation could have taken place at the station and that her desire to see a friendly face had bypassed her professionalism. 'I wanted to get your local knowledge first thing,' she said, thinking fast.

'Why, of course,' said Thomas, smiling.

'Have you ever seen a case like this before?' The question sounded awkward and Thomas looked confused. Louise didn't know why she'd asked it. She knew the stats and murder cases in the whole of the south-west of England by heart.

'In Weston? Not sure I've ever seen anything this nasty, certainly not since I've been in CID. We've had a few murder cases, but this is particularly brutal. And the age of the victim makes it that much stranger. If it was a robbery gone wrong, for instance, I could understand it, but why go to the bother of moving the body? Why would you want to do something so horrendous to someone that age?'

'A grudge?'

'That's one hell of a grudge.'

'What's everyone saying?' asked Louise.

Thomas paused. 'Everyone?' he asked, amused.

'What's the word on the street, DS Ireland?'

'The street is spooked, boss.' Thomas's smile broadened. 'I don't know. It was too early to tell yesterday. That article in the *Post* will get everyone talking, I guess.'

'Don't remind me.'

'And your discovery, of course,' said Thomas, his eyebrows rising.

'It strike you as odd, a woman that age having heroin in her possession?'

'Nothing surprises me any more in this town. I've seen all ages on it. The one thing that was curious was how well maintained her house was. Not the typical habitat for a user,' said Thomas.

Louise agreed. It suggested the habit was either a new one, or that Veronica had been managing to function despite taking the drug.

They sipped at their drinks, Louise thankful when Thomas interrupted the silence. 'Is Dempsey doing the autopsy today?' he asked.

Louise paused before answering, searching for a hint of subtext in his words. Thomas would know about her fling with Dempsey, but nothing in his manner suggested his comment was anything but professional. 'The case is a priority, so he's agreed to do late afternoon, around 5 p.m. FIU are pushing things through too.'

'Let's hope we get something from the Forensic Investigation Unit. From yesterday, I'm struggling to see a potential motive beyond the dealer. Some DNA would come in handy.'

'Wouldn't it just.'

They left the place, the owner's lips curving upwards as Louise followed Thomas out of the restaurant. 'I'll see you at the station,' said Louise.

A car horn blared as she walked across the road and she turned around in time to see the smiling face of DS Farrell in his police-issued car. As he drove off, she looked back and noted that Thomas would have been in full view. Thomas shrugged his shoulders, as if Farrell seeing them wasn't important, and Louise turned away towards her car.

If she could have chosen one person not to see her leaving the restaurant with Thomas, it would have been Farrell.

DS Greg Farrell was a young officer going places. He'd joined CID straight after his probationary period three years ago and had received his promotion to sergeant shortly after Louise joined the department. She couldn't question the man's work ethic. He was professionalism personified. His clothing was always immaculate – tailored suit, crisp shirt, tie level with his top button – and she'd never known him to miss any paperwork deadlines. He was out to impress and had been noticed by DCI Robertson and those higher up. But she'd yet to connect with the man. He was always personable, albeit with a more aloof manner than Thomas, and treated her with respect, at least to her face, but she remained wary of him. This wasn't unusual. Being in a police squad was akin to being in a family. You didn't get to choose who you worked with, and although you pulled towards a common goal, you didn't always like your colleagues.

Maybe it was simply the annoying way he appeared to be continuously smiling. Whatever, she imagined it would be a long time before she ever fully trusted him.

Louise decided to take a drive before heading back to the station, not wanting to arrive at the same time as Thomas.

Her position in Weston was complicated by the reason for her appointment. She tried not to act like the move was a demotion, but everyone knew why she was no longer in Bristol. She shook her head, driving thoughts of Max Walton and his depraved farmhouse from her mind, and drove towards Uphill, past the General Hospital and around the back roads of the Oldmixon estate, stopping outside Veronica's house.

A curtain twitched as she stepped out of her car three doors down, the inhabitant retreating from sight before Louise could make eye contact. This part of Weston was still alien to her. The Weston she knew was the sun-kissed town of her childhood. Her memories revolved mainly around the seafront. Donkey rides on the beach, avoiding the cracks of the wooden boards as she walked along the pier, hot afternoons at the Tropicana, the town's now defunct open-air swimming pool. Those memories were now tarnished by her recent history, and although she'd explored every corner of the town in the last eighteen months, it still felt unfamiliar. She envied Thomas and Farrell their connection to the town, and was torn between wanting to extend her knowledge of the place and the desire to get out as soon as she could.

Her team was waiting patiently for her in the incident room when she arrived twenty minutes later. Farrell's permanent smile was seared to his face and he stared at her as if they were co-conspirators with an illicit secret. She studied the murder board before speaking. The pictures of Veronica Lloyd matched those in her living room and were surrounded by photos of those closest to the woman. It looked like the cast list for *Cocoon*. No one on the board appeared to be under sixty.

'What have you got for me?' she said, to the silenced room.

'I'm meeting with the chairman of the tennis club,' said Thomas. 'Then I'm off to see the parish priest of St Bernadette's, where Veronica volunteered.'

'Busy boy,' said Farrell, before Louise had a chance to respond.

'And you, DS Farrell?' she said, distracted by her fantasy of ripping Farrell's smile from his flesh.

'I've got a possible lead for Veronica's dealer. Trevor Cole. Known to occasionally deal out of the Cartwheel, the local pub on her estate.'

Louise knew the establishment and couldn't quite picture Veronica entering it, let alone buying drugs there. 'We're twenty-four hours in now. Finding this supplier has to be our number-one priority,' she said, adding, 'some of the preliminary forensics should come back to us today as well.'

'And the pathologist?' asked Farrell.

Louise studied the grinning face of the DS, trying to ascertain if he was alluding to her fling with Dempsey. Farrell maintained eye contact, as if the question were innocuous. 'Autopsy is this afternoon,' she said, her tone signalling that there would be no further discussion on the matter.

She assigned the day's duties and dismissed everyone before returning to her office. She'd considered joining Thomas at St Bernadette's but didn't want to give Farrell any more ammunition that morning. For now, she had to trust her team to make the right decisions while she waited for forensics and the autopsy that afternoon.

News was drip-fed to her through the day: Thomas's report of his meeting with Father McGuire at St Bernadette's Church and his encounter with the tennis community; an update from Farrell on the dealer, who he'd as yet been unable to locate.

Lunch was a dry sandwich from the canteen eaten at her desk. When her internal phone rang sometime later she was surprised to see it was already 4 p.m., an hour before the autopsy. The day was fading and so far she had little to show for it. 'DI Blackwell,' she said, picking up the receiver.

'Louise, it's Simone. I've got a lady from Hengrove School in Bristol. Won't tell me what it's regarding. Should I put her through?'

Louise's heart skipped. Hengrove was Emily's school. 'Put her through. Louise Blackwell.'

'Hi, Ms Blackwell. This is Caroline Travis from Hengrove School in Bristol. I have you down as an emergency contact for Emily Blackwell?'

'That's correct, she's my niece,' said Louise, her hand gripping the phone.

The woman paused before speaking, sighing as if what she had to say was an inconvenience. 'Emily was supposed to be collected at three fifteen today as usual, but no one has collected her and we can't reach her father.'

Chapter Seven

Geoffrey Simmons finished the last of his work at 4.30 p.m., giving him over two hours before evening Mass.

Earlier that morning, he'd taken the boat back under the cloak of autumn darkness. His mooring spot was by the old lifeboat station at the end of the derelict Birnbeck pier – known by the locals in Weston as the old pier – where he was able to drag his small boat out of sight beneath the rotting timbers and steel girders.

He'd felt different this morning. The nagging feeling in his stomach had unravelled and in its place came a sense of clarity. He'd felt no guilt as he'd taken the gag from his prisoner and fed him bread and water. At one point the man had begun to plead his case, but Geoff placed the gag back on and returned his attention to the stillness of the early morning. Before leaving, he'd covered the man with his sleeping blanket – he had shivered through breakfast and Geoff couldn't let him slip away before it was his time.

He'd waited for his mum to leave the house that morning before returning. He kept his bedroom door locked so she would presume he'd returned late the previous evening and was sleeping in. Not that she ever checked on him. He stayed in the house out of necessity alone. He couldn't afford to leave and she couldn't bring herself to make him. They barely spoke any more. She would prepare him his dinners and would do his laundry if he left it outside his room, but Geoff couldn't remember when they'd spent time in the house together, and was thankful for the fact.

He'd grabbed an extra hour of sleep before heading out in the van. In his planning, he'd read that keeping a routine was important in evading detection, and he'd managed to complete three jobs during the day. All simple removals, cash in hand, meaning he could now treat himself to a meal from a local pub in Uphill before Mass started.

The low-ceilinged bar was all but empty. A lone man with a flat cap and a walking stick sat reading a newspaper, a warm-looking pint of dark-red bitter untouched in front of him, while the young barman fed coins into the fruit machine. That was something Geoff had discovered about the pubs in Weston. Unless it was high season, they were nearly always deserted, except at the weekends. He'd always wondered how so many of the places survived, but there they were year after year, somehow getting by.

The barman stopped wasting his money and smiled at Geoff. 'How can I help you, sir?'

Sir. It wasn't often he was called that. The young man had a pleasant way about him. Geoff imagined, and hoped, that the desolate pub was merely a stepping stone for him and that in years to come he would escape the clutches of this dying town. 'You doing food?'

'Sure are,' said the barman, moving behind the protective solid wood panelling of the bar and handing him a menu.

Geoff ordered a steak and ale pie, with a cola to drink – he rarely drank alcohol after seeing what it had done to his dad – and took a seat at the other end of the bar from the old codger with his newspaper, keeping his head down as he waited for his food to arrive. The smell of stale beer from the carpet was familiar but unwelcome, and his thoughts returned to Steep Holm and his prisoner chained to the wall of the cave.

He needed to be strong, to fight the conflicting desires within him. It would be easy to finish it now, return to the island and put the man out of his misery, and that nagging doubt, which he thought had been banished, tried to convince him that this was exactly what he should do. But he had to ignore such negativity.

He had to save his father.

The pie wasn't a pie. It was a bowl of stale meat coated in a rich, salty sauce and covered by a lump of puff pastry. Still, it did the job. He washed it down with the cola, swiping the back of his hand across his mouth to cleanse it, and left the pub, thanking the barman. He'd parked the van in the car park. It was a two-mile walk to the church, but the vehicle was conspicuous and he couldn't risk it being spotted.

Winter was definitely coming. He'd felt it on the island – the ground frost hard beneath his tent in the morning, the air dropping close to freezing at night – and it chilled him now as he walked the back streets to St Michael's Church. He was concerned about his prisoner, though only in the sense that he needed him to survive for the next few days. He'd wanted him to stay in the cave for the duration but was worried it would soon be too cold and that he would have to move him to the visitor centre on the other side of the island.

The seasons affected Weston more than other towns, as if it were two very different places. Late spring through summer, the town seemed to double in size. The tourists would arrive from nowhere, like hermit crabs emerging from their shells, and take over everything, only to scurry back to their cities when the winter weather arrived. Geoff preferred the town like this, the quiet and desolation when Weston was returned to its residents.

By the time he reached the church gates the skin on his hands was numb from the cold. The sensation, although painful, was also enjoyable. He loved these nights, the darkness already descended and the air crisp but still. The scent of lit candles filled the air as he opened the old church doors. A familiar tremor ran through him as he stepped into the open space. His body hummed, as if accessing an invisible set of vibrations that enveloped the church. It took him back to his first memory of visiting a church, walking hand in hand with his father through the doors of St Bernadette's. He could have been no more than four at the time, but he remembered that feeling of shock and awe that had momentarily made him speechless, his mouth hanging open as if he were trying to catch something within it. All week his dad had been telling him about God's house, and there he was, standing within the place where God lived. Of course, he had only a rudimentary understanding of what that meant at the time, but he'd felt God's presence then as surely as he felt it now.

Like the pub, the church was empty. After genuflecting, the drip of holy water from the font at the entrance to the pews clinging to his forehead, he made his way to the front of the church.

As Geoff got older, his dad never understood why his son still wanted to go to church. 'After what happened. After what you did,' he would say. But his words were never accusatory and he'd never once tried to stop his son attending. Geoff understood his dad's confusion, and he wished he could have explained what the church meant to him, and that no one, not even the man they never discussed, could take that away.

Parishioners, all women, began shuffling into the empty pews. Geoff didn't recognise any of their faces – this wasn't his church and so he'd never been to a Mass here. None of the women looked younger than sixty, possibly seventy, which for an evening Mass was the norm. He presumed they were all widows and would light a candle for their dead spouse at some later point. It was sad in its way, but they would find some comfort from the act, so who was he to question them?

Five minutes later, the priest made his way to the altar. It wasn't a Sunday so there was none of the usual pageantry. No incense wafted from the golden chalice, no altar boys leading the procession around the church pews. During Geoff's first time as an altar boy, he and his friend Gregory hadn't realised they were supposed to follow the priest for a circuit of the church and had taken a seat at the altar while the priest had made his lone journey. Geoff had struggled with the giggles at that point, but the smile had faded when his dad reprimanded him afterwards.

This priest was as old as his parishioners. His movements were slow and measured, his bones creaking as he held the chalice of wine and blessed it.

Geoff let the old ladies take Communion first. It was rude not to, and he wanted to be the last to accept the offering. He knelt before the altar and held his tongue out as the priest mumbled, '*Corpus Christi.*'

'Amen,' said Geoff, blessing himself and returning to his seat.

Had the priest recognised him? He doubted it. They'd both changed so much in those years and Geoff had studiously avoided attending the same Mass as the old man until today. Yet hadn't there been a tremor to his hand as he'd placed the Communion wafer on his tongue?

Back at the pews, Geoff prayed. He asked for the strength to carry out what he had planned, to see things through to the end. He'd learnt as a boy that these were the most realistic things to pray for. God didn't grant wishes like a genie, but He could help you get things done.

Geoff continued kneeling, pretending to pray, when Mass ended. The little old ladies lit their candles and said their prayers, and Geoff was thankful that he would never be one of them. He sat up when the last of them left, alone in the coldness of the church. When Geoff was a boy, his local church was left open all the time – at least Dad had told him that; he'd never put it to the test – but as an adult he'd learnt that they always locked their doors at some point, which meant someone would have to ask him to leave.

The priest stuck his head out from the vestry twice before approaching. His footsteps echoed as he shuffled towards Geoff and leaned against his pew. 'I'm afraid I have to close the doors, my son. Is there anything I can help you with?'

The words were so kind and genuine that Geoff hesitated before answering. Again, he questioned himself, like a true doubting Thomas.

And then he remembered his quest.

'Yes, Father, I think we need to talk.'

Chapter Eight

Louise placed the receiver down and rubbed her eyes. This was the last thing she needed. Although she'd agreed to be an emergency contact, she wasn't Emily's parent. Paul couldn't keep doing this; it wasn't fair on anyone. Although the idea of being a mother one day still appealed to Louise, the possibility was fading with every passing year. Occasionally, she would fantasise about Emily moving in with her. They could live together in Weston. She could drop her at school in the morning, find a childminder to look after her until she returned home. They could start a new life together, free at last from the past. She pictured Emily sitting in her living room, content and happy. Then reality would dawn on her. She remembered the pictures hanging on her wall of Veronica Lloyd's dead body. Her lifestyle wasn't compatible with bringing up a young child.

Her parents' phones went straight to voicemail. They'd been better of late but, by default, their mobile phones were usually switched off. As her mother explained, there was no need to have them switched on if they didn't need to call anyone.

She stopped at Thomas's desk on her way out of the office and asked him to be present for the autopsy in her place.

'Everything okay?' he asked.

Louise nodded and left, not offering an explanation.

She was heading out of town, along the seafront, when her mother returned her call.

'Sorry, Louise, we were at the cinema,' she said, her voice tinny and distant on the car's speaker system.

'It's okay for some. Did you get the message from the school?'

'Yes. We're on our way now. Should be there in five minutes. Sorry you had to be called out.'

Louise sighed. 'Do you know where he is?'

'We'll talk about it later.'

She knew her mother didn't like talking about Paul in front of her father. He had less patience with her brother's antics and felt that nothing good would come of discussing it after the event. No doubt Paul had got drunk and somehow forgot he was supposed to be picking Emily up from school. As she hung up, she felt guilty for not continuing to Bristol. She reminded herself that Emily was not her responsibility, that Paul had caused her to miss the autopsy, but still she had to fight the urge to go and check on her niece.

She turned the car around and parked along the seafront, opposite the area where Veronica's body had been discovered. Thomas would already be on his way to the autopsy and she could trust him to see the job through properly.

The sky was darkening, her view obstructed by the fog rolling in from the distant sea. She left the car and made the short walk to the beach, receiving an odd look from a couple walking a pair of Labrador puppies, as if the fog-strewn shore were the last place on earth she should be visiting.

Fifty metres in and it was as if the beach had swallowed her up, the fog now so thick she could see only a few metres in any direction. She stumbled forwards, the sea a distant sound, until she thought she was close to where Veronica's body had been found. She turned around to face the clouded lights of the seafront. Had the killer experienced this same feeling of isolation when he or she had carried Veronica's body? And why leave her in such an exposed space?

In her experience, there were usually three reasons why a murderer would leave a victim in a very public place: one, due to a mistake, bad timing, that meant they'd had to flee the scene; two, because they were proud of their handiwork and wanted to show off; and three, because part of them, conscious or not, wanted to be stopped. Often, reasons two and three were interchangeable. Louise didn't think the killer had made a mistake and was convinced the positioning of the body was significant. But whether the killer was showing off or wanted to be caught, her major concern now was that they were not going to stop.

She fought the urge to start running as she headed back to the car, ignoring as best she could the childish fear of being lost in the fog. Nevertheless, it was a relief to be free of the shifting sand, and she let the car's heater warm her as she read a message from her mother to say Emily had been collected and Paul located at his house. Louise didn't need any help to deduce the true meaning of her mother's explanation that he'd been 'worse for wear'.

Her dad had asked her not to see Paul, to let him sleep off what must have been one hell of a hangover, and she'd reluctantly agreed. She called Thomas.

'Hi, Louise, everything okay?'

Louise didn't have any time for small talk. The office would already be awash with rumours about why she'd not been able to make the autopsy, why she'd had to rush back to Bristol after receiving a call from a school. 'Fine. How did the autopsy go?'

'Usual stuff. Lots of things I didn't want to see or smell,' said Thomas, making light of the ordeal.

'What were Dempsey's findings?'

'As he'd suspected on the beach. The bastard had put her through some awful shit before killing her. Multiple fractures to the

51

legs and shoulders. Both ankles were broken. It appears he tied her up and tortured her before taking her life. Dempsey found some fibres on the incisions to the wrists and ankles that are off to FIU.'

Louise closed her eyes, battling with the images in her mind. It was impossible to comprehend the motives that would drive someone to inflict such harm on another human being, whatever their age, but somehow Veronica's seniority made it that much harder for Louise to understand. The sequence of events suggested the kill had been planned and organised. Now they had to determine if Veronica was the intended target, or if the killing had been random. 'Cause of death?'

'As Dempsey thought. Something was driven into Veronica's right wrist. There are multiple incision marks, as if the killer was trying to find the right spot. It created quite a hole, a couple of centimetres in diameter. Eventually the killer sliced the radial artery and Veronica bled out. Dempsey is sure she was moved post-mortem.'

'So we don't even have a murder scene,' said Louise, sighing.

'I can go through the report with you tonight?' said Thomas.

Louise thought she'd heard something in his inflexion, as if her DS sounded hopeful about meeting her. 'Email it to me.'

'Everything?'

'Everything is fine, Thomas. Thank you,' said Louise, hanging up.

She didn't want to go back home just yet; the thought of her bungalow, resplendent with images of Veronica Lloyd's corpse on the wall, unappealing. She called one of her old colleagues, Tracey Pugh, and arranged to meet her in Clifton in Bristol. Tracey had been a DS on her team in the city and still worked in the same division as DCI Finch. She'd been promoted to DI when Louise left, effectively taking her position.

Tracey was already waiting for her in the bar they had agreed on, a large glass of Prosecco in her hand. 'Hey, boss, great to see you,' she said, getting to her feet and giving Louise a hug.

Momentarily overwhelmed by the odour of nicotine and perfume on Tracey's neck, Louise hugged her back. She was surprised how good it was to see her. When she'd left Bristol, she'd decided to cut herself off as much as possible. Tracey had been the only person she'd kept in contact with, and even then she'd kept that to a minimum. It had been a coping strategy, but Tracey's welcome made her wonder if she'd made a mistake.

'What you having?' said Tracey.

'Just a small one. I'm driving.'

Tracey smiled, and ordered her a glass of white wine. She was in her fifties, a loud, confident woman, her hair an unruly sweep of curled black hair. She'd received the unfortunate nickname 'the hairdresser' in the office, not because of her hair, but due to the stereotype, among the men at least, that Tracey was a hairdresser's name. Not that anyone would call her that to her face. Tracey was a force that couldn't be tamed and was not to be messed with. Tracey had been her confidante at Bristol, and there weren't many people alive who Louise trusted more.

'So how's Weston-super-Mud?' asked Tracey as they took a seat in a small booth to the rear of the bar. Unlike Louise, whose accent was faint to the point of being almost non-existent, Tracey's was full Bristolian. She dropped the consonants at the end of words as a matter of course, and occasionally Louise found herself straining to understand what she was saying.

'Same as ever. You've heard about the body, though?'

'Of course. Your news has reached us. I was going to call you about that. Sounds like a horror show.'

Louise wanted to unburden herself, tell Tracey all about the late-night text messages from Finch, the sorry state her brother had got himself into, and her poor niece, but didn't know where to begin, so she stuck to work. 'Veronica Lloyd's body was left on the beach – the killer did a number on her beforehand. Looks possibly like torture,' said Louise, lowering her voice.

Tracey shook her head. She didn't need to say any more. They'd both reached the stage of their careers where they understood the world was full of sick bastards, and there was very little left that could shock them. 'Anyone in line?'

'No family. Some friends in the tennis club,' said Louise.

'You think it's a random?'

Louise sipped her wine, the drink overly sweet and lukewarm, and thought about the question some more. She felt guilty for being in the bar when she could be back in Weston, doing more work. 'No, I don't think it was random,' she said, glad to give voice to her thoughts. After reading Thomas's report on her phone before joining Tracey at the bar, she'd decided there was something personal, almost intimate, in the way the killer had interacted with Veronica before taking her life. The wounds were specific, to the wrist and ankles in particular, and in her experience, random attacks were more chaotic than that.

'I'm not sure if that's a good thing or not,' said Tracey, her voice loud enough to attract some unwanted attention from their fellow drinkers.

'It depends on the killer's motive,' said Louise, trying to lower the sound of their conversation again. 'If it was isolated, then fine, but . . .'

'You think they might strike again?' said Tracey, unable to contain the excitement in her voice.

Louise forced a second swig of the wine down, the taste improving slightly. 'It did cross my mind. The kill was reasonably efficient and they managed to dump the body at the beach undetected. If the killer gets a taste for it, then this might not be the last.'

'This is why I love meeting you, Lou. You're always cheering me up,' said Tracey, the sarcasm hidden behind her deadpan delivery. 'Another?'

'I'll get these,' said Louise.

She returned with a Prosecco for Tracey and a glass of sparkling water for herself. 'Enough shop-talk. What's going on with you at the moment?'

'You know me, Lou, fun-loving and free. Though . . .'

Louise sipped at her water, smiling as she waited for Tracey to reveal some salacious gossip. 'Yes?'

'I may have taken one of the new batch of PCs under my wing, if you know what I mean.'

Louise's expression said she knew exactly what Tracey meant. 'How old?'

'Late twenties,' said Tracey, with a look Louise could only describe as enigmatic.

'Serious?'

'Well, you know I don't do great with serious. It's very casual at the moment, but he seems a nice guy.'

Louise felt Tracey was doing herself a disservice. There was nothing her ex-colleague would have liked better than finding someone to settle down with, but she didn't always make the best choices.

'What about you?' said Tracey. 'Any hot blood in Weston?'

'You have been to Weston, Tracey?'

'There's a few lookers down there, I'm sure. Who've you got your eye on?'

It came as no surprise to Louise that her thoughts automatically turned to Thomas. She'd felt an immediate attraction to him on her first day at the station that hadn't faded with time. But the little issue of his wife and three-year-old meant she would never act on it. 'Nope, no one of interest at the moment.'

'What are you hiding, lady?'

Louise shrugged. 'Nothing. The last thing I need at the moment is—'

'Do not finish that sentence until I'm back from the bar,' said Tracey, downing the rest of her Prosecco in one gulp. 'One for the road. Sure you don't want anything stronger?'

Louise shook her head, marvelling at Tracey's alcohol consumption. As she watched her walk unsteadily to the bar, she wondered why it was only in hindsight that she remembered what fun it could be to spend some time with her friends. She'd met up with Tracey on a handful of occasions since leaving for Weston, and being here, she didn't understand why they hadn't met up more. They lived only about twenty miles apart, yet that distance between their worlds often felt like an unbreachable gulf.

'Before I forget, Tim Finch was asking after you today,' said Tracey, returning.

'Oh?' said Louise, trying not to sound downbeat as her heart pumped furiously.

Although Tracey had never taken sides on the Walton case, she'd always offered Louise her full support. But she had to work with Finch, and Louise was reluctant to involve her any more than necessary.

'He was trying to sound casual, asking about your case, but I could tell he was just interested in you.'

Louise nodded but didn't respond, her thoughts still on the text message she was sure he'd sent last night.

Tracey didn't seem to notice. 'You ever hear from him?'

Louise laughed. 'Let's talk about something else, shall we?'

Tracey looked crestfallen. 'Sorry, Lou, I didn't mean to upset you.'

'No, no, you haven't. I'm just beat. You know how it is. SIO on this sort of case.'

'Of course. Let's forget about work while I finish this, and then I'll walk you to your car.'

They embraced in the car park, the awkwardness over Finch having vanished.

'It was great seeing you again, Tracey. You sure you don't need a lift back?'

'No, I'll get the bus,' said Tracey, slurring a little. 'Might make a quick call to my young PC first.'

Louise chuckled. 'You be safe. We need to do this more often.'

'I agree. I might pop down to the seaside soon, if you'll have me?'

'I'd love to. See you soon.'

'See you soon, beautiful,' shouted Tracey as Louise pulled away in the car.

It was a shame Tracey had mentioned Finch. Now it was all she could think of as she made her way back to Weston. Was there no escape from him? She'd hoped that her transfer to Weston would have been the last of it. He'd won the battle, forced her out of his life, so why was he still hounding her? In her anger, her foot pressed down hard on the accelerator as she made decent time along the deserted M5. As she took the exit into Worle, she slowed down and tried to organise her thoughts. There were so many distractions in her life at present. Aside from Finch, she had to deal with her messed-up brother and make sure he was properly parenting her young niece, all the while trying to keep focus on the Veronica Lloyd case. She owed it to the woman. Veronica was the victim of a horrendous crime, one that had robbed her of her dignity so late in her life. Of course she wasn't going to turn her back on Emily. She would be there for her, and her parents and brother, when needed, but for now, everything had to be about Veronica.

Back inside her bungalow, she made some milky tea and sipped it while staring at her home-made murder board. Every now and then she checked her phone for her nightly message from Finch, but it never arrived.

Chapter Nine

Up close, the priest looked frailer than Geoff expected. It shouldn't have surprised him – he'd been a boy when he'd last been face to face with the man – but the change in his appearance was unnerving. His skin was a greyish colour and seemed devoid of elasticity. It flaked over his bones, sagging in sheets from his neck. His eyes were a similar colour, the faded whiteness pitted with tiny streaks of red. The nagging feeling returned to Geoff's stomach and once again he doubted himself. He remembered the priest's crimes as he tried to convince himself he was worthy of his vengeance. 'Do you remember me, Father?' he asked, his voice echoing in the empty church.

The priest studied Geoff, his head unsteady as he tried to recall where he'd seen the man before. Geoff doubted anything in his features would remind the priest of the boy he'd once been. In puberty, his face and body had transformed him into something different. His nose, like his limbs, had elongated. His face was stretched and gaunt, his skull covered by the thinnest of coverings, his hair snaking behind towards his shoulders. The only clue would be his gloved hands, hiding his disfigured skin.

Shaking his head, the priest said with a smile, 'I'm sorry, son, my memory is not what it once was. So many people, you understand. I can hardly recall what I had for my breakfast.'

The priest still had a way about him. A rich Irish brogue to his voice despite his age. The feeling in Geoff's stomach intensified at the kind words.

'What is your name, son?'

'That doesn't matter, Father.' Geoff hesitated, knowing this was the defining moment. He glanced at the crucifix high above the altar, the white Jesus hanging in perpetual agony, and recalled what he'd seen all those years ago. How he'd gone to this priest for help and how he'd been pushed away. Decision made, Geoff acted. 'I know it's late, Father, but I need to go to confession.'

The priest blinked, his eyes widening as if he'd just recognised the man before him. 'Of course. Here, or would you like the privacy of the confessional?'

Geoff stood up. 'I'll follow you.'

The priest pushed himself to his feet using a creaking wooden pew for leverage. Geoff reached out to help him, the pair of them genuflecting in front of the crucifix like two old maids.

It was a long, slow walk, the priest shuffling his feet as if trying to hold back time. It reminded Geoff of the times he'd visited St Bernadette's with his dad, when they'd walked the Stations of the Cross together. He must have only been four or five when he'd been allowed to watch a mini-series on television about Jesus's life. He hadn't understood much of it at the time, but the show had caught his attention like no other.

His dad could often be stern, but when it came to the programme he indulged Geoff, keeping his patience as Geoff asked question after question. In particular, Geoff was fascinated by the Crucifixion scenes. He'd quizzed his dad as to why Jesus was carrying the cross, why the crown of thorns was placed on to his head, and why the guards were whipping him as he struggled to carry his burden. When it came to the Crucifixion itself, his mother had tried to stop him watching, but his dad insisted he be allowed to, despite his tender age. He explained how Jesus was saving everyone's souls by being crucified, and although Geoff winced as the nails were hammered into Jesus's flesh, as if the wounds were happening to him, he marvelled at the miracle. He cried as Jesus hung on the cross, and in one of the very few times he could remember, his dad hugged him.

A week after the show ended, his dad took him to St Bernadette's Church again, and together they walked the interior of the church as his dad showed him the Stations of the Cross, making comparisons with the television series. There was Jesus falling for the first time; there was Jesus seeing his mother, Mary; there was Simon of Cyrene helping to carry the cross.

They made the pilgrimage around the church at least once a month together, Geoff experiencing something new each time. As he grew older, Geoff understood the meanings of the stations more. His favourite image was always when Jesus was nailed to the cross. At first the sight had brought back the tears, but he grew to understand the sacrifice Jesus was making for all mankind and to him it became a beautiful vision.

He would have shared his memories with the elderly priest, but Geoff didn't think he would understand. When they reached the confessional, the priest gestured for Geoff to enter. The confessional was divided in two compartments, so priest and parishioner were separated from one another. When Geoff had made his First Confession as a child, he'd been in the same room as his parish priest. He recalled his embarrassment at listing his sins – lying, cheating, being rude to his parents, not going to church on a Sunday – and the sense of relief once it ended, and the feeling of lightness as he said his penance. One Hail Mary, one Our Father, and his sins were lifted, erased from his soul.

He stopped going to confession soon after. The rules were plain, simple enough that a child could understand them. You had to confess every sin or you were not truly forgiven. Sure, you could bundle them together, like all the lies he told, but some sins were so important they had to be stated specifically; and some of Geoff's sins even at that tender age couldn't be shared, in the confessional or anywhere else.

The priest gestured that he should enter through the door on his left side, but Geoff waited for the priest to enter on the right side, before following him in.

It surprised Geoff how much simpler it was this time. The old priest had less fight in him than Mrs Lloyd but it was something more than that. Geoff didn't hesitate as he tied the priest to the chair, despite their location. Each time doubt troubled him, he reminded himself why he was there, why the priest had to suffer, and that made everything easier. Even when he showed the priest the nail and the hammer, and the old man started crying and babbling in Latin, he didn't waver.

Afterwards he sat in the pew studying the Crucifixion, the angle of Christ's limbs and the points where they joined the wooden cross. He should have fled the scene – at any moment someone could walk through the door and see what he'd done – but it was peaceful being alone in the church. He considered falling on to his knees and repeating his penance from his First Confession all those years ago, but he wasn't sorry for what he'd done, so he knew it wouldn't count. Instead, he stared at the various wounds on the Christ figure and the crown of thorns that bit into his scalp.

He was uninterrupted on his walk back to his van and still had a few hours before the tide would be high enough for him to journey back to the island. He couldn't return to the same pub where he'd had dinner so he drove into town.

The bright lights guided him along the seafront, the grand pier stretching into the wasteland of mud towards the incoming sea. He pulled up outside the Smiths Hotel, the rush of sea air as he left his vehicle sending him back to long summer evenings as a child sitting in the beer garden with his parents and relatives, sipping Coca-Cola in a glass bottle. He hadn't appreciated those times then but missed them once they'd been taken away.

He walked inland to a bar he knew would be busy this time of evening. It wasn't somewhere he wanted to be, but his research told him it was good to be seen on a night like this. Loud music greeted him as he entered the bar, the chimes and squeaking lyrics discordant to his ears. A young barmaid looked him up and down as he ordered a lager shandy, as if he didn't have the means to pay for his drink. 'And some dry-roasted peanuts,' he said, when she returned with it.

'All right, love,' she said, not once breaking eye contact with him.

He took his drink to the corner of the bar. He tried to blend in, but he was the only person alone. Everyone ignored him, but he was sure he was the topic of their conversations. Each time someone laughed, he felt it was aimed at him. *If they knew what I've just done, they wouldn't be laughing*, he thought as he drank his over-sweet drink.

'Simmo!'

Geoff lowered his eyes as the cry rang out across the bar, causing some of the banter to stall momentarily. The source of the shout waved over at him, and Geoff had no option but to make the painful walk through the bustling bodies to the other side of the bar.

'Malc,' he said to the smiling man who'd beckoned him over.

Malcolm Harris had been in the same year at secondary school. He'd always been loud, in and out of class. He smiled at Geoff now, as if he were pleased to see him, but he'd never paid him any attention at school. 'Look at you,' he said, looking him up and down, just like the barmaid had.

Geoff didn't know what to say so he just smiled. Malcolm was with three friends he didn't recognise. The four of them were wearing the same get-up – dark jeans and crisp designer shirts – and Geoff felt out of place in the tatty clothes he'd changed into after the church.

'It's great to see you, man,' said Malcolm.

'And you.'

'Just finished work?' he asked, nodding towards Geoff's overall. Geoff had never met anyone who grinned as much as Malcolm. It was as if his face was stuck that way. There was no humour in the gesture. Geoff understood the man was smiling at him, not with him. At school, Malcolm had never spoken to him except to make some crass comment about his hands.

'Yes,' said Geoff, trying not to stare down at his gloves.

'What you up to now?' said Malcolm, grinning as he glanced at his friends.

'Removals.'

'Removals, hey? Good for you, mate. Good money in that?'

Now Geoff knew he was being ridiculed. Malcolm was still smiling, but his eyes lacked any warmth. In primary school, Geoff had once made the mistake of telling his dad about a bully at school. A boy in the Junior Two class, John Maynard, had been taking some of his lunch every day and he hadn't known what to do. Geoff's right hand unconsciously touched his left wrist as he recalled his dad grabbing him there and pulling him close. Geoff had flinched, not so much from the firmness of his grip but from the sourness of his dad's breath. He couldn't look away from his dad's eyes, from the sadness and rage emanating from them. As his dad pulled off his belt to teach Geoff the lesson he needed to learn, he'd told him that no son of his would ever be bullied again.

Geoff's revenge on Maynard had been short and swift. As he'd been bending down at a water fountain, Geoff had pushed his head forwards, at first tentatively but then with enough force that Maynard smashed two of his front teeth against the metal urn. No one in the school ate his lunch again, but the bullying didn't really end. It changed to something else he didn't understand, then or now. The strange glances, the whispered name-calling. He thought attacking the bully Maynard would have made him a hero, but it had only made him more of a victim.

'Get you a drink, Geoff? You look like you need one,' said Malcolm, receiving some muted laughs from his friends.

'I need to go.'

For the first time since he'd walked over, Malcolm scowled. 'I offered you a drink,' he said.

Geoff looked at Malcolm's friends, who'd all stopped smiling, like their leader. Geoff wanted to leave the bar and return to the safety of the van. He'd seen Malcolm start fights before and didn't want to offend him. He'd cleaned up after the church, but the priest's DNA would still be on him. 'Okay, I'll have a drink,' he said.

Malcolm stared at him, stone-faced, before breaking into a malicious grin. 'Simmo,' he shouted, slapping Geoff on his back, his friends relaxing.

Geoff managed to escape just before eleven. By this stage, Malcolm and his cronies had lost interest in him. They'd already managed to upset two groups of men and were now chatting to some women as drunk as they were. Geoff went to the toilet, before slipping out of the bar.

The air outside made him nauseous. Malcolm had plied him with shots of dizzying colours that all tasted the same, and his stomach was rebelling. He found a side street and vomited, intrigued by the luminous shades he expelled on to the pavement.

He would have to retrieve the vehicle. He had to return to the island. Leaving the van on the front would result in a parking ticket, and he shuddered to think what would happen if someone looked inside at the evidence he'd yet to dispose of. In the driver's seat, he forced down a kebab with the aid of bottled water. His head thumped and he could think of nothing he'd like more at that moment than going to sleep. He could go back to his mother's but that would mean another day without seeing his prisoner and he wasn't sure the man would survive without him.

The pubs were kicking out, people spilling on to the seafront in packs, heading for the nightclubs or home. Geoff glanced at them through the tinted windows of his van, oblivious to their motivations. He'd drunk more tonight than he'd ever done, and couldn't see the attraction. There was something pathetic in the way the drunken meandered on their way, arm in arm, shouting and singing. It wasn't the way they would behave in the daytime, so why did they think it was acceptable now?

Once the crowds had dispersed, and the lights from the seafront bars and restaurants had dimmed, Geoff set off in the van. He was careful to keep close to the speed limit as he exited the seafront at Knightstone and up the hill towards Birnbeck pier. He was pleased when his usual parking spot was free, finding it difficult to concentrate with the noise reverberating in his head.

The alcohol continued to affect him. He struggled to control his heavy limbs as he strolled towards the old pier, the dark scenery flicking in and out of his vision as the cold wind billowed around his face. He stopped more than once, convinced he was being followed. Had Malcolm seen him leave the bar? He wanted to be sick again but only managed to dry-retch into the bushes before climbing over the wall to the fenced-off entry of the derelict pier.

Even as a child, the old pier had only occasionally been open. He'd been taken there a couple of times and everything about it, even then, had felt antiquated in comparison to the gleaming shininess of its sister pier, the grand pier in the centre. He'd been scared walking the loose boards of the old pier itself, and he'd been disappointed with the arcade machines on offer – mainly ancient penny machines that didn't work.

Now it was simply dangerous to step on to the derelict structure. He shone his torch on the wooden boards as he made slow and uneasy progress across the walkway, clinging tight to the rusted sides as he avoided the loose boards and the gaps where the panels no longer existed. Through the holes, he heard the sound of water spilling in towards the shore.

He'd never been more pleased to reach the relative safety of the end of the pier. He sat on the concrete and closed his eyes, willing the dizziness to fade. In all the drama of the last few hours, he'd somehow forgotten about the priest at St Michael's Church. Had his body been discovered yet? Had they started making some sort of connection between the victims? He couldn't focus on that now. He located his boat, which was moored at the pier, and dragged it to the end of the slip, almost losing his footing as he eased down the slick runway into the sea.

The sound of the small outboard motor roared in the silence of the night and Geoff headed off into the darkness, guiding himself by the lights of the retreating town and the vague silhouette of Steep Holm protruding from the water in the distance.

Chapter Ten

For the first time, Louise ordered food with her morning coffee at the Kalimera. Sleep had been slow to arrive, her mind racing with worries about Emily and Paul, how her parents were coping, and of course Finch. It was absurd, but the lack of a text message troubled her. After hearing from Tracey that Finch had been asking after her, she was confused as to why he hadn't texted. It wasn't as if he'd sent her a message every night since she'd left for Weston, but the omission last night felt strategic.

As usual, the owner looked at her as if they'd never met, only to surprise her by starting a conversation. Perhaps it was because Louise had ordered eggs on toast. 'Your friend not joining you?' she asked, clearly meaning Thomas.

It was the most she'd ever heard from the woman. 'Not today,' she said.

'Attractive man,' said the owner, grinning as she ground the beans for Louise's Americano.

'Work colleague,' said Louise, amused by the woman's statement.

The owner laughed as she placed the coffee on the counter. 'If you say so,' she said.

Louise took her usual seat, looking out across the road towards the sea. Somewhere, the sun was rising, the darkness of the morning fading to grey. It was mornings like this – the desolation of early winter, the coldness exacerbated by the chill of the sea air – that made her miss Bristol. It was like two completely different towns sharing the same geography. There was the summer Weston of her childhood, sunny and swarming with day tourists, and this, its ghost-town doppelgänger. *How do people live like this?* she thought, before remembering she was now one of them and that this was her second winter in the town.

The owner placed her breakfast on the table. Louise cut into the eggs, ravenous, and finished the meal within minutes, surprised by her hunger.

Two hours later, Louise was at Uphill Marina. Following the morning's briefing, the desk sergeant had told her about an altercation in the station the previous evening when one of Veronica's tennis friends, Estelle Ferguson, had demanded to speak to someone in charge.

Louise parked up next to a number of glamorous-looking cars and made her way to the marina. Estelle had told the desk sergeant that she would be working on her boat that morning. Louise identified a likely figure standing on the deck of a small white craft, smoking a cigarette.

'Estelle Ferguson?' she asked, approaching the boat.

The woman took a long drag before replying, the gesture ageing her as a patchwork of wrinkles broke out on her face. Beneath a long designer raincoat she was wearing training gear. Her face was flushed, as if she'd just stopped exercising. 'Yes,' she said, as if annoyed by the question.

'DI Blackwell.' She showed the woman her ID. 'I'm following up your visit to the station yesterday evening.'

Estelle's expression shifted. 'Good, at last. Are you in charge of this investigation? No one last night would tell me what the hell is going on.'

'I understand you were a friend of Veronica Lloyd.'

The woman scowled. 'Of course I was. Why else would I have gone to your station? I was extremely disappointed not to have been notified about Veronica's death. Instead I had to hear it from the chair of the tennis club this morning.'

'Can we go somewhere to speak about it?'

Estelle lit another cigarette and took a drag before replying. Louise wouldn't usually let such rudeness slide but she knew that grief affected people in different ways and she was willing to be patient for the time being.

'I'll join you,' said Estelle. 'You don't have the correct shoes for the boat.' The woman sprung from the deck on to the jetty. She was surprisingly agile for her years, cigarette still in hand. 'Why wasn't I told?' she said, invading Louise's space with the smoke from her cigarette. 'Imagine finding out that way. A body found on the beach and I'm told by the bloody chairman.'

Louise kept her footing, ignoring the smoke lingering in the frosty air. 'You were close?' she asked, choosing not to engage Estelle in an argument.

'Yes, we were bloody close. We played tennis together three times a week.'

'Listen, Mrs Ferguson, I appreciate you are upset, but you were one of many contact numbers on Veronica's phone. There were no direct messages from you or from Veronica to you. That's why you weren't personally contacted by the police.'

Estelle frowned, her tone softening. 'Well, Veronica didn't like using the phone that much.' The woman's initial abruptness had faded, the hand grasping her cigarette trembling a little. She leaned back against one of the cars parked on the road, a white Mercedes convertible, the colour draining from her face as she took another fierce drag on the cigarette. 'I told her to move out of there,' she said eventually, a hint of tears in her eyes.

'There?'

'That bloody place. The housing estate where she lived.'

'And where would she have moved to?'

'Near me. Somewhere safe.'

Although Veronica's estate wasn't the most salubrious place in town, there were worse places in Weston. 'What makes you think it isn't safe?' asked Louise, thinking about the heroin kit she'd discovered in Veronica's room.

'You only have to look at the place,' said Estelle, her face full of disgust.

Louise ignored the comment. 'You may be able to help us, Mrs Ferguson. Do you know if Veronica had any close family or friends?'

Estelle frowned and took a step back as if suspicious of the question. 'She was her mother's carer until five years ago. She was Veronica's last close relative, and when she died, I suggested she move away from here, nearer to us.'

'Us?'

The woman stood straight, frowning as if she'd spoken too much and wanted to take back her words. 'A few of us at the tennis club live close to here. It's a quiet, peaceful place. None of the trouble that goes on elsewhere.'

'Why didn't Veronica take you up on the offer? Cost?'

'Perhaps, although I think she could have afforded it. She bought her house off the council in the eighties and even those places are worth something nowadays, and I imagine she had a decent enough pension.'

Louise struggled to hide her disdain while wondering if Veronica's money had been lost to her habit. 'Maybe it wasn't the right crowd for her.'

'Who would want to do this to Veronica?'

'I was hoping you could answer that for me.'

'How the hell would I know?'

'Did Veronica have any enemies, any grievances we should know about?'

'Veronica?' Estelle paused, and looked towards the dirty-brown water where the boats bobbed. 'She could be a bit of a handful. Very forthright. It was the teacher in her. She could rub some people up the wrong way.'

'Anything specific?' asked Louise.

Estelle finished her cigarette and carelessly ground it into the ground with her tennis shoe. 'There was an incident with one of the tennis coaches.'

'An incident?'

'Some of us were not happy with the lack of time he was spending at the club.'

'And?'

'And Veronica and I made a formal complaint. Some of these coaches think they can come and go, work when they like. We needed someone committed to the club, someone willing to help out.'

'What was the name of the coach?'

'Matt Lambert.'

'He's still at the club?'

'Unfortunately, yes.'

'So he's employed by the club?'

'No, self-employed.'

'Let me get this straight,' said Louise slowly. 'You tried to get the coach sacked because he wasn't at the club enough, yet no one would be paying him for the extra time?'

'You don't quite understand.'

'I think I do. You think this coach would feel so aggrieved as to brutally murder Veronica and leave her body on the beach?'

'How the hell would I know?'

The interview was going nowhere fast. Louise didn't like to pigeonhole people on first impressions, but she could see Estelle was a spoilt, privileged lady used to getting her own way. It saddened her to think that Veronica might have been the same, not that it made the hunt for the killer any less urgent.

'One last thing. Did you know of any complications in Veronica's life?'

'Complications?'

'Drinking problem, addictions, that sort of thing.'

Estelle looked shocked. 'No, no. Veronica enjoyed the occasional glass of wine, but nothing stronger. She was a very sensible woman.'

It appeared Estelle didn't know her friend as well as she thought. That, or she was lying.

Chapter Eleven

From a Thermos flask, Geoff poured coffee into a steel mug. He sat in the camping chair surveying his kingdom in the early-morning light. Save for the man chained to the interior of the cave, he was the only person on the island of Steep Holm, and the place felt like his home. The island was only six miles from the mainland, but he could have been in the middle of nowhere. The solitude was something he'd been striving for his entire life. He'd been here as a child, making the occasional journey with his dad, who'd captained the small ferry from the mainland, but only now had he come to fully appreciate the true beauty of the island. It would be his perfect place to live. He could walk around the whole place in less than an hour yet it felt like his own little country.

The ferry still ran. In the summer months it would transport a handful of tourists every few weeks, trapping them on the island for twelve hours until the tide returned. But for now, it was all his.

Geoff enjoyed solitude, even if, in part, it had been forced on him from an early age. It wasn't just the Maynard incident. His classmates had always treated him differently, even before he'd broken the bully's teeth. He was always separate from them, unable to join in their silly break-time activities. Although, like him, most of them went to church every Sunday, they never wanted to be there. He would watch as they entered the church – he was always there first with his dad at the front of the pews – and he never saw the sense of wonder that he felt on their faces as they stepped through the church doors. Geoff took it seriously, but they were there mainly through coercion. He pitied them for that, and maybe that was why they resented him.

It only became worse as he'd grown older. When he tried to be part of the crowd – going to the arcades or the beach after school, trying to join in the lunchtime games of football, and latterly the teenage forays on to the pier, and, when night came, beneath it – he was tolerated but never accepted, as if they didn't want him around but were too scared to tell him.

He threw the remains of the coffee on to the hard ground and inhaled the still air. Biting his thumbnail, he turned his attention to his companion. 'How did you sleep?' he asked, after battling his way through the bushes to the cave and removing the man's gag.

'Why are you doing this?' said his prisoner immediately. His complexion was now as grey as the rock of his shelter.

'Sit up,' said Geoff, dragging him upright.

'At least have some decency,' said the man, his voice coarse and gruff. 'I'm sitting in my own waste.'

Geoff grimaced. It wasn't something he'd planned for. From his pocket he took out a hunting knife, the rippled metal more for show than use but enough for the man to cower. 'I am going to undo your ties. Let you stretch. Remember, you are weak, and if you try anything, I will not hesitate to use this.'

The man trying to run didn't bother Geoff. He was too old to get far and his shouts would be snuffed out by the solitude of the island. He was more concerned about using force before it was necessary. He didn't want the man to fade before it was his time.

Geoff dragged the man through the branches. He cut his arm as he caught it against a particularly stubborn vine. 'Sit there,' he said, pointing to a patch of ground next to his camping chair.

He poured the man coffee and offered him the remains of his breakfast, which he picked at as if it were poison. Geoff spread the man's sleeping bag out on to the ground, recoiling from the smell. The man's clothes were sodden, but he didn't have any replacements. 'If you behave yourself, I'll get you more clothes tonight when I return.'

'Why are you doing this?' repeated the man, as if his words were caught in some eternal loop in his mind.

Geoff closed his eyes, the play of the seagulls filling his senses as he tried to drive down his anger. 'You know who I am. What you did to me.'

The man looked at him with genuine confusion. 'That was so many years ago now. I can see how it hurt you, damaged you more than we could ever have anticipated, and I'm sorry for that. Your mother is too.'

Geoff sprung to his feet, the knife in his hand, and charged at the man. 'Don't,' he began, his words increasing in sound and vehemence, 'ever speak of my mother.'

To his credit, the man held his ground. He remained on his chair, his eyes matching Geoff's gaze. 'I'm sorry,' he said. 'Sorry that we did this to you.'

Geoff squinted, sunlight glinting off the blade of his knife. 'We?'

'You know what I mean, Geoff. People should have looked after you better. And everything that happened afterwards – the accident – that was you as well?'

Geoff understood the insinuation but pleaded ignorance. 'Finish that up and you can get back inside.'

'I'm sorry, Geoff, I really am. Can I stay here for a while? I presume we're alone on the island?'

'You are alone, yes. But I'm afraid I have work to do.' The man whimpered as Geoff tied his hands and pushed him towards the cave, where he chained and gagged him again. He returned minutes later and threw his own sleeping bag over the man, deciding he would burn the other one. 'I'll check in on you before I leave tonight.'

Geoff took his time walking to the visitor centre in the middle of the island. The island itself was only a half-mile long and Geoff liked to savour these moments. It would be dark before the tide was high enough by the old pier for him to make his return journey. He scanned the building before approaching. Although the ferry didn't run during the autumn and winter months, there was a possibility that a lone boat could navigate the journey.

Satisfied he was alone, he walked over to the centre. From his pocket, he took a key to one of the working sheds and opened the door to reveal his partially finished creation. He ran his hand across one part of the object, pleased with the feel of the smooth surface against his scarred skin. It almost seemed a waste to join it together. But given its intended purpose, that would be glorious.

He busied away until lunch, securing the joins where the sections would interlock. Although he wanted to fix the sections together, he would have to wait until nearer the time to complete the object.

For lunch, he ate a limp cheese sandwich, nearly twenty-four hours old, with bottled water. Lethargy crept over him after eating and he spent another hour working on the object before locking up. Dark clouds were rolling in over the horizon. They loomed like mountains and he feared it would be too dangerous to return to the mainland later.

Back at the camp, he checked on the man, allowing him some sips of water. He needed to let him exercise at some point or he would lose all his strength. Geoff had already noticed the difference in him, the weight loss in his face, the greyish patches of skin and the faraway look in his yellowing eyes. He didn't protest this time as Geoff took the water from him. The time would come soon when Geoff would have to move his prisoner to the warmth of the visitor centre. The place was sheltered, with electricity and hot running water. He'd avoided keeping him there on the off chance that someone made an impromptu visit to the island, but the old man wouldn't be able to go on like this for much longer.

Geoff tried to get some sleep in the tent, but his mind was busy. The next part would be the hardest, and he should really return to the mainland now. He'd already made mistakes and couldn't leave anything to chance. He changed into his wet-weather clothes, urinating in a bush near to where the old man was being held, before setting off to his boat.

He reached the top of the stone steps leading to the pebble beach where his boat was moored before throwing himself to the ground at the sight of a dazzling light. His heart hammered in his chest as he peered over the cliff edge. It was what he'd feared, what he'd really been unable to properly prepare against.

Two canoeists were circling the area close to shore. The light he'd caught came from the high-powered torches on their respective helmets. They were weaving in and out, still a hundred or so metres from shore, and appeared to be talking to one another. Geoff could only hope they weren't preparing to approach the island.

Chapter Twelve

The call came in as Louise left the marina. A second body had been found, at St Michael's Church in Uphill, less than a mile from her current location. Disturbed by the proximity and with half a mind to go back and check on Estelle Ferguson, she set off.

A small group of emergency services personnel had formed at the church, a skeleton crew of paramedics and two uniformed police officers. Louise recognised the disgruntled officer, Hughes, from the beach.

'Where?'

'Inside, ma'am. In the confession-box thing.'

'You seen the body?'

'I was the first on the scene, ma'am. I didn't need to take a pulse to tell he was dead. I haven't let anyone else in, not even the paramedics.'

'Good work, Hughes,' said Louise, receiving a surprised look from the PC.

From the back of her car, Louise took out the SOCO uniform she always carried with her. She dressed in a hurry, trying to control the adrenalin in her system. More police vehicles arrived as she made the walk across the stone pathway to the church. She pulled at the heavy wooden door, keen to see the body before the SOCOs arrived and took over. St Michael's was worthy of a picture postcard; the lone village church had barely changed in the last hundred years. Like St Bernadette's, the church was Catholic, and already she was wondering if the connection was significant.

She walked across the polished wooden floorboards and glanced up at the stained-glass windows depicting pictures of saints and angels. A draught billowed through the high-ceilinged room and Louise imagined there was always a chill to the place. She pictured a group of shivering parishioners in the winter months, huddled together as they listened to the week's sermon.

As she approached the confessional, the smell of the body reached her. Although less pungent, the odour reminded her of those first moments at Max Walton's farm. There, decay had emanated from every centimetre of the derelict building, but here it was isolated. Louise paused before edging forwards.

The door of the confessional was open, Hughes having placed police tape across the threshold. Louise prepared herself as she peered through the opening, holding her breath as she stuck her head beneath the plastic tape.

An elderly man, a priest by the look of his dog collar, was pushed up against one corner of the small space. Louise understood why Hughes hadn't checked the man's pulse. His lifeless eyes stared back at her, wide open, as if still in shock at what had happened to him, every part of him draped in blood.

Louise stepped back. Even though she was wearing her protective uniform, she didn't want to take the chance of contaminating the crime scene. It was too coincidental for this to be anything other than the handiwork of Veronica Lloyd's killer. Beneath his blanket of blood, Louise could see the bind marks around the priest's ankles and wrists. His left hand was in pieces, the hole in his wrist having gone straight through to the other side.

As the SOCOs arrived, Louise could only hope that the killer had slipped up this time. They hadn't moved the body so the team had an effective crime scene to work with. She had to determine if the killer had left the body here on purpose, or if he or she had been forced to change their plans.

DCI Robertson was waiting outside. Louise sensed the tension in the growing number of uniformed officers at the scene. Robertson had a way of instilling a respectful fear in his officers. He called her over and began walking to the cemetery at the rear of the church.

'Louise,' he said, his gruff accent making her name sound like an accusation.

'Sir.'

They stopped by a dilapidated grave. A slab of grey concrete grew from the overgrown grass at a lopsided angle. Louise read: *Elizabeth Bailey, beloved Mother of Robert and Mary. Died 1932. Age 58.*

'Same killer?' asked Robertson, ignoring the tombstone.

'There's little doubt. There is a deep wound to the victim's wrist. It's the left one this time, but it looks very similar to the wound on Veronica Lloyd.'

'Jesus. In a church,' said Robertson, with no irony. 'He's definitely a priest?'

Louise nodded.

Robertson handed her a sheet with two pictures. 'The church has two parish priests,' he said, but Louise could already tell which one was the victim.

'That's him,' she said, pointing to the picture of Father Mulligan.

'You sure?'

Mulligan was the older priest. There was no mistaking the shock of grey hair, the deep incisions that age had carved into his features.

'There's a lot of red on him now, but that's him,' said Louise, irked at having to repeat herself.

Robertson ignored her tetchiness. 'Do we even have a credible suspect for Veronica Lloyd?' he asked, knowing the answer.

'Not beyond her drug dealer, and he doesn't really have the wherewithal for something like this,' she said, repeating the information Farrell had given her that morning at the briefing. She thought about the tennis coach but didn't think he warranted a mention.

'Is that right?'

'Yes, Iain, it is. Look, let's get to the point. This killing is going to open the investigation. We have a connection to investigate, a modus operandi for the killing.' She hated speaking this way with the priest's corpse still residing in the confessional, but they both knew she was right. There were already a number of connections. The age of both victims, the possible link of the Catholic churches, and they hadn't even begun to look into Father Mulligan's private life. 'What is it, Iain?' she said, when her boss didn't respond.

Robertson shook his head. 'This is going to get messy. Two brutal slayings within days of each other. One on a beach, one in a godforsaken church.'

Louise frowned, wondering if the DCI appreciated his choice of words. 'I've worked on cases like this, Iain. You know I have the experience.'

'I'm not doubting you, Louise. No one is,' he added, a little too quickly for her liking.

'What, then?'

'You may have worked on cases like this, but this town hasn't experienced anything like it in living memory. We're going to receive a lot of attention. I would be shocked if this isn't national news by the end of the day. I even had the local MP on the phone earlier, asking me how the investigation is progressing.'

Louise appreciated the pressure coming Robertson's way, the attention they would all be facing. 'Maybe it will be, but my focus is on Veronica Lloyd and Father Mulligan and finding whoever is responsible.'

'That's admirable, Louise, but you need to get realistic. As SIO, you will be the main focus.'

Something was being left unsaid, but she didn't push it. 'Don't worry about me, Iain.'

Robertson nodded and walked back towards the church.

Louise watched him leave. The wind had picked up. Carrying the scent of the sea, it stung her ears and numbed her flesh. What wasn't Robertson saying? She conceded the case would probably prove to be the most high profile the town had seen for some time, but that didn't fully explain Robertson's behaviour. Ever since that first afternoon, following Veronica's murder, he'd been treating her as if she were some inexperienced rookie. She guessed it came down to what had happened during the Walton case and wondered if that millstone would ever leave her.

A commotion was waiting for her as she returned to the church a few minutes later. A middle-aged man wrapped in a long black overcoat was arguing with PC Hughes outside the church door.

'Ma'am, this is Father Riley. I've explained to him he can't enter the church at the moment, but . . .'

'Father Riley, DI Blackwell. You're the parish priest here?'

'That is correct, and if something has happened, I should be informed,' said the priest. The man looked a good thirty years younger than his departed colleague. He was tall and slim, his features sharp and angular. He struggled to hold eye contact with Louise as he answered her, his tired eyes betraying his exhaustion.

'Is there somewhere we can go to talk?' she said.

'The rectory. Please, follow me,' said the priest, making long strides towards a small building behind the church. 'Please excuse me. I've been up all night,' he said, opening the door.

The air felt colder inside than out as Louise followed the priest to a small kitchen area, where he switched on a kettle. A moment of realisation came over the man as the kettle boiled and he looked at her, his face draining to a ghost-white shade. 'Father Mulligan,' he muttered, wavering on the spot.

Louise rushed to the man's aid, pulling out a rickety chair for him to sit on. 'Are you okay, Father Riley?'

'I knew something serious must have happened. Why all the police? Why wasn't I allowed in the church?'

'I'm afraid Father Mulligan was the victim of a serious assault, which has resulted in him losing his life.'

He stared at her. 'He's been murdered? In the church?'

Louise placed her hand on his shoulder. He was frailer than she'd imagined, and shook as she touched him. 'I'm afraid so.'

'Why, for heaven's sake? He's in his late seventies. Why would someone do that to him?'

'I'm afraid that's what we have to find out. You mentioned you've been up all night?' asked Louise, making some sweet tea for the priest.

'Yes. I was at the General all evening. I'm afraid we lost one of our parishioners, Gladys Vernon, last night. It was a horrendous time. Her family were there. I gave her the last rites, and offered my support to the family during the night.'

'When was the last time you saw Father Mulligan?'

'Yesterday, early evening, before I was called out.'

'Early evening?'

'About 5 p.m. Father Mulligan was due to take his Mass.'

'There was a Mass yesterday evening?' asked Louise.

'Yes. Father Mulligan runs a Mass every Tuesday evening at 7 p.m. We rarely get any more than six or seven attending, but it's good to keep these things going. Helps to maintain a sense of community. Do you understand?'

Louise was surprised by the direct question. 'Yes. I know this must come as an awful shock to you, but could you give me the names and addresses of the parishioners who attended last night?'

The priest eased himself off his chair and walked over to the sideboard. 'We have a computer system, but I'll be damned if I can work it. I'll write you a list, but I can only hazard a guess,' he said, pulling out an A4 pad and blue biro. His hands shook as he wrote, his eyes close to tears.

'I could write the addresses for you?'

'No, that's fine.' He paused, rubbing the pen under his nose. 'How . . . how did it happen?'

Louise pictured the dead priest, the thick grooves on his arms and legs, the savage hole through his wrist. 'That's what we're trying to understand now,' she said.

'I will need to see him before he is taken away.'

'That can be arranged,' said Louise, taking the list from the priest. She hesitated before adding, 'I'm afraid this isn't the first killing. You heard about the lady found on the beach?'

'My goodness, yes. Terrible business. You're not saying . . .'

'We believe the deaths are linked in some way. The other victim was called Veronica Lloyd. Does that name mean anything to you?'

'No,' said the priest, without hesitation.

Louise nodded. 'Veronica was an active member of St Bernadette's Church.'

Father Riley furrowed his brow, confused by the statement. 'I am sorry to hear that.'

'So you know the church well?'

'Naturally. It's the closest parish to ours, and of course Father Mulligan was the parish priest there for twenty years.'

Chapter Thirteen

Nervous excitement ran through the incident room as Louise started her briefing. It was as if the whole of the station's personnel had been crammed into the space, many of the uniformed officers standing as Louise told them to focus their energy on the links between the two victims and the churches of St Michael's and St Bernadette's.

'Thomas. You met with the priest from St Bernadette's yesterday?'

'Yes, Father McGuire. Young guy. Had only good words to say about Veronica Lloyd. He appeared to be devastated about the news. He'd lit a candle and already started praying for her by the time I'd left.'

'Set up a meeting for me in the next hour.'

Back in her office, Louise stared at her phone. She'd waited for Dempsey to arrive before leaving the site. He'd promised to call her if he discovered anything of significance, but that would be some time yet. So why was she so distracted? She hadn't heard from her parents that morning and would have liked an update on how Emily was, but it wasn't that either. It was hard to admit, but part of her was waiting for a text message from Finch.

'Louise?'

She flipped the phone over and looked up to see Thomas in the doorway.

'Yes?' she asked, her tone harsher than necessary.

'Father McGuire is waiting for you at St Bernadette's. He was already aware of the incident at St Michael's.'

'Okay, thank you. I'll head over now.'

'You need me to join you?'

Although it would have been good to have the company, she wanted to view St Bernadette's alone. 'No, that's fine. Thanks, Thomas.'

St Bernadette's was only a five-minute walk away, so she left the car, regretting the decision as she walked headlong into a biting wind billowing in from the shore. Louise didn't pass anyone on her walk to the church, and it felt as if there was less traffic on the roads. The town was still reeling from the death of Veronica Lloyd and Louise imagined news of Father Mulligan's fate had likely already spread. Were people keeping themselves inside, fearing they could be the next victim?

Situated next to a primary school of the same name, St Bernadette's was a simple yellow-brick building. She stepped inside and looked around, trying to pinpoint why the place didn't feel like a church. The interior had the atmosphere of an office block, despite the religious imagery hammered into the walls and the depiction of Christ's Crucifixion above the altar.

'It's the lack of windows,' said a voice.

Louise swivelled on her heels to face the source of the statement, a rake-thin man with a mop of dark hair. He smiled at her, the gesture so innocent and welcoming, the man's face so fresh and young, that it took her a few seconds to register that he was a priest.

'Father John McGuire,' said the priest, holding out his hand. 'But please, call me John.'

'DI Blackwell.'

'Yes, I understood from your colleague that you'd be visiting.'

'Is there somewhere else we can sit?' said Louise, uncomfortable in the surroundings.

'Please, the rectory is through here,' said Father McGuire, guiding her around the pews.

Louise had been baptised as a Catholic and recognised the Stations of the Cross as she followed the priest towards the rectory. The paintings of Jesus carrying the cross were modern, close to abstract, and Louise couldn't help but wonder if a child had painted them.

Unlike St Michael's, the rectory at St Bernadette's adjoined the church. McGuire led her to his office. The room had a cold feel, with bare floors and white painted walls. A wooden desk took centre stage, and behind that was another crucifix.

'Can I get you a tea or coffee?' said McGuire.

'No, thank you. I understand from DS Ireland that you've heard about the murder of Father Mulligan at St Michael's?'

McGuire's smile crumbled and she noticed that his hands were trembling. He reached under his desk, from where he produced a pack of cigarettes. 'Do you mind?' he said, fumbling with the packet.

'Please, go ahead.'

He lit the cigarette with an addict's care and Louise wondered what other vices the young man might be hiding. 'How long have you been working here?' she asked, once he'd taken his first long drag.

'Five years.'

'You're the parish priest?'

'Yes, all alone, actually. My last colleague left two years ago and we've yet to find a replacement.'

'That must be difficult.'

'It can be, but I get support from the other parishes. We get by.'

'I imagine the news about Veronica Lloyd came as a terrible shock,' said Louise, keeping her tone gentle.

'You can only imagine. One of the unfortunate side effects of being a priest is that you become accustomed to death – but something like this, and now Father Mulligan . . .'

Could I ever become accustomed to death? she thought. There was a clear parallel between the priest's work and her own but she wasn't sure 'accustomed' was the correct word. 'I have to ask you this, Father. Can you think of anyone who would want to hurt Veronica and Father Mulligan?'

The priest didn't hesitate. 'No one would ever want to hurt Veronica. She was the gentlest soul I've ever met, and as for Father Mulligan, he was an old man. Why would anyone do this to him?'

Louise gave the young priest some time, allowed him to drag further on his cigarette before asking her next question. 'Again, this is something I have to ask. We will have to look at Father Mulligan's past. Is there anything we're going to find?'

It took a few seconds for Father McGuire to understand the question. She hadn't liked asking it, but with all the historical sex scandals that had affected the Church over the years, it wasn't something she could brush over. If there was ever going to be a motive for committing such an atrocious act, then a victim of child abuse avenging themselves had to be a consideration.

Father McGuire started to shake his head. 'How can you even suggest that? That poor man has only just lost his life.'

'I appreciate that, Father, but I have to ask the question. Was Father Mulligan ever accused of anything inappropriate? We're going to find out one way or another, but if you can point us in the right direction now, it could aid us in finding his and Veronica's killer.'

'Believe it or not, Inspector Blackwell, not all of us are sexual deviants.'

'No one is suggesting that, Father McGuire.'

The priest held his hand up. 'No. No. I will not accept this. Father Mulligan was found murdered this morning, and you're already here besmirching his name.'

Louise frowned. She had sympathy for the priest, and respected him for defending his colleague, but the investigation had to proceed. 'No one is besmirching his name, but it is a question that needs to be asked. And needs to be answered,' she added, holding his attention and leaving McGuire in no doubt as to his duty.

The priest sighed. 'I have never heard of any accusation about Father Mulligan, and frankly, the suggestion is ludicrous.'

Louise decided to leave it for now. She would have the team look into it as soon as she returned. 'He used to be the priest here?'

'Yes, so I believe.'

'Why did he leave?'

'Unfortunately, that is rarely our decision. I believe when he was here he was one of three priests. As you can see, there is only one priest here now. Falling congregation. He's been at St Michael's for thirty years.'

'Would he ever have encountered Veronica Lloyd?' asked Louise.

'I imagine it's possible. Veronica was very active in the parish and we would occasionally host joint events with St Michael's. I can't recall seeing them together, though. Father Mulligan's health has not been great over the last few years so he hasn't been able to get around as much as he would have liked.'

Louise decided to ease back on her questions about the murdered priest, sensing Father McGuire's mounting distress. The conversation was reaching its conclusion. 'Regarding Veronica, did she ever confide in you about personal matters?'

'She would attend confession, if that's what you're asking.'

'I guess you can't elaborate on that.'

'Of course not, the seal of the confessional is sacrosanct.'

'Outside of the confessional, though, did you know of any personal issues Veronica had to contend with?' she pressed.

'Obviously, she was devastated by the death of her mother, but that was some time ago and she was an older lady . . .'

Louise came to the point. 'We found heroin in Veronica's house.'

'Heroin? No, no, no. Veronica would never. She's not that sort of person.'

Louise had heard such denials countless times before. 'Sometimes it's hard to detect when people are using,' she said.

'Perhaps, but I think I would have noticed. Veronica was the most productive and valuable member of our volunteers. In all the time I knew her, she never cancelled an appointment, was never late. I find it impossible to believe she was a drug user.'

Louise decided not to push the young priest any further. 'Thank you, Father McGuire, you have been very helpful.'

'Please, let me show you out,' said the priest, stubbing out his second cigarette.

He led her back through the church, and the abstract Stations of the Cross.

'Interesting architecture,' said Louise, as they stopped by the church's door.

McGuire nodded, his manner sober. 'Yes, it's not ideal. I imagine in the eighties it was all the rage.'

'The eighties?' said Louise.

'Didn't you know? There was a fire in the eighties and the majority of the church was burnt down. Some of the structure survived, but it was too unsafe to keep. Hence we have this . . . modern building.'

'When was the fire?'

'Nineteen eighty-three,' said the priest.

'Father Mulligan was a priest here in 1983?'

The priest looked momentarily confused. 'I guess he must have been, yes.'

Chapter Fourteen

Louise took the short walk from the church to the seafront. The tide was fully out – it could stretch up to a mile from shore at low tide – leaving mud in its wake. People were always getting stuck in the dangerous mudflats, and since Louise's arrival in the town two people had died, despite the numerous warning signs along the beach.

From the sea wall, she gazed out towards the spot where Veronica Lloyd's body had been discovered. It was hard to believe it was only two days ago. A dog walker trampled the ground where the SOCO tent had been pitched, his grey whippet sniffing at the patch of sand as if it sensed what had occurred on the spot. The sea had washed away their chances of finding further evidence and Louise could only hope the SOCOs had collected everything necessary. She expected to hear from the Forensic Investigation Unit in Portishead today. It was possible, though unlikely, that the case could be all but over once their report came back. All it would take would be a trace of DNA on Veronica's body from someone on their database and they would have an active suspect.

However, although Louise was sure there would be traces of the killer's DNA on both Veronica and Father Mulligan, she doubted there would be a hit with the database. It felt unlikely to her, not because she thought the killer was too organised, too professional, to leave their DNA at the scene, but because she suspected Veronica was the murderer's first kill. As he or she had done with Veronica, the killer had left the body of Father Mulligan in a public place where he would be discovered. It was inconceivable that someone known to the police would do this unless they wanted to be caught, and she didn't think this killer wanted to be caught.

At least, not yet.

Her phone rang as she ordered a coffee from a kiosk on the seafront. She glanced at the screen: her brother. With everything that had happened today, she hadn't been distracted by thoughts of what he'd done yesterday. She'd yet to speak to her mother, who had texted earlier to say that Emily would be staying with them for a few days. Paul would be calling either to blame her or to persuade her to help him in the fight against their parents. Either way, Louise wasn't willing to get involved. A man had died yesterday on her watch and she had to find out who was responsible.

She let the phone ring out before walking back towards the line of amusement arcades on Regent Street. They were increasingly empty in the winter months, becoming a haven for local drug dealers, and she often wondered how they could afford to keep the flashing lights of the arcade games and the slot machines running. She marvelled at how excited she'd been as a child, passing this very row of buildings. Then, the arcades held all the anticipation of a fairground; now, they seemed tawdry and cold. Vacant, sad places.

It made her think of the church of St Bernadette's, its enforced modernity in stark contrast to the olde-worlde atmosphere of St Michael's and the priest who ran the place. Priests. She'd seen three of them today, though only two of them had been alive. Like the churches, Father Riley and Father McGuire were polar opposites. Riley, the old, solemn type of priest she remembered from her childhood; McGuire, young and innocent. She couldn't imagine confessing her sins to a priest that age. Maybe it was because she was older now, or because she hadn't been to confession since she was eleven.

Not that McGuire was completely devoid of gravitas. When Louise raised the suggestion of child abuse, he'd been very quick to jump to Mulligan's and the Church's defence. Had he been toeing the company line, or had he been hiding something? She didn't like the idea of it, but they would have to investigate both parishes for instances of suspected abuse, and with her experience of the Catholic Church, she imagined it would be problematic. She'd worked on abuse cases before, in Bristol. The Church liked to keep things in-house and it was difficult to get any direct answers from them. That was one of the main problems in dealing with an organisation that believed all your crimes could be forgiven if you just prayed hard enough.

And then there was the fire. McGuire hadn't mentioned that there was anything suspicious about it, but it was also something she was keen to investigate.

She saw Farrell as she was entering the station. He gave her his customary smirk as he said, 'Ma'am.'

'Where are you off to, Farrell?' she said, not willing to engage in civilities.

'I've had a sighting of Veronica Lloyd's suspected dealer in a bar over in Hutton. I'm going to bring him in, question him about Father Mulligan.'

'Take some uniform with you.'

Farrell frowned. 'I don't need any. I know this guy, real low life, he's going to do what he's told.'

'Just do it in case.'

Farrell went to say something else then just shrugged. 'Okay, you're the boss,' he said.

Louise didn't like the way he'd said 'boss', or his accompanying shrug, but she let it slide.

She sensed the tension as soon as she entered the office. Her officers were busy working, but there was an unusual silence in the area. Robertson's door was shut, his blinds pulled down. 'What's going on?' she asked Thomas.

'Not sure,' he said, looking up from his screen.

'Who's Robertson got in there?'

Thomas frowned, looking guilty, as if he'd been caught out in a secret. 'Someone from HQ.'

'Portishead?'

'I think so.'

Louise went to her office, sat at her desk and closed her eyes. It couldn't be, not so soon into the investigation. She switched on her screen and ran a search on the fire at St Bernadette's in 1983 but couldn't focus on the results. She had to see who Robertson was talking to, had to make sure it wasn't *him*.

She felt all eyes on her as she made the lonely walk to Robertson's office. It could be something innocuous, a routine visit, but the hushed atmosphere suggested otherwise. She knocked on the door.

'Yes,' she heard Robertson say.

Louise took a deep breath and eased open the door, trying her best to control her furious heartbeat. She glanced first at Robertson, and then at his companion, keeping her face neutral.

Now she knew why there hadn't been a text message on her phone last night or this morning.

DCI Finch had decided to bypass his usual secrecy and pay her a little visit instead.

Chapter Fifteen

The canoeists had been circling the island for thirty minutes now. What were they waiting for?

Geoff had remained rooted to the spot, lying on the cliff edge of the island since their arrival, watching them turn and bob, head towards the shore, only to retreat. They wouldn't be able to see his boat on the pebble beach, but they weren't leaving, the torches on their helmets dissecting the darkening sea. He couldn't let them discover he was on the island. The prisoner was safely hidden away, and technically, Geoff was allowed to camp on the island, but if they found out and talked about having seen anyone here, it could put everything he'd been working towards at risk.

Fortunately, Geoff had two things on his side: the increasingly bad weather and the dangerous tides surrounding the island. The tide could reach up to seven knots. Such was the force of the water, it was hard enough getting to the island even with the aid of an outboard motor. For the canoeists, it would be suicidal to get any nearer, and with darkness approaching it would be foolhardy for them to try to reach the shore.

But what would he do if they did? In all his planning, he'd never considered this scenario. The canoeists were innocents. The deaths of Mrs Lloyd and Father Mulligan had been just, but he couldn't harm these two people, could he?

Geoff was overcome by a moment of pure loneliness. A desperate part of him wished to end it now, to reveal himself to the canoeists and to stop the whole sordid business. He was transported back to the previous night and his feeling of isolation in the pub when he'd been forced to drink with Malcolm and his friends. Had that been a warning? A punishment for the killings and the deeds he was yet to commit?

God, he missed his dad. He would have known what to do. After Mass each Sunday he would discuss with Geoff the content of the service. He would quiz him about the sermon and the various Gospel readings, pointing out themes and motifs, lessons he may have learnt. Now and again, he would lose his temper when Geoff misinterpreted something. Geoff shivered at the memory of such encounters. He closed his eyes, fighting the remembered sound of his dad's belt on his flesh, and tried to summon the old man's wisdom.

He was being tested. He'd known it would happen at some point, and he would have to deal with it. John Maynard had been a test, and he'd passed that. Before losing his front teeth, the boy had been a tyrant, an evil that haunted everyone in Junior One and below, but Geoff had rescued him. Although they'd never been friends afterwards, the boy was irrevocably changed after that moment. He'd never thanked Geoff, but Geoff liked to think that Maynard would occasionally look back on his life and see the incident by the water fountain as a turning point.

As if understanding Geoff's new-found certainty, the canoeists made one more attempt to reach shore before spinning around and heading back towards the mainland, the light of their torches ripping through the sea. Geoff watched them retreat until they were pinpricks in his vision before struggling to his feet.

He sat on the cliff edge and stared across the sea towards the shore. Weston was clouded in mist. He strained his eyes, as if he could make out the tiny figures busying away on the mainland. The police would have found the priest by now, and the thought made his stomach lurch. He'd been careful last night but had taken a risk by going to Mass first. The grieving widows would have noticed him, even if they'd refused to acknowledge his presence. He doubted their recall abilities were up to much, but between them, there was a chance they'd come up with some form of description of him. And now, with the canoeists' arrival, he had to be doubly careful on the island.

Time was running out. He would need to finish the next two as soon as he could.

Chapter Sixteen

DCI Robertson looked like a guilty schoolboy caught doing something he shouldn't, while Finch's smile snaked on his face, charm personified. She couldn't deny that his smile used to keep her off-guard, and that she'd found his streak of arrogance attractive. He hadn't changed much in the last couple of years. Finch had eased into the role of DCI as if it had been his destiny. His dark navy suit was perfectly tailored, and as he spun his chair around to face her, his hand running through his thick, dark hair, he exuded the confidence of someone entitled to be sitting in her boss's office, when the truth was he was merely an interloper.

Louise held his gaze, even matched his smile.

'You know DCI Finch,' said Robertson, his Glaswegian growl lacking its normal intensity.

'Tim.'

'Louise, how are you?' said Finch.

For one horrendous moment, she thought he was going to embrace her. He held out his hand and she shook it, not flinching as he squeezed it hard. 'I'm fine,' she said, fighting the urge to unleash the full canister of pepper spray in her jacket into the man's eyes as she pictured him at Walton's farmhouse warning her, ordering her into action. 'So what brings you here, Tim?'

'Please, join us,' said Robertson, acting as if nothing unusual was happening.

Louise took the seat next to Finch, ignoring the waft of his go-to aftershave. She was prepared for what he was about to say but struggled to control her quickening pulse.

'DCI Finch is here at the behest of Assistant Chief Constable Morley,' said Robertson.

'This is about the Veronica Lloyd case,' she said, keeping her tone neutral for the time being.

'Terrence asked me to come here to offer assistance, if needed,' said Finch.

Louise almost laughed at Finch's casual use of the assistant chief constable's first name. It lacked subtlety, but he said it convincingly. He was on first-name terms with Terrence Morley, but because of her rank, she wasn't. Morley had been instrumental in her departure from the MIT. He was an old-school copper in his late fifties, yet to fully integrate modern police practice and office politics. He was still quick with the occasional risqué joke or lewd comment, but never did or said anything that would get him into trouble. In her few dealings with the man, he'd treated her respectfully enough, but she'd sensed he'd just been playing the game. He had his favourites – one of them the man sitting next to her – and the rest he tolerated. She knew that Morley blamed her for what had happened at the Walton scene, viewed her with contempt for having a different story to Finch.

'And what does Terrence have to say for himself?' she said, noting the upward twitch of Robertson's upper lip at her own use of Morley's first name.

Finch acknowledged the slight and turned to Robertson for support.

Her boss lifted his hands from his desk and sighed. 'DCI Finch is here with an offer of help, Louise. No one is trying to take the case away from you.'

Finch smiled. 'You know the resources we have in Portishead, Louise. And with the discovery of Father Mulligan's body, it is arguable that the MIT should be investigating this.'

Louise glared at Robertson, her sense of indignation in little doubt. She stared at him after he'd looked away, purposely making the silence in the room uncomfortable. In her peripheral vision, Finch tapped a pen against his left thigh, a nervous tic she hadn't noticed before. She knew the moment was pivotal, would define not only this case but her working relationship with Robertson and possibly her future in the police force. 'Thank you, Tim, for your kind offer, but we have everything under control at the moment. Perhaps if you could hurry up FIU with their results from the Veronica Lloyd scene, that would be helpful, but other than that, we're okay for now.'

A second wave of silence descended over the room. As the lowest-ranked officer present it wasn't her decision to make, but she wasn't prepared to work with Finch and certainly wasn't about to give the case over to MIT on the suggestion of Terrence Morley, whatever his rank.

Finch's lips were tightly shut. He looked at Robertson, eyes wide, as if he'd already predicted everything Louise had just said and the phrase 'Told you so' was dying to leave his lips.

Robertson began nodding his head to an inaudible beat. The pause before he next spoke felt like an eternity to Louise. 'Okay, thank you. We have things covered for now, Tim, but appreciate the offer. Naturally, we'll be in contact, should the situation change.'

Louise hid the smile threatening to blossom on her face. She'd never admired Robertson more than she did at this moment.

Finch pretended to take the rejection in good spirit but couldn't hide the agitation in his hard eyes. It wouldn't be the last they heard from him, Louise felt.

'Okay. I think you're making a mistake, Iain, but thank you for your time.'

Both men stood and shook hands. 'Inspector,' said Finch, as he headed for the door.

Louise remained seated. 'Tim.'

After watching Finch leave the office, Robertson returned to his seat.

'Thank you, Iain, I do appreciate it.'

'Don't thank me yet. Finch won't let this rest. He's got the ear of the assistant chief. We'll need to be able to show them something soon, or I won't be able to stop them taking over.'

'What do you know about the fire at St Bernadette's?' she asked, changing the subject.

'It was before my time,' said Robertson, caught out by the question. 'Why?'

'I'm not sure. Veronica Lloyd used to volunteer there, and the church has a strong link with St Michael's. It's likely Father Mulligan knew Veronica, one way or another.'

'It's flimsy, but it's something. Here,' he said, handing her a business card. 'The editor at the *Mercury*. He'd have been working as a journo when that church burnt down. Give him a call. You'll have to ply him with alcohol, but if there's a story, he'll know it.'

'Thanks again, Iain,' said Louise, getting to her feet.

'Don't thank me yet, Louise. It's all borrowed time.'

She composed herself as she returned to her office. She could still smell Finch's aftershave. It clung to her skin – the memory of his scent now forever entwined with those last moments at Walton's farmhouse – and she wanted to shower, to scrub herself clean of the lingering aroma. She'd always feared this day, and now it was here she could either dwell on Finch's planned interference or try her best to ignore him and to solve the case without his help.

A high-pitched whistle jolted her from her thoughts. It was the office manager, Simone. 'Who was that hottie?' asked the woman.

Louise looked at her as if she were an aberration. 'What?' she said, a bit more sternly than she intended.

'That guy from Portishead? Finch, wasn't it?'

Louise couldn't recall Simone making a comment on any man's appearance before. They didn't have a close relationship and their interactions could occasionally be fractious, so it surprised her to hear the woman speaking as if they were gossipy friends. She wondered if Finch had put her up to it. 'Someone I used to work with,' she replied.

Simone raised an eyebrow. 'I'm surprised you got anything done.'

Louise frowned, hoping Simone would back off.

Simone mirrored Louise's frown. 'Anyway, this came in for you when you were in with Robertson,' she said, handing Louise a phone number. 'FIU. Toby Farley. Says you can call him, but he's emailed over the details.'

'Thanks, Simone.' Louise turned away from the office manager and logged on to her laptop. She scanned through the email from FIU, before rereading the document in greater detail. As she'd expected, the DNA samples found at the site were numerous. The hits from Veronica's body were much lower, but none of the DNA found on her person matched anything on the PND, the Police National Database. So either the killer didn't have a DNA record on the database, or they'd somehow managed to avoid contaminating the crime scene. The latter was so unlikely that Louise could almost dismiss it out of hand. Forensic detection had developed so much even in the last few years that it was close to impossible for a killer not to leave some mark at a scene.

She closed the report. The only positive of having the second body was that they could match the DNA reports at both scenes.

Of course, it meant nothing if they didn't have a legitimate suspect they could test, but it was a start. Now all she had to do was find out who would want two people, both around seventy, one a priest, dead. The age of the victims was the closest thing they had to a pattern. The old were not immune to falling prey to violent death, but this usually coincided with failed house burglaries or muggings. The elderly were rarely victims of such targeted killings, and that suggested their ages were significant. Couple that with the tentative link to St Bernadette's Church, and they had something to investigate. Veronica Lloyd would have been thirty-two at the time of the church fire, Father Mulligan thirty-five.

Louise tried to ignore the doubting voices in her head telling her that the ages of the victims, and the fire, were irrelevant as she picked up her mobile and called the number given to her by Robertson.

'Dominic Garrett,' said the well-spoken man who answered.

'Mr Garrett. DI Louise Blackwell. I was given your name by Iain Robertson.'

'Ah, Iain. Very kind of him. Louise Blackwell. Now that name rings a bell,' said Garrett, who sounded full of humour, and possibly alcohol, if his slurred consonants were anything to go by. 'Ah, yes, you're in charge of the beach body. Veronica Lloyd, I believe?'

'That's correct, Mr Garrett, I was wondering . . .'

'Recent developments, I hear. A priest from Uphill,' said Garrett, interrupting. 'Father Mulligan?'

'That's correct, Mr Garrett. I was—'

'I didn't do it.'

'Didn't do what, Mr Garrett?'

'The killings, naturally. I have a full alibi.'

Louise sighed, holding the mouthpiece away from her. It was only three in the afternoon. 'I'm sure you do, Mr Garrett, but that's not what I was calling about.'

'How intriguing.'

Louise considered ending the call. The possible link between the fire and the killings was so fragile it hardly warranted pursuing, and she didn't want a drunk journalist printing unhelpful information in the local paper. 'This is off the record, but I was hoping to get some information about the fire at St Bernadette's Church that took place in 1983.'

The line went quiet, then Louise heard the man swallowing. 'You are intriguing me, DI Blackwell,' said Garrett, breathless. 'Tell you what, buy me a G'n'T and I will tell you everything. Say, in an hour at the Royal Oak Hotel?'

Louise agreed and hung up.

As she was putting on her coat, Farrell returned. His usual smirk was missing as he threw his wallet and mobile on to the desk with attention-seeking force.

'Everything okay?' asked Louise.

'The dealer is a no-go. Cast-iron alibi on the night Veronica Lloyd died. In Bristol with his mates until the early hours. By the state of him, he wouldn't have been capable of anything. I'm going to follow it up now, but it's not promising.'

'What did he say when you questioned him about Father Mulligan?'

'The little shit was amusingly indignant. Said he would never sell to the clergy, as if he was morally against it or something. We don't think Mulligan was a user, though, do we?'

'We'll find out soon enough.'

It was already dark outside, the clocks having gone back an hour the previous weekend. She walked along Walliscote Road towards the Odeon cinema, noting a homeless person huddled beneath a mound of sleeping bags in a disused shop front. She made a mental note to get some of the uniformed officers to check the current shelter situation, before crossing the road towards the high street. The lights of the Silica – a thirty-metre work of art that served as a bus stop and information kiosk – stretched into the gloom of the night at the top of the pedestrian zone. It was nick-named 'The Carrot' by some of the locals, and to Louise its location in the town always jarred. To her mind, the thinning concrete spire looked out of place and lacked purpose. Although it had been in the town for over thirteen years, it had gone unnoticed by Louise while she'd been in Bristol and reinforced how much she'd lost touch with the place she'd visited so frequently as a child.

The walk down the pedestrianised high street was usually a depressing prospect and, under the shadowy streetlights, the drab shop-window displays looked worn and tired, the area desolate, as if long ago abandoned. Again, she had the feeling that people were staying inside, hiding from the unpredictability of a killer on the loose and that she was indirectly responsible for the wave of fear in the town.

She found Dominic Garrett with little difficulty, in the hotel bar. He was the sole customer, holding court with a bemused-look-ing young barman.

'Ah, DI Blackwell, I thought you'd jilted me,' he declared, as if addressing a theatre audience. His size matched his voice. He was gargantuan, his suit, stretching across his vast chest and stomach, containing enough material to cover three average-size men. 'Same for me, barkeep. What can I get you, Inspector?'

'Just a spring water for me, thank you,' said Louise.

'Nonsense. I will not drink alone,' said Garrett, with a long, theatrical sweep of his arm. 'Now what will you have?'

Louise lacked the energy to argue. She never drank on duty, and didn't plan to start, but she could at least order a drink to placate the editor. 'White wine, please,' she said to the barman, who looked pleased not to have to deal with Garrett on his own any more.

'Shall we take a seat?' she said.

'Yes, why not? After you.'

Louise headed to a table and chairs, before changing course towards two brightly decorated sofas, fearing Garrett wouldn't be able to fit within the confines of the wooden seats. She sat opposite the man as he lowered himself on to the sofa. 'Not sure I'll be able to get back up,' he said, smiling. 'So, how are you enjoying life in Weston-super-Mare, Inspector?'

She couldn't help but warm to Garrett. He was confident and self-deprecating, if a little loud. 'You can call me Louise.'

'Louise it is,' he said, raising his glass for a toast. 'Dominic, please.'

Louise clinked glasses with him and took a small sip of wine as he swallowed half the contents of his drink. 'It's a bit of a cultural shift,' she said as Garrett lay back on the sofa.

'I can certainly imagine. You were in the MIT, I believe?'

'That's correct.'

'So who did you piss off to end up here?'

Louise laughed. Garrett would know all about the Walton case and she appreciated his approach. 'Who *didn't* I piss off?'

Garrett's laugh echoed around the bar as a group of office workers quadrupled the customer base. 'I suspect we are kindred spirits, Louise,' he chuckled, before pausing. 'And this new case. The body on the beach, and this priest over in Uphill?'

She hadn't met up with the editor to discuss the case, but doing so was unavoidable. The *Mercury* was a weekly local newspaper for Weston and the surrounding areas, unlike the daily *Bristol Post*, which covered much of the south-west. A murder story like this wouldn't be featured in as much detail by the local paper, but she had to offer him something. 'Tania Elliot is covering the story for you?' she asked.

'You've done your homework. Good.'

Louise had talked to the young journalist on a few occasions at the magistrates' court and the county court building in Worle. However, she had yet to speak to any journalist about this particular case, having successfully forwarded all enquiries to the PR team in Portishead. 'Perhaps I could sit down with her at some point?'

'How would tomorrow morning suit?' said Garrett, before swilling back his gin and tonic.

'It's certainly a possibility.'

'Grand,' said Garrett, shuffling around so he could face the bar. 'Same again, barkeep,' he hollered to the startled youth behind the bar. 'So, this fire at St Bernadette's?'

'Yes.'

'This is obviously related to the case?'

'I would prefer it if we keep this off the record for the time being,' said Louise. She'd learnt from the past that such a caveat was always important when talking to the press.

'As I said, my lips are sealed.'

Louise told him about her meeting with Father McGuire at St Bernadette's, how Veronica Lloyd had volunteered at the church and that Father Mulligan used to be the parish priest.

'I can see the dots you're joining,' said Garrett.

'Just a line of questioning at this point,' said Louise.

The barman returned with his drink. 'Good man, keep the change,' said Garrett, handing him a five-pound note. 'Okay, Louise, the fire. I confess, I was intrigued when you called me, as I remember the fire at that church very well. I was a cub reporter then, doing some secondment work for what used to be the *Bristol Evening Post*. There was talk of me going to Fleet Street, would you believe. I would hate London, I'm sure. But I digress,' he said, his voice rising like a pantomime villain's. 'So, being a local boy, I was given the chance to run the story. The official line was that the fire was an accident. A lit candle catching some loose material, the fire building up over the evening until it reached the pews and the wooden structure of the roof.'

'You didn't think it was an accident?'

Garrett leaned forward, his voice dropping a notch. 'I was suspicious, Louise, let's say that. And not only because the building had almost burnt to the ground before the fire services arrived. Accelerant was found at the scene, petrol that was used for a back-up generator for the rectory and the church itself. Conveniently stored in a small enclave.'

'The damage must have been severe?'

'The church had been refurbished at some point, so although its base was stone, some of which remains, much of the structure was wood. The place was gutted, hence the rebuild.'

Louise took another small sip of her warm wine. She could smell the fire at the church, could see the black smoke billowing in the church rafters. 'I couldn't see any mention that arson was suspected in the records,' she said.

'That line of investigation was nipped in the bud pretty quickly. I was convinced there was a story, but no one was talking, and I mean no one. Not the police, not the Church. I took my suspicions to my editor both here and at the *Post*, but they weren't interested. That's when I lost my innocence, Louise.' Garrett paused, his face deadly serious, before bursting into laughter. 'I jest about the last bit. My innocence had long been destroyed by then. This was the eighties. I'd seen enough corruption and cover-ups to last a lifetime.'

'Why would someone cover up an arson attack on a church?'

'Depends on the reason behind the attack, I suppose. People forget the power these organisations have. They may have dwindling numbers in this country, but the Church, Anglican or Catholic, still have one hell of a voice. The day after that fire, Church officials swarmed the place. I half-expected the Pope to pay a visit. I've never seen anything like it. They closed in on themselves, wouldn't speak to me, and a few days later the official explanation was that it was an accidental fire.'

The group of office workers had left without ordering, and once again they were the only customers in the bar. Louise drank more wine, trying not to wince as the sharp liquid dribbled down her throat. 'You don't strike me as the kind of person who would give up so easily, Mr Garrett.'

Garrett raised his glass to her and smiled. 'I made some enquiries, but the news moves on and there were no resources for an investigative piece. Not my finest moment, granted.'

'You must have had your suspicions, though?' said Louise, concerned the editor wasn't going to provide her with anything of use.

'To return to your question, who would set fire to a church? The obvious answer would be someone truly pissed off with it, wouldn't you agree?'

'And why would someone be pissed off with a church?' said Louise, thinking aloud.

'Exactly. The first thought would be abuse scandals and that sort of sordid thing, but it could be anything. I don't have a faith, but people believe, more than you would imagine, and when things go wrong it's easy to blame the big man up there. Death in the family, chronic illness, marriage breakdown . . . the list is endless. But I think you may be on the right track, Louise. It could be coincidence, but by the sounds of it, these two victims have a link to St Bernadette's. Maybe their killer also had something to do with the fire.'

'If only it was that easy, Mr Garrett.'

'Well, where would the fun be in that, Louise? Can I tempt you to have one for the road?'

She stood up. 'Thank you for your time, Mr Garrett.'

He pushed himself off the sofa, struggling to maintain his balance. 'It's been entirely my pleasure. Shall we say 9.30 a.m.?'

'Nine thirty a.m.?'

'Your appointment with Tania tomorrow.'

Louise smiled, though the last thing she wanted to do was to speak to the young journalist. Tania Elliot wouldn't be able to give her any more information. 'Okay,' she said, conceding defeat.

'Bravo, Louise. Looks like we may have a story for her to get her teeth into, after all.'

Louise left the editor approaching the bar for another refill and pushed through the door in time to spot a familiar face. She went to call Thomas's name but held her tongue when she saw that he was carrying a small holdall and heading up the staircase towards the hotel's bedrooms.

Chapter Seventeen

Louise waited outside for five minutes before returning to the police station. She was a little out of breath, the sight of Thomas filling her with conflicting emotions.

Thomas was married to a lovely woman called Rebecca, whom Louise had met on a few occasions at police social functions. Thomas didn't talk about her much, but they'd always appeared to be happy together. Maybe they'd had an argument and he'd chosen, or been forced, to stay the night at the hotel? The reason was irrelevant. What troubled Louise was her own reaction. She'd fooled herself for some time now that, beyond a basic attraction, Thomas was just another colleague to her. But if she was being honest, a place within her, a place she didn't care to acknowledge, wondered if he was back on the market. And although she would never do anything to act on it, a guilty part of her was excited by that possibility.

A pair of drunk men, dressed unseasonably in shorts and T-shirts, accompanied her along the high street back towards the station. They didn't pay her any attention, too engrossed in a slurred conversation about the merits of certain motor vehicles they'd almost definitely never driven. When one of the pair began a squeaky rendition of 'Danny Boy', Louise sped up until she was out of earshot.

Only DCI Robertson was still at the station, the dim glow of his desk light spilling out into the dark shadows of the open-plan office. A couple of reports had been uploaded to the IT information system – HOLMES 2 – that they used for major investigations. Thomas had worked through the list of parishioners given to Louise by Father Riley. Louise's attention was piqued as she read the account from three of the elderly women about a lone male who'd been in attendance. None of the women had recognised the man, and it was the most positive lead they had to date. Thomas had arranged for the women to attend the station in the morning to go through a face-recognition questionnaire. Louise was surprised Thomas hadn't presented this information to her directly, but she had barely seen him that day. If they could identify the man, they could start looking for more eyewitnesses, and might even be able to get a hit from CCTV cameras in the vicinity. There was also the update from Farrell on the drug dealer, and the result of an interview with the tennis coach so despised by Veronica Lloyd's friend, Estelle Ferguson. Neither line of investigation appeared to be going anywhere.

Louise turned her attention back to the fire at St Bernadette's. She located an old article in the *Mercury* from after the fire, and laughed as she saw the picture of a much younger, and infinitely slimmer, Dominic Garrett under the byline. She'd read the piece before, but it had a different resonance after what Garrett had told her. As he'd stated, the official line had been that the fire was accidental. The photograph on the front page showed the remains of the church. A bewildered group of people milled about on the forecourt, including at least three priests, forever caught in a snapshot of confusion.

There was no mention of an accelerant being found at the scene, and when she cross-referenced the police and fire reports, both stated that the fire had started accidentally. It was disappointing, yet although it didn't help her directly, Garrett's revelation gave her something to work with. If his suspicions about a cover-up were correct, it suggested a conspiracy between the Church and the police authorities. Such things were less likely to happen nowadays, but she could easily imagine it happening then. It could have been a means of protecting the Church, or protecting someone senior. If she had any evidence at all that the fire had been started deliberately, then it could possibly be a case for Anti-Corruption, but for now she could only consider how it affected her case; how, and if, it had any connection to the deaths of Veronica Lloyd and Father Mulligan.

Thirty minutes later, she left DCI Robertson alone in the office. She felt physically drained by the day's events, and the wine she'd drunk with Garrett had made her sleepy.

She wanted to go straight home, to collapse into bed and sleep the memories of the day away, but despite her tiredness, she couldn't rest. On autopilot, she found herself driving to St Michael's Church in Uphill. She parked outside, the glare from her headlights the only illumination in the area. When she switched them off, her car was enveloped by the dark. She was surprised by the lack of streetlights, only a solitary glare above the police barrier tape covering the church entrance. Thomas's report had said there were eight people at last night's service, seven elderly women and a lone man. Louise pictured the women shuffling out of the church into the gloom. She needed more information. Had they driven to the church? Were they local? Did they have to walk alone under this cloak of darkness? It didn't seem safe to Louise, and she wondered why the church hadn't done more to protect its congregation.

If the killer had been present the previous night, it would have been easy for them to slip in and out of the church unnoticed, but the area was residential and it would only take one neighbour glancing out of their window, shutting their curtains, taking out their recycling bins, to have spotted someone suspicious. It was often these small chance happenings, events that couldn't be accounted for, that undid the most meticulous of plans. The residents had been canvassed today, but Louise would insist that the operation was repeated again in the morning with specific attention paid to the lone man at the Mass.

The tide was in as she headed home along the seafront. In the darkness, with the glimmer of the streetlights reflecting on the rippling surface, the water looked enticing, its mud colour hidden by the night sky. Louise slowed down as she approached the marine lake at Knightstone. The quickest way home now would be to take the old toll road via Kewstoke back to Worle, but she found herself turning right and driving inland towards the Boulevard and the Royal Oak Hotel.

She had no illusions about why she was here, but that didn't make her feel any better. *You're being pathetic*, she thought to herself as she slowed down outside the hotel, searching for a glimpse of Thomas. She was just in time to see the staggering figure of Dominic Garrett being helped out of the bar by two men and placed into a waiting taxi. No sign of DS Ireland.

Louise floored the accelerator, a cold sweat coating her skin. What the hell had she been thinking?

She was home ten minutes later, her breath visible as she left the car, the front windows of her bungalow beginning to frost over. The inside of her building was little warmer than outside. She switched on the gas fire in the living room and retreated to the kitchen to microwave a ready meal as she waited for warmth to seep back into the walls.

She was in time to catch the ITV local news, which led with the murder at St Michael's. The camera crew must have reached the scene just after she'd left. The pictures showed a number of uniformed officers and the lone figure of Stephen Dempsey standing outside the church. A few local residents were quizzed close to the high street about the murders, their responses edited perfectly to maximise the confusion and fear in their faces. A local butcher claimed his trade was already suffering, that people were scared to leave their homes. The local MP who Robertson had spoken to reiterated the concern of local businesses and residents, stressing that everything was being done to catch the killer. The report made it seem like the town was under siege and Louise sighed as she thought of the mounting pressure that would come her way because of it – just as Robertson had warned her.

After finishing her bland meal, she turned her attention to her home-made murder board, adding the pictures of Father Mulligan and drawing a line between the two churches of St Michael's and St Bernadette's. She'd just written '1983 fire?' under 'St Bernadette's' when she heard her phone ping.

She moved towards it like an addict, partly appalled by her desire to see the message, partly intrigued to see if Finch would accidentally reveal himself after seeing her today.

Her pulse quickened as she saw the name Thomas on the screen, her hand trembling slightly as she unlocked the screen to read the message:

> *Hi Boss, hope all is well. Was wondering if you fancied a coffee in the morning before work?*

Chapter Eighteen

Rescuing Maynard had done little to boost Geoff's standing at primary school. If anything, he was viewed with more suspicion by his classmates. Geoff was sidelined with a cruel efficiency. It was never stated officially, but after the incident he wasn't allowed to join in the group activities at playtime or lunch. While the others were playing football, or giant games of tag on the field opposite the school, Geoff would sneak off to the adjoining church. No matter how many times he entered the building, he still experienced the same tingle of anticipation as the large wooden doors eased open and he was presented with the inside of the church. He wasn't supposed to be in the church alone, but there was rarely anyone else there during the day. Energy roared through him as he genuflected and made his way to one of the pews, the beautiful Christ figure watching over him like a guardian.

His prayers had been jumbled back then, lacking the sophistication he'd developed of late. He'd taken to reading a junior Bible with its paraphrased Gospel stories, but his understanding was still vague. He knew Jesus had died on the cross to save mankind from their sins, but he didn't understand exactly how that worked. When he thought about the classmates who'd isolated him, he wondered why Jesus had bothered. They were mean and selfish. He'd snuck a look at the Revelation of St John the Divine in the grown-up version of the Bible, but it hadn't made any sense at all. The words were too long and foreign-sounding. His dad had given him a basic grounding in its meaning, though. One day, everyone would be judged, and sometimes, sitting alone in the church, Geoff couldn't wait for that time to come. Fire featured prominently in the book of Revelation, that much he did know. The priests would hint at it during Mass, and when Geoff pictured the devil, he was always awash in a sea of cleansing flames.

The crossing was the hardest Geoff had faced so far. As a boy, he'd travelled with his dad to the island many times, but his dad avoided the journey during the winter months and would never have travelled at night. Once, Geoff had begged him to take him for the weekend in winter. Despite his dad's protestations, Geoff had insisted that the sea was calm and that they would have the island to themselves. He'd whined too much and had rightly been punished for his disobedience.

After feeding and securing his prisoner, enduring the man's pitiful attempts to bargain with him, he set off from the shore. Even with his outboard motor, he'd struggled with the strength of the tide. By the time he'd breached the last of the waves he was drenched. And then the rain began to fall. He crouched inside the boat as it veered up, crashing down on the dark sea and sending a line of water into the vessel. It was a risk, travelling by night, but he had no option.

The tide at the old pier was little better than at Steep Holm. He made a makeshift mooring from an old steel girder but was waist-deep in the freezing water as he jumped from the boat. His hands were numb as he pulled at the metal, hauling the boat beneath the ruins of the pier and out of sight. Collapsing with exhaustion, he lay on his back on the wooden structure, the breeze skimming the sea and sending a fine drizzle over him.

It wasn't how he had imagined it. He'd managed to romanticise his plan, picturing perfect moonlit boat journeys and nights on the island under the stars. The other things he had to do were necessary, were *just*, but the island had been the one thing he'd shared solely with Dad and he hadn't been prepared mentally for the toil the journeys would involve.

He shuffled up the bank to the disused interior of the pier. The wind billowed through the gaping holes in the structure and it wasn't any warmer inside than out. He picked at the lock of his bag, wanting to cry out at the cold locking his fingers in place and making his body tremble. He stripped naked and put on his spare dry clothes, wrapping himself into a tight ball until the warmth began returning to his blood.

As the tide was still in, it was another two hours before he could return to the van. He had to contend with the unlit rotten wooden boards of the pier. Even as a child, he'd been on the old pier only a handful of times. It always seemed to be shut, or unsafe to cross. He couldn't remember much about the few times he'd managed to visit it. He had a dim recollection of a car museum and some ancient penny slot machines before it shut permanently in 1994. There had been continuous noise about its redevelopment, but nothing had happened and now it was slowly fading away into disrepair. As a teenager, he would sometimes walk along the stony beach when the tide was out and try to gain entry to the small rock of Birnbeck Island, where the main part of the pier was situated. Even now, teenagers occasionally tried their luck. A few months ago a group had to be rescued after becoming stranded by the oncoming tide, but thankfully, no one was here now. Geoff's route along the decrepit walkway was well practised; he felt as if he knew every rotten board, yet it still took him a good thirty minutes to manage it, and to clamber over the barbed wire at the pier's entrance.

In the van, he switched the air conditioner to the maximum heat as his body thawed. He wasn't sure how many more times he could do this. It was a miracle he hadn't been spotted or had an accident. And his prisoner was suffering. How many more nights would he be able to spend on the island without succumbing to the cold?

As Geoff set off for his mum's house he decided there would be only two more crossings. He would scope his two victims over the next day before returning to the island to check on the man. He would then return for one last time to finish his work.

Mum had left for work by the time he arrived at the house in the early morning. He felt like a stranger as he opened the front door. Welcoming the blast of heat from the central heating, he dumped his soiled clothes in the washing machine and made himself a breakfast of scrambled eggs and beans, washed down with coffee. His mind could play tricks on him when he was here. The warmth and security made him sentimental, made him forget what his mother had done.

He allowed himself a couple of hours of sleep as his clothes dried before setting off in his van.

His first job was in town, a bedsit removal from a flat in Jubilee Road. The client was a woman in her twenties who was moving back in with her parents. Geoff struggled to engage her in conversation as he lifted her meagre belongings into the back of the van. She was pretty, and on a couple of occasions he found himself staring at her slim figure and long hair, her big eyes, which failed to conceal her sadness. He turned away swiftly when she made eye contact and he wished he had the nerve to speak to her. He'd never had a girlfriend, had no idea where to begin. He recalled the women from the other night at the bar, the easy way Malcolm and his friends had talked to them and the welcoming smiles the women offered in return. They'd been impossibly beautiful, as was this woman.

He'd made some clumsy attempts to communicate with girls as he'd grown older, but they didn't want anything to do with him. He was always on the fringes. He'd tried changing his haircut, the clothes he wore, but they would always see through his disguise. There'd been a stigma to him ever since primary school that he'd never been able to shrug off. He wasn't good at sports, he wasn't particularly academic, and he simply didn't know how to speak to people. His only real talent was woodcarving, but that didn't get the girls.

Even at church they'd ignored him. When his dad had stopped attending, Geoff went alone – always sitting in the front pew. He'd tried to explain to some of the younger members of the congregation what he experienced being there, the visceral feeling running through his body when he sat in the church. He soon learnt their smiles were from politeness. Their eyes would wander towards his gloved hands and Geoff could tell they were thinking of the rumours that had plagued him ever since he'd been forced to leave St Bernadette's in Junior Five.

'You can follow me, but here's the address in case you get lost,' said the woman, handing him a piece of paper.

Even from the distance of her outstretched arm he could smell her perfume. The scent was exotic and ignited a desire in him he thought was long extinguished. He opened his mouth and considered asking her out. How hard could it be? He could ask if she fancied going for a coffee afterwards. There was nothing creepy in that, was there? She could say no if she wished, and that would be the end of it. His heart felt as if it were trying to free itself from his body. It raged within him, faster even than the times he'd been alone with Mrs Lloyd and Father Mulligan.

A sound fell from his lips, but it made no sense.

'What was that?' asked the woman. She was smiling, and Geoff couldn't quite understand her kindness.

'Nothing,' he said, turning away and climbing up into his van.

He didn't see her again. Her parents were waiting for her at their house in Bleadon, her father insisting on helping him move her belongings into the house. The man tipped him after he dropped the last box into the front hall, as if he were desperate for Geoff to leave.

Dad always told him he had nothing to worry about, that he was better off being alone anyway. Geoff had seen first-hand how relationships could destroy someone, but now and again he wished he had the chance to spend some time with a woman, even if it was just for one night.

He recognised the woman from his next job. Her name was Katherine Huddleston and they'd been in the same year at secondary school. They'd even shared some classes together. She was called Mrs Watson now, and she either didn't recognise him or pretended not to as she answered the front door of her house in Winscombe.

'The sofa is in the front room. I can get my son to help you, if you like?'

Geoff nodded, and she turned away and called upstairs for her son. 'We have a new sofa arriving tomorrow so need to create some space,' she added.

'Oh, that's nice,' said Geoff.

She smiled, but the gesture was uneasy. He could tell she was trying to place him. It had been over twenty years since school. The two children they'd been no longer existed. He saw the girl she'd been in her plump features and wondered if she was seeing the boy he'd been in him.

A teenage boy, almost the same height as Geoff, shouted down from the top of the stairs. 'What?' he demanded.

'Hi, darling. Please could you help this gentleman move the old sofa?'

The teenager sighed and shot Geoff a look of contempt as he reached the bottom stair. 'Come on, then,' he said.

Katherine sighed too, shrugging her shoulders at Geoff in lieu of an apology for her son's behaviour and leading him through to the living room. She'd done well for herself. The room was warm and well decorated, and Geoff caught a look of pride on her face as she pointed to the sofa. It was clear now that she recognised him.

'We have a leather sofa from John Lewis to replace this tatty old thing,' she said.

Geoff nodded. The sofa looked fine to him and he couldn't understand why she needed to replace it.

The boy grunted and moaned all the way to the van, despite the size of him. 'There,' he said, as he pushed the sofa into the back of the van.

'It's to be dropped off at the British Heart Foundation, as we discussed on the phone,' said Katherine, standing in the doorway of her house.

Geoff wanted to ask her if she remembered him, but kept silent as she gave him the cash. What would she think if he told her about his prisoner on the island, the two people he'd killed? Would that impress her? *How would it compare to a brand-new sofa from an overpriced department store?* he wondered.

'Thank you,' said Katherine, edging her door shut.

'Thank you,' repeated Geoff.

Inside the van, he switched on the heater and gazed at the sofa in the back. It looked good there and he was too tired to go to the charity shop, so he decided he would keep it. It would be his little secret. A point scored against Katherine Huddleston-Watson and all the people like her.

He bought dinner from a fish and chip shop on the Boulevard, and managed to find a space across the road from where the woman volunteered. Geoff had known her as Mrs Forester at school. She was the head teacher's wife, and the school secretary. Some things you didn't fully understand until you grew up. The way adults treated children, humouring them, promising them love and protection when it wasn't always theirs to give. Geoff had liked Mrs Forester. Once, in school, he'd fallen over on the hard concrete, reopening a scab on his knee, and she'd treated him with great kindness, cleaning the wound and offering him a juice as he'd sat in the nice-smelling office. He'd missed at least thirty minutes of class that day, and she'd been so kind he wished he could hurt his knee every day.

And perhaps she still was kind. People made mistakes, Geoff understood that now, and a person couldn't be judged solely by just some of their actions. God would have forgiven her by now, and until recently, Geoff would probably have done the same. He hadn't thought about her that much over the years, but after what happened to Dad he understood that she was, in part, to blame.

God may have forgiven her, but he couldn't. It was the only way he could save his dad from the damnation he faced.

She was older now, of course, but still had that skinny frame. They'd called them Little and Large at school – her husband, Mr Forester, was an obese man who always wore his trousers stretched over his gut, as if only the girth of his stomach held them in place. Geoff watched her leave the charity shop, the streetlight highlighting the wrinkles and over-indulgent make-up on her face, and walk the twenty metres or so to the bus stop.

She hadn't recognised him the other day when he'd bought a used paperback from the shop. She'd smiled at him as she'd taken the money, but he'd seen the lack of humanity behind the gesture. Her smile, like so much of her, was a mask she hid behind. It had fooled Geoff as a child but didn't fool him now. He finished his meal as she boarded the bus, before starting the engine and following her home.

Chapter Nineteen

Rain lashed the windscreen as Louise drove along Locking Road. Her wipers were on their fastest mode, but no sooner did they clear the water than her vision was once again impaired. The traffic out of Weston was at a standstill, the ghost-like figures within the vehicles staring forlornly towards the sign for the M5 as the downfall continued unabated.

Louise edged towards town, the text message from Thomas still fresh in her mind. The message itself was innocuous, but the lateness of its delivery, coupled with her sighting of Thomas in the hotel, changed her interpretation of it. But maybe she was reading too much into it. He could simply want to meet early to discuss the case, and hadn't she been the one to invite him for coffee only a couple of days ago?

She sighed as the rain finally relented. She'd hardly slept since Veronica Lloyd's body had been found on the beach, but she had to be careful not to let recent events overwhelm her. For the second night in a row, Finch hadn't sent her a message. In a way, the radio silence was more troubling than the constant texting. It didn't make her think he was finished with her. At least when he'd been sending her a text every night she'd sensed what he was up to, what he was thinking. Now she had no idea what he'd do next. There was one thing she was sure of, however. She needed a coffee.

The owner of the Kalimera greeted her with a smile. 'Your friend is already here,' she said, pointing to the corner, where Thomas sat nursing a coffee, staring out towards the rain-swept seafront.

Louise wasn't sure if she liked this new, talkative version of the woman. She realised she almost missed the sullen looks, the woman's veil of silence. 'Coffee, please,' she said, ignoring her insinuation.

Thomas glanced up at her as she sat opposite him. She couldn't recall ever seeing him look so dishevelled. He was clearly enduring a hangover. His face was pitted with grey and black stubble, heavy bags beneath his eyes. He was wearing the same suit as yesterday, with a fresh shirt and tie. 'Everything okay?' she asked.

'Yeah. Bit of a late one,' he replied, wincing as he sipped his coffee.

Her working theory was that he'd been kicked out of, or left, the marital home for the evening and had spent the time drowning his sorrows. Not that she was about to quiz him. He didn't know she'd seen him last night, and she wasn't about to let on just yet.

'Thanks, Georgina,' he said as the owner placed a chipped china cup brimming with coffee in front of Louise.

As the woman retreated to the counter, Louise shook her head. 'You know, I've been coming here ever since I moved to Weston and until now I didn't even know that woman's name.'

'Call yourself a detective?' said Thomas, squinting as if it pained him to laugh. 'I sort of know her. Used to go to school with my older sister. St Bernadette's, funnily enough.'

Even hung-over, there was still something about him – the darkness in his eyes, the roundness of his lips – that she didn't want to drag her eyes away from. 'You went to St Bernadette's?'

Thomas shook his head. 'No, we moved a bit further out once my sister went to secondary school, so I went to Balgowan in

125

Worlebury. I could have caught the bus in, but we're not that big on the whole church thing so there wasn't really any point.'

'You're a fellow lapsed Catholic?'

'Is there any other type?'

Louise drank her coffee; the liquid felt like nectar as it hit her bloodstream. 'I guess those who attended Father Mulligan's last Mass would disagree.'

Thomas could barely hold his head up to look at her. 'They're just lonely old women. I doubt they believe any more than we do.'

'I see you're all sunshine and light this morning,' said Louise, taking another hit of coffee.

'Sorry. I should have learnt when to stop at my age.'

'Anywhere nice?'

Thomas looked up at her, his eyes bloodshot.

'Last night. Where were you drinking?'

The hesitation lasted a split second, but she noticed it. To his credit, he didn't lie. 'The Royal Oak,' he said.

Louise feigned surprise as she told him she'd met the editor, Dominic Garrett, at the same place earlier in the evening.

'So you must have left him there. He was still in the bar all evening.'

'You know him?' she asked.

'Our paths have crossed. I know he likes his drink. Could have done without him in the bar last night, though. The man's voice doesn't half carry.'

Louise wanted to ask him who he'd been out with but didn't want to catch him in a lie. If he wanted to tell her why he'd been there, he would do so at some point. Instead, she asked, 'Any particular reason you wanted to see me?'

'Oh yeah, sorry about that as well. I was just thinking about the case and thought it might be worthwhile meeting up first in peace and quiet. But we could have discussed it at the station.'

'You don't need to apologise, Thomas. If there is anything you need to talk to me about, I'm here for you.'

'I appreciate that, boss.'

'But, Thomas.'

Thomas gazed at her, his eyebrows raised quizzically.

'If you call me boss again, I won't be responsible for my actions.'

This time he managed a smile. They briefly discussed the case before leaving, trying not to get too hopeful about the sighting of the lone male at the church. Louise left money for her coffee on the table.

'Thank you, Georgina,' she called out as she left the restaurant.

On the way back to the station Louise called the journalist, Tania Elliot, and postponed their meeting, excusing herself with the pressing concerns of the case. Louise was surprised by the vehemence of the journalist's response. 'I'm sure our readers will be very disappointed you don't have the time to discuss their concerns over safety,' she said.

Louise pulled over and put the phone to her ear. 'That's a bit of a low blow, Tania,' she said. She was experienced enough never to mistake a member of the press as a friend, but she'd always got along well with Tania so the implied threat felt disproportionate.

'You agreed to meet me, Louise. This is the biggest thing to have ever happened in this town, and yet you haven't even spoken to the local newspaper about it. I'm not sure if you're aware, but our town is in crisis. The winter is hard enough, without the threat of a serial killer walking the streets.'

'I think you're being a bit dramatic.'

'Two killings in three days. That's not dramatic? Is that a direct quote?'

'No, it isn't, Tania,' said Louise, remembering that she was talking to a journalist. 'Of course, our priority is keeping the town safe, but there is no direct threat to the general public at the moment.'

'Are you saying that the killer is targeting specific victims? There seems to be a link between the churches of St Michael's and St Bernadette's.'

'I can't comment on that at the moment, and I would appreciate it if you didn't allude to it in your reports.'

'The link is an obvious one. Why shouldn't I mention it?'

'The link could quite easily be coincidental and I think it would be irresponsible to print speculation. I will naturally keep you, personally, up to date with the latest developments.'

This appeared to appease the journalist for the time being, and after answering a couple of further questions about what the police were doing to solve the case, Louise promised again that she would keep in contact.

The first of the *old ladies*, as they were being called in the office, arrived at 9 a.m. Louise watched on video link as Thomas worked with an E-FIT specialist to try to identify the man who'd been at the Mass on the evening of Father Mulligan's death. They were in for a long day. One woman, Edith Case, was in her eighties, and her recollection was, at best, hazy. She kept describing the man as being big with hunched shoulders. By the time she'd left, the most significant feature they had was long, greasy hair which was somewhere between lower neck and shoulder length.

The final two women were little better. Like Edith, they both confirmed the man they had seen was big, but neither mentioned his greasy hair, long or otherwise. In the end, the E-FIT became a pointless exercise. None of the three women seemed to agree on anything. When, out of desperation, Thomas showed them photos of known local criminals, they shook their heads at each photo. Louise wondered if they had any idea what the man looked like, and if they'd agreed to attend out of anything more than sheer loneliness.

'So we're looking for an overweight tall short guy who may or may not have shoulder-length greasy hair,' said Farrell at the beginning of a midday meeting called by Louise.

Even Louise stifled a laugh. Recollection was difficult at the best of times, but when you didn't even know you were witnessing a crime, it could be impossible. That didn't change the fact that the lone man was still their most promising lead.

'We need to intensify the search. Go door to door again, and check for any suspicious sightings. Mention the man's size, and his hair, if necessary. He had to get to the church somehow. Was he driving? If so, what was he driving? What route did he take? If not, how did he get there?' Louise was doing little more than thinking out loud, but it was good to give voice to her thoughts. She ignored the collective groan from her audience and decided not to share her information about the fire at St Bernadette's for the time being. Then she assigned tasks, reminding everyone that they had a potential link now. Two victims, two possible motives. She drew a line in red on the murder board in the meeting room between Veronica Lloyd and Father Mulligan and placed a question mark beneath it. 'Let's find out, shall we?' she said, before dismissing the team.

She was troubled that Robertson had stayed in his office during the briefing, and was about to go and see him when she received a text message. Not Thomas or Finch this time, but her old colleague Tracey Pugh. She hadn't spoken to her since their drinks the other night in Bristol and it felt good to hear from her – until she read the message. Louise read it a second time, trying to work out if there was some hidden code she hadn't noticed:

Looks like they're getting the team back together. See you at yours this afternoon. T x

DCI Robertson was standing by his door as she looked up from her phone, trying to contain her growing anger. 'Louise, a word,' he said, retreating into his office.

Louise took a deep breath, glancing around to gauge whether anyone else was in on this, before walking slowly towards Robertson's office.

'Take a seat,' he said.

'Did you not think you should run this by me first, Iain?' said Louise, holding her phone up.

'Oh, you've heard,' he said, reading her. 'It's just been signed off now. The assistant chief constable thought we needed help, and who am I to argue?'

'That's fine, Iain, but what exactly is this help?'

'Just one officer from head office. Your old colleague, DI Tracey Pugh. DCI Finch thought it would be a good fit, as you used to have a sound working relationship, so I understand. Is this not the case?'

Louise knew it wasn't Tracey's fault, and if she could have picked anyone from her old team to work with it would have been her. What troubled her was the involvement of Finch. 'Tracey is great, but that's not really the point, is it?' she said.

'I don't understand your problem here, Louise. Our team is not really set up for this kind of thing. If it wasn't for your experience, then this would have been passed over to MIT already. I thought you'd welcome the opportunity of having one more experienced officer on your team.'

She glanced out of the window, trying to keep a lid on her emotions. Despite their friendship, Tracey would be duty bound to report everything she found out to Finch. That in itself shouldn't have bothered her – he could get all the information he wanted easily enough – but it did. Finch was worming his way into the investigation, and with Tracey in place he already had a foothold for when he decided to take over. She wanted to tell Robertson her fears, but it would only make her sound weak, if not paranoid. 'Okay, on your head,' she said.

'What does that mean exactly?'

'I thought you'd want this case, Iain. Now you're going to let it be taken away from you.'

Robertson's eyebrows narrowed, his anger palpable. In the time she'd known him, she'd never had a reason to question his professionalism, but now she wondered why he hadn't put up a bit more of a fight. If HQ took over, then they would take the plaudits for any results. Maybe there was a reason he'd been in the same rank for so many years.

'You're upset. I don't know why, but you are, so I will let your last comment go. But let me be clear, nothing has been taken away from me, or us. We are part of a bigger picture here, Louise. Maybe that is something you should consider.' He emphasised the 'you' with a Glaswegian growl and returned to the paperwork on his desk.

Louise stood, acknowledging the dismissal. He wouldn't expect an apology so she didn't offer one.

Back at her desk, she replied to Tracey, confirming that she was looking forward to seeing her. Tracey was an excellent detective with a great eye for detail, Louise reminded herself. Furthermore, she had a way of galvanising any team she was part of. Louise hadn't met anyone who Tracey couldn't get along with, and it was a quality she admired. Hopefully, Tracey would help to bring the team together.

She called a meeting for when Tracey was due to arrive. At present, the place was empty, save for Simone and a couple of admin staff. Louise took the time to update her HOLMES record. Putting the investigation in writing highlighted the precarious state they were in. Two bodies, and the closest they had to a suspect was an unidentified lone male at a church service.

Was the positioning of the two bodies significant? Both victims had been left in places where they could easily be discovered. Did the locations mean anything? Was there significance to the beach and the church? The more she examined the evidence, the more chaotic the incidents appeared. Veronica Lloyd's body had been moved, but Father Mulligan was found in situ. Both victims were bound and seemingly killed by an object forced into their wrist, but on Lloyd it was the right wrist, Mulligan the left.

She was considering the endless anomalies when Simone called to say she had Stephen Dempsey on the line.

Louise picked up her phone. 'Stephen.'

'Louise. I've managed to move my backlog so have been able to focus on my autopsy of Father Mulligan.'

'Great, what have you got for me?' asked Louise, wondering how you moved a backlog of dead people.

'I still have some work to do, but I believe the cause of death to be the severed radial artery on the victim's left wrist. An almost mirror copy of what happened to Veronica Lloyd. In fact, after measuring the wound on Father Mulligan's wrist, I would hazard a guess that the same object was inserted into his wrist. The measurements are identical, but I am hypothesising at this point.'

'Do we have any idea what this object would be?'

'Hard to say for sure. The incision itself is not that large, a diameter of thirteen millimetres. We will cross-check with Veronica Lloyd to ascertain if there are any matching fibres in the wound. What is interesting – very interesting, I believe – is the positioning of the wound. As I said, it's identical to the positioning found on Veronica Lloyd, and I do not use that term loosely. The entry point is through the bones of the forearm, close to the wrist. With Mrs Lloyd's body, I thought it was perhaps a fluke, but the killer has managed to drive whatever object he used between eight small bones in both cases.'

'That sounds very specific.'

'Yes. I have some ideas but will need to get back to you.'

'Thanks, Stephen, keep me updated,' said Louise, hanging up before he had time to engage her in small talk.

She should have been happy with the revelation, but for the time being it raised more questions than answers. It appeared they were looking for someone highly skilled and precise, and this troubled her. If the killer was already so accomplished, it was possible Veronica Lloyd hadn't been his or her first kill. It also indicated that Father Mulligan would not be their last.

Tracey was waiting for her in reception. Louise greeted her with a hug, and although she had only seen her the other evening, it felt reassuring, seeing a friendly face again.

'So this is your new patch?' said Tracey, glancing around at the dull interior of the reception area.

'It's been eighteen months, but yes.'

'Buy me a coffee?'

'I'll get you a coffee from the canteen, but I can't guarantee you'll like it.'

'Lead the way,' said Tracey.

The canteen was a small kitchenette in the heart of the building. Louise poured them coffee from the machine, which, thankfully, used real coffee beans, and they took a seat on the plastic chairs in the main dining space. 'So this is a surprise,' she said.

'Tell me about it. Finch only told me this morning. Apparently, you have some staff shortages?'

Louise shrugged but didn't elaborate. She didn't want to get into a discussion about DCI Finch with Tracey. She was a loyal friend, but she didn't have the same toxic relationship with the man. 'We can always do with the help. As you know, the CID department here is very small and this case is growing in importance,' she said, choosing her words with care.

She spent the next thirty minutes updating Tracey on the case and her new colleagues. The lack of progress was evident as she spoke, but Tracey didn't comment, understanding that investigations often had their own momentum and the focus could change within hours.

By late afternoon the team had reassembled and they presented their daily reports after Louise had introduced Tracey to the team. The only decent news came from Thomas. A local resident on Clarendon Road, fifty metres from the church, had reported seeing a lone male walking towards St Michael's on the evening of Mulligan's murder.

'The witness described him as being between six foot two and six foot four. He was wearing a long trench coat, had a thick, heavy-set body. Commented on the weird way he walked – his shoulders were hunched and he limped slightly on his left leg,' said DS Ireland.

Louise pointed out that this account resonated with some of the descriptions from the old ladies at Father Mulligan's Mass. 'Thomas, work with Tracey on this,' she said. 'We need to work out a route that he could have taken to the church, so backtrack from the sighting, follow all possible roads and pathways until we start hitting CCTV. See if we can spot him. Usual thing: check all shops, pubs, restaurants. Someone else must have seen him.'

Again, she decided not to share her investigation into the eighties fire at St Bernadette's just yet. It was something she could handle alone for the time being, but she wasn't finished with Veronica Lloyd's old parish. She instructed her team to repeat the interviews with parishioners of the church and to cross-reference their knowledge of St Michael's and Father Mulligan. 'Remember, Mulligan used to be the priest at St Bernadette's. Let's find out what people know about him. If there is any suggestion as to why someone would want him dead.'

As the team went to work, she returned her attention to the fire. She was concerned that she was giving it more attention than it deserved, but after speaking to Garrett it still nagged at her. The police report of the incident wasn't digitised so she had to order paper copies from head office. She wanted to speak to the investigator in charge and to determine for herself if, as Garrett had insinuated, the case had been improperly investigated.

That evening she was the last person to leave the office. Robertson said goodbye to her at eight, but she stayed on for another hour to update HOLMES and to read through the ongoing reports from her team.

She spotted the man as soon as she left the main building. He was loitering on the pavement outside the car park, ten metres from her car. Dressed in a long black coat, he was at least six feet tall but didn't match the heavy-set description put forward by Thomas. His coat fell from narrow shoulders, his body rake-thin and angular.

The car park was well lit and cameras pointed towards it from various directions, yet she kept one hand on her pepper spray while she freed her baton from her belt and approached the man. Five metres from him she stopped. 'Can I help?' she said.

As the man turned, she saw the dog collar across his neck. *Great, another priest*, she thought as the man smiled at her. He was older than he'd looked at a distance, the streetlight highlighting the thick grooves in his forehead. 'DI Louise Blackwell?' he asked.

'That's me,' said Louise, her fingers tensing on the baton.

'My name is Monsignor Ashley, Inspector Blackwell. I think we need to talk.'

Chapter Twenty

Another restless night. Sleep had been difficult for years but over the last few evenings Eileen had struggled to get more than a couple of hours. She was too preoccupied with thoughts of Mr Lanegan. It was probably nothing, but she couldn't get the idea out of her head that something had been wrong at his house. *You're just a foolish old lady*, she would convince herself every night before going to bed – Mr Lanegan could have time away, even if he had forgotten to mention his departure to her – but the darkness would reignite her fears, and by morning she was sure something bad had happened.

But what could she do, who could she tell? There was no one closer than Mr Lanegan in her life, and she didn't even have a phone number for him. And even if there were anyone else to tell, what would she say? That something had been off about the house, that there was a coldness present that she'd never experienced before? Fat chance. They would lock her away in some God-awful retirement home, or possibly a nuthouse. She had no option; she had to return to his house to find out where he was.

She set off in the early-morning darkness after managing a few spoonfuls of warm porridge and lemon tea for breakfast. The temperature had dropped a few degrees since the other morning and the cold wind stung her eyes and clouded her already poor vision. 'They should put me down like the lame horse I am,' she mumbled as she walked down the hill to the sea wall. The next bus wasn't for two hours so she took her usual route. The tide was high and she stopped by the RNLI Lifeboat Station to marvel at the shifting water, a sight even her old eyes would never grow tired of.

Going up the hill was harder than ever. It was the first time she'd walked the incline twice in a week in twenty years, and her body wasn't ready for it. The pain was tremendous and left no part of her untouched. The clicking of her joints was audible as she struggled forever upwards, and her inflamed muscles ached as if they'd been torn from her bones. Yet the satisfaction when she reached the summit was second to none. She gazed back down at the town of her birth – the sun rising behind the thick plumage of grey sky – in victory, before continuing the walk to Mr Lanegan's.

Only when she arrived at his door did she realise that it wasn't a very neighbourly time of the day to be calling. If Mr Lanegan was at home, and had any sense to him, he would, most likely, still be in bed. She peered through his front window and then the letterbox before deciding to open the door using her copy of his front-door key. If he was asleep, then let him be. She had to find out if he was okay.

The cold, and something else deep within her blood that she couldn't identify, made her hand shake as she placed the key into the opening. She couldn't unlock it on her first attempt and had to use her spare hand to force the key to turn. She eased open the door. 'Mr Lanegan,' she called, even though she was now convinced no one was in the house.

Inside, she peered at the electric thermostat on the wall. The house needed heat almost as much as she did. After a few minutes of study she pressed the '+' symbol on the screen, marvelling as the number rose from fifteen to twenty-two and the boiler ignited in the kitchen.

As the radiators grumbled she took herself upstairs, calling out Mr Lanegan's name as she made her slow progress. She had to rest at the top of the stairs. Everything looked the same as she'd left it the other day, but still she hoped to see Mr Lanegan fast asleep as she opened his bedroom door.

But she was disappointed. His bed was made; it looked like he hadn't returned since she'd been here last. It felt a little disrespectful, but she took a seat on Mr Lanegan's bed, the speed of her ascent and her growing concern leaving her breathless. Why did this bother her so? For all she knew, Mr Lanegan could be on holiday.

She moved from room to room, trying to understand why she was getting herself into such a state. She tried to rationalise the situation, but her thoughts kept returning to the overwhelming fact that Mr Lanegan had never gone away before without telling her. And that could mean only one thing: he'd been taken sick and had gone to hospital.

She dialled 999 from the landline, an indignant woman informing her that she shouldn't call emergency services to check if someone had been admitted to hospital.

'But it *is* an emergency,' said Eileen, confused by the heartless way the woman spoke to her.

'It isn't an emergency, I'm afraid. You will need to call the local hospitals.'

'But that's what I'm trying to find out. What hospital was he taken to?'

The woman sighed, as if speaking to a child. 'Where are you calling from?'

You'll be like me one day, thought Eileen. 'St Ives,' she said.

'I would suggest you try West Cornwall Hospital. They will be able to guide you further.'

'Do you have the number?'

The woman sighed again before rushing through a number of digits and hanging up.

Eileen spoke to three more people before a man told her that Mr Lanegan hadn't been admitted to any of the hospitals in Cornwall in the last month. 'You could perhaps try the police if you think your friend is missing,' said the man, who was infinitely more helpful than the first woman she'd spoken with.

By this time, Eileen was too tired to ask for a phone number. There was a local police station in town and she decided it would be easier to wend her way downhill than go through another round of phone calls.

She needed a pick-me-up first. Back in the kitchen, she filled the kettle, and as she waited for it to boil she searched through Mr Lanegan's kitchen cupboards, hoping for some biscuits. She found a tin of shortbread in one of the drawers. He was always so generous that she was sure he wouldn't mind.

The tea was heavenly, and she treated herself by dunking a second biscuit into her cup. It was a peaceful area where Mr Lanegan lived, the quiet welcome. Her thoughts turned, as they always did at times of silence, to her son, Terrence. After leaving Mr Lanegan's house the other day, she had wanted to call him, but she didn't know how much it would cost to call Australia. Not that she needed a phone. Terrence never called her. The only calls she ever received were from people trying to sell her things, or convince her she'd once been involved in an accident. Now and again, she got angry. How hard could it be to pick up a phone and call your own mother? He'd never been the most affectionate of children, and had been a difficult teenager, falling in with the wrong crowd, but he was a man now, and she'd thought he would at least spare her a thought in her old age.

She shook her head, and it was only as she stood to rinse her teacup that she noticed the lock of the back door was broken.

Chapter Twenty-One

'It is rather late, Monsignor Ashley. Could we meet tomorrow morning?' said Louise. The day's events had drained her and she lacked the energy for another meeting.

'I think you would appreciate what I have to say,' said Ashley.

'I'm sure it could wait until the morning,' said Louise, clicking open her car.

'What if I were to tell you that I believe there will be three more killings?'

Louise stopped. Sighing, she shut her car door. 'I'd say we'd better get a drink.'

She took him to a small bar near the station, which was emptier than usual. 'Excuse my ignorance, but what exactly is a monsignor?' she asked, once they were both sitting in the snug. Although she would have loved something alcoholic, she ordered a sparkling mineral water, while the monsignor drank a pint of Guinness, the white of the foam catching on his greying beard.

'It's just a title. I'm basically a priest with a fancy name, not as grandiose as a bishop, I'm afraid.'

'You're here in an official capacity?'

Ashley smiled, his eyes full of warmth. 'I'm just a concerned citizen.'

'So this isn't a premonition or something like that?'

Ashley chuckled and took another sip of his drink. 'We can be mystical in the church, but premonition is beyond us at present.'

'So why do you think there will be three more killings?' asked Louise, lowering her voice.

'Are you religious, DI Blackwell?'

'Does it matter?'

'I suppose it doesn't. I imagine you've heard the story of the Passion of the Christ?'

'You mean when Jesus was crucified?' said Louise, recalling the crude rendition of the Stations of the Cross at St Bernadette's.

The monsignor smiled in acknowledgement. 'What can you tell me about the manner in which your two murder victims died?' he asked, his voice a rich baritone.

'I can't tell you any more than is public knowledge.'

Ashley nodded, as if he'd expected her answer. 'An object was driven into the right wrist of Veronica Lloyd, between the eight bones of her forearm towards the wrist. The same fate befell Father Mulligan, only to his left wrist. Is this correct?'

Louise tried to hide her surprise. 'You seem to know more than the public. How did you come by this information?'

Ashley held his arms out. 'Two murders, two Catholic churches – we were likely to find out.'

'Remind me in what capacity you are speaking to me?'

Ashley chuckled. 'As I said, Inspector, unofficial. What I'm about to say is not something you want going public.'

Louise was intrigued. She couldn't help a nervous laugh slipping out as she imagined the priest telling her about some Old Testament curse. She was about to ask if it was the end of days, but didn't want to sound disrespectful. 'Okay, you've piqued my interest.'

'Wonderful,' said the monsignor, taking another sip of Guinness. 'Not a bad drop. So, the mystery of the Passion.' Ashley unclasped the chain around his neck and showed it to her. 'Do you know what this is?' he asked her.

'A rosary,' said Louise. She'd never had one herself, but remembered the older parishioners from her church wearing them. It consisted of a number of beads. As far as she was aware, she told him, each bead represented a prayer.

'Very good,' said Ashley, playing with the beads. 'These smaller beads are arranged in what we call decades, ten beads, which represent ten Hail Marys. Basically, they are counting devices so that one can focus on prayer rather than counting. These larger beads are intended to honour the five holy wounds Christ suffered when He was crucified,' he added, before pausing.

'Five holy wounds?' asked Louise, experiencing a sinking feeling.

'For the Catholic Church, these wounds have great significance. The first two holy wounds are the nails inserted into the hands or wrists of Christ.'

Louise stared at the monsignor, trying her best to assess the man. He sounded sincere, but she only had his word that he was even a priest. She ordered another round of drinks, this time getting herself a gin and tonic.

'Let me get this straight. You think Veronica and Father Mulligan were crucified?' she said when she returned from the bar, lowering her voice.

'Not exactly, but I believe your killer is re-enacting the wounds suffered by Our Lord. I'm afraid we've seen similar things before.'

'Similar, how?'

'You've heard of stigmata, Inspector?'

'Yes, of course. But that is self-inflicted. Unless you believe in magic.'

Ashley began laughing just after taking another swig of Guinness. He coughed and excused himself. 'We don't call it magic,

Inspector. As you know, stigmata is the manifestation of bodily wounds which correspond with the wounds suffered by Christ on the cross. Namely, the five holy wounds. Although you are right that these are often self-inflicted, some believe these marks appear, or manifest, without any outside influence.'

Louise tried not to sound incredulous. 'And you believe this?'

'As a Church, we do like our miracles,' said Ashley, with a hint of mischief.

'How is this related?'

'While the majority of cases are, indeed, self-inflicted hoaxes, it has been known for other people to inflict these wounds. In the early twentieth century, a cardinal in Italy was discovered to be drugging the Communion wine and wounding his unsuspecting congregation.'

'But this is more than stigmata. Whoever is doing this isn't stopping with a simple wound.'

'Yes, of course. I think what is of significance is the placement of the nails.'

She paused, her glass mid-air. 'No one has said there were nails.'

'No, but whatever has been inserted into the victims' wrists has been done so with exact precision. If you look at most images of the Crucifixion, the nails holding Christ in place are positioned through the palms of his hands and feet. But in truth, had the nails been placed in such a way, the sheer weight of his body would cause his hands to have been ripped off. The Romans were, alas, very good at this sort of thing. Your killer could have simply hammered the nails through the victims' palms, but the fact that both incisions were so specific suggests they know what they're doing. And there are five holy wounds, which means there are three to go.'

'So the next victim will have a nail driven through their feet?' said Louise, struggling with the absurdity of her own words.

There was no levity to Ashley's stare. 'If your killer continues in the same fashion, then yes. Two of the holy wounds were to Christ's feet or ankles.'

'And the fifth?'

'Any good doubting Thomas should know the fifth holy wound, Inspector,' said Ashley, his grin returning.

'Not this one.'

'The fifth holy wound was to the side of Christ's chest. The Romans would pierce the body to make sure that their victims were dead. It is believed Christ showed the wound to Thomas after His resurrection.'

'I see,' said Louise, taking a long drink. Although she was already convinced the killer hadn't finished, the thought of three more killings was hard to fathom. 'Okay, so that's the bad news. What else do you have for me?'

'I'm afraid that's it, DI Blackwell. A friendly pointer in the right direction.'

Louise sighed. 'Well, thank you. It's something we can work with, I suppose. What can you tell me about the fire at St Bernadette's in 1983?' she added, trying to catch the priest unawares.

Ashley appeared unruffled, though she noticed he reached for his drink before answering. 'A tragic accident. Why do you ask?'

'Do you really believe that, Monsignor Ashley?'

'I'm afraid I have little knowledge of the incident. As I recall, there was a safety issue and, thankfully, no one was injured. We have over three hundred thousand churches worldwide. These things do happen. Why do you ask?' he repeated.

It was Louise's turn to be coy as she sipped her soothing gin and tonic. She didn't want to share Garrett's theory that the fire hadn't been an accident, but from Ashley's responses she suspected he knew more than he was letting on. 'Father Mulligan was working at the church at the time of the fire. Coincidences happen, but

145

with Veronica Lloyd being an active member of St Bernadette's, I have to wonder if the events are related.'

'That is why you are the detective, and me a mere priest. I wish you well on your search,' said Ashley, standing up and stretching out his long, thin hand for her to shake.

She watched him leave and ordered another drink before closing time, no longer in a rush to return home to the emptiness of the bungalow. She could picture the headline now: 'The Crucifier', or some other such religious connotation. The wounds on Veronica's and Father Mulligan's wrists were consistent with Ashley's theory, but that alone wasn't enough to base an investigation around it. It would be a hard sell to Robertson and her colleagues, but at that precise moment, it sounded like the best line of enquiry. Forgetting for the time being how the priest had come about the information, she considered the precision of the incisions on the victims' wrists. That in itself was a potential lead. It was possible the killer might have a medical background of some sort.

Placing her empty glass on the counter, she left the bar feeling light-headed as she walked headlong into the cold breeze back to her car. She'd only had two shots of gin but felt guilty as she set off for home in case she was over the limit. Locking Road was deserted, the majority of the town's inhabitants safe behind the stone walls of their homes.

On the way home she thought about the monsignor and the light-hearted way he'd presented his theory. Perhaps it was just his manner, the practised way he gave out bad news. Her phone pinged and she glanced down to find that the message was from an unknown caller. Her heart leapt. She couldn't explain why, but she preferred it when Finch was in contact with her. Maybe it was something to do with the old adage about keeping your enemies close.

She waited until she was home before opening the message. She glanced at the murder board first, noting the injuries to Lloyd and Mulligan. What at first looked like a frenzied attack was now revealed to have been premeditated and precise.

'Okay, Finch, what do you have for me this time?' she said, touching her phone's screen.

Chapter Twenty-Two

Sergeant Joslyn Merrick had already finished the morning's briefing at St Ives police station and assigned duties to her small team of police staff and community officers by the time PC James Lewis arrived for work.

'A word,' she said, interrupting the young man as he began to speak.

In her office she instructed him to sit down before she closed her office door. She stayed by the door for thirty seconds, daring him to look round at her.

'How old are you, James?' she asked, when she eventually took her seat behind her desk.

'Twenty-five,' said the police constable, who was only six months into his probationary period.

'Do you know how old I am?'

James's mouth hung open as the implications of answering the question ran through his mind.

'I'm forty-five years old, James.' She held up her hand. 'I know I don't look it. But I'm twenty years older than you.'

The PC looked bemused, so she continued, enjoying the roll she was on. 'You're single, aren't you, James?'

'Well, sort of,' said James, a nervous twinge to his voice.

'But you're not married?'

He shook his head.

'And you don't have children?'

'No.'

'Oh, really, so you don't have a seven-year-old and a nine-year-old who go to different schools?'

'No.'

'Oh, that's interesting, James. Guess what? I do. And I got them out of bed this morning, made them breakfast, got them changed and took them to their separate schools – don't ask – and I still managed to get here thirty minutes before my shift started.'

If anything, James looked more relaxed now, as if he thought she was simply offloading about her home life. Joslyn changed that assumption with a stern drop in her voice. 'Sit up, Constable, when I'm talking to you.'

James sat bolt upright, his cheeks reddening.

'Now, if at the grand old age of forty-five, and with two young children, I can get to work on time, can you explain to me why you cannot?'

'Sorry, Sarge, I overslept.'

Joslyn snorted out loud. It was getting harder and harder to get recruits this far south-west in Cornwall, let alone quality ones, but sometimes she was mystified by how some of these young officers managed to succeed at training college. They were relying more and more on the community liaison officers as it was, and the ones she had at her disposal were of greater use than the young man in front of her, who was as green as she'd ever encountered.

She opened his file on her iPad as he played with his fingers. The lad was exceptionally bright, had a first-class degree from Durham University, so she didn't quite understand his ineptitude. 'Listen, James, this is the fourth time this month you've been late. I want you to succeed in this role, but you have to give me something. If I'd given that excuse for being late when I was a probationary, I'd have been out on my ear. Is there something you're not telling me? Anything I can help you with?'

'No.'

It was true, she wanted to help him, but he had to give her something to work with. 'In that case, I'm writing you up. This can't go on. This isn't a normal nine-to-five job, James, you know that. From now on, you are to arrive at work thirty minutes before your shift starts. Am I clear?'

James began to shake his head, and she thought for a second that he was going to dare to argue with her.

'Yes, Sarge.'

'Good. Don't fuck this up, James. Cornwall and Devon have invested a lot of money in you and I don't want to be blamed for it all getting pissed against the wall. Do we understand each other?'

'Sarge.'

'And as an extra treat, you can work with me this morning. I'll meet you outside in five.'

As PC Lewis slouched away, Joslyn uploaded the file from yesterday. An elderly lady, Eileen Boswell, had reported a missing person by the name of Richard Lanegan. Lanegan employed the woman as a cleaner, which, considering her age, surprised Joslyn. According to Eileen, Lanegan was always home when she cleaned, but he hadn't been in this week, and when she'd returned three days later she'd noticed the lock on the back door was broken. The cleaner had no number for Lanegan or any emergency contacts, so Joslyn had agreed to look into it but hadn't the time or the resources yesterday to visit the place.

'Listen, Sarge, I'm sorry about this morning. I promise it won't happen again,' said James in the car park outside the station.

Joslyn looked at him. He was a good enough kid, but she feared he was still too naive to be on the beat. The best she could do for him was to lead by experience. 'Good, James. Don't let me down.'

They drove to the house, Joslyn switching on the car radio to drown out the awkward silence. Lanegan's house was on a small estate near the fire station. The elderly woman had given her a key, but Joslyn didn't want to open the door unless it was absolutely necessary. After knocking, she peered through the front windows before instructing James to go around the back.

He returned a few minutes later to say the back door was open and the lock appeared broken.

'Okay, make a note of the time. We're going in.'

They stepped inside the front door. The first thing to hit her was the heat. The thermostat was stuck on twenty-two and she switched it off as sweat prickled her brow.

'Something feels wrong in here,' said James as he walked through to the kitchen and the broken back door.

Joslyn snorted. She had no time for how things felt. That was for television. All she had to work on was a busted lock and an overheated house. The cleaner had been in twice in the last week so she could have put the heating on and forgot about it, and the broken lock could be innocuous. 'Don't start jumping to conclusions, James. We need to find some contact details for this Mr Lanegan. See if you can find an address book, or anything with a phone number.'

Either Lanegan was meticulously tidy, or the cleaner had done a great job. The place was spotless, everything in perfect order. Joslyn opened the drawers in Lanegan's bedroom, and found everything arranged in an almost obsessive way. Even the man's underwear was folded and arranged neatly. If the cleaner was responsible for this, then it might be worth chatting to her. Joslyn's house was the antithesis of this place. Her husband worked shifts at a factory in Falmouth and it was hard enough for them to arrange having one parent present at home at any given time, let alone keeping the place in order. But where her house was full of love, Lanegan seemed to live a life of solitude and simplicity. There were no photos in the house, no books – other than copies of the Bible and a few other religious texts spread through the rooms – and no television. Joslyn tried not to judge other people by the way they lived, knowing most would condemn her as a slob if they could see the mess she lived in. People managed in different ways, and Lanegan could well be happy in this minimalist setting.

She tried his bedside cabinet, and beneath the King James Bible she found what she'd been after, an old-fashioned address book with small alphabetical indents. She flicked through the contents, keen to depart the house, noting the immaculate calligraphy of the man's writing style. There was enough here to be going on with, so she called down to James. 'Let's get back to base. You have some phone calls to make.'

Chapter Twenty-Three

The message from Finch was anti-climactic. No mention of his visit to Weston, or the ongoing case, just a familiar refrain:

Good night, Louise. Sleep tight x

Anything else may have given him away, but still she was disappointed that he hadn't revealed himself. She recalled the way he'd looked at her in Robertson's office as if nothing had happened between them, as if it wasn't his fault she was stuck in this town. He could certainly play the part when warranted. It had taken her years to see through him, so she couldn't blame Robertson and the others for being taken in by the man. But he would slip up, she was convinced of that, and she would be ready when he did.

Robertson called as she was heading into Weston the following morning. It was as if the man didn't sleep.

'When will you be gracing us with your presence, Inspector Blackwell?' he asked, his voice gruffer than usual on the car's internal speaker system. It was 7 a.m.

'Ten minutes.'

'Don't be any longer,' said Robertson, ending the call.

And good morning to you, thought Louise. The clouds were low and black as she swung her car around Walliscote Road into the car park, as if the sky were falling in. The desk sergeant greeted her with a minuscule nod as she entered the main office, and the muted atmosphere in the building was almost enough to send her back through the doors. The place was always dull in comparison to Bristol, but at this hour it had all the energy of a morgue, and this while in the middle of a high-profile multiple-murder case.

She poured herself a coffee before heading into Robertson's office. He tried his usual power play of keeping his head down, pretending to read the notes in front of him, as she entered the room.

'Coffee, Iain?' she said, placing a cup in front of him.

He surprised her by handing her a copy of a national tabloid newspaper. 'Page seven,' he said.

'Not your usual reading material, Iain.'

'No. I wouldn't normally wipe my arse with it, but I like to keep up with things that are happening in my town.'

Louise opened the paper to page seven, screwing her eyes up as she saw the headline: 'Pensioner Killer hits seaside town.'

'It lacks spark,' said Louise.

'Does it now?'

'It's not much of a nickname, is it?'

'Stop fucking deflecting, this is important. Read the bit where it says we have no suspect. And then you can go and have a quick look online, see the outpouring of grief, especially for the bloody priest.'

Louise read the article. The murders had been sensationalised and it was poorly researched. It suggested the town was almost in a state of lockdown, and indicated that the already struggling tourism industry would be hit further by the killings.

'Come on, Iain, that doesn't affect the way we run the case. I want this bastard caught as much as anyone. I've seen first-hand what he did to Father Mulligan and Veronica Lloyd. Moaning about us in the press and online doesn't change anything.'

'Don't be so fucking naive. You and I are meeting Assistant Chief Constable Morley this morning. He's coming here. He's never once visited this station in all my years in this town. I'm getting shit from all angles, Louise, and I'm afraid to say I can't see this being our case by the end of the day, unless you come up with something fast.'

Louise placed the paper down, when really she wanted to throw it at her boss. She repeated the manoeuvre with her cup of coffee. This had Finch's hands all over it. He had excellent contacts in the press, even the nationals. She'd watched him charm them in the past, keeping the local reporters topped up with beer, passing on information when it suited him and his investigations. What better way to take the case from her? 'What do you want me to say, Iain?'

'I want you to say you have a suspect. I want you to say you have something I can offer the assistant chief constable.'

Louise understood the pressure Robertson was under, but he knew as well as she did that it wasn't that easy. Everything changed when you were dealing with a multiple murderer. The normal avenue of first exploring family, close friends and work colleagues was altered when there was more than one body. Focus changed to finding a link between the victims and establishing a motive. Although they didn't understand the killer's motive at present, the probabilities were high that his or her victims had been specifically targeted. Their age may have been an issue, but Louise thought the links to the churches was just as important, especially after her conversation with the monsignor. It had become clear that the killer knew what they were doing and was precise in their manner of execution.

Louise took a deep breath and told Robertson about her meeting with Monsignor Ashley. She explained about the five wounds, and Ashley's theory that there would be at least three more killings.

Robertson looked at her as if she were deranged. 'This is fantastic. Morley will love this. Three more killings and we can wrap this up.'

'It gives us a clear angle to investigate.'

'Unless this monsignor – is that even a thing? – is some nutjob. Have you looked into him yet?'

'I only met him last night. I have all his details so will verify him this morning.'

'This is a flimsy premise to move on, Louise.'

'Yes and no. We have an active parishioner of one Catholic church, and the priest of another one as victims. The method of the killings is consistent with the historical method of crucifixion as explained by Monsignor Ashley.'

'That is to be determined.'

'Yes, but the information does come direct from the autopsy, and the doc's report confirmed that the incisions missed the eight bones in the hand on both victims. Surely that is too much of a coincidence. I believe the killer is obsessed, one way or another, with the Crucifixion of Christ.'

Robertson swigged the coffee, glaring at her all the while. 'Are you kidding me, Louise? That's not a motive.'

'No, but it's a line of investigation.'

'Let's hope the assistant chief sees it that way.'

'File's just arrived for you from HQ,' said Simone as Louise returned to her office. Louise nodded her head in acceptance, her energy drained from the early-morning meeting with the DCI. She was about to open the document when Tracey arrived.

'What's up, boss?' she said, in an overdone American accent.

'You seem happy?' said Louise, noting the smell of nicotine and a faint whiff of alcohol behind the almost overwhelming perfume. 'Good night?'

'You could say that. I'll tell you later. I made some inroads into the St Michael's congregation yesterday, though it's hard to get a word out of anyone. There is a distinct mistrust of the police force in this area, I would say. From the people I did speak to, the general feeling was of utter shock, as you would imagine, but also genuine grief. There's definitely a high level of feeling for Father Mulligan in that community. And that's despite the fact that he only did one service a week. They're holding a Mass for him this Sunday. Might be worth a visit.'

That's if I'm still working on the case by then, thought Louise. 'Thanks, Tracey. I'll be holding the briefing in thirty minutes.'

'Boss,' said Tracey, giving her a quick salute.

Louise watched her friend circulate among the other officers, each seemingly pleased to see her. Louise admired the easy way Tracey had with people. Not having the baggage of leadership made it easier for her, but Louise had to work much harder to develop such relationships and she wondered if that was the reason she'd yet to be promoted beyond inspector.

She tore at the large manila envelope left by Simone, pleased to see the old-fashioned case notes from the fire at St Bernadette's. The brown card, dated May 1983, had a musty scent and was layered with a fine film of dust. The lead officer at the time was Detective Sergeant Ben Farnham. Louise wasn't familiar with the name, or the paperwork itself. From what she could ascertain, the investigation had been thorough. Farnham made reports on a daily basis that contained witness statements as well as details from the other emergency services. The photos she'd viewed in the old copy of the *Mercury* were present, as were a number of other black-and-white images.

She left her office to grab a coffee. Thomas was standing in the small open-plan kitchen waiting for a kettle to boil. 'Morning,' he said, as she approached.

'Hi, Thomas. Quick one. You remember a DS Ben Farnham?'

Thomas's eyes twitched, a slight down curve to his mouth. He was wearing a clean suit and fresh shirt. His face was still drawn, but he looked better than he had when she'd met him at the Kalimera. 'I remember him,' he said with a sneer.

'Sounds positive.'

'Never saw eye to eye with the man. He was a year off retirement when I started in CID, and acted like it. I worked with him on a number of cases, but he was counting down the days. Not much use to me at the time.'

'Anything else you can tell me?'

'Not really. I heard he'd been good, once. Had a purple patch in the late eighties, bringing in a number of drug runners who'd infiltrated the town from Bristol. He was also a bit of a hard case, by the sound of it. Ex-boxer, though he'd turned to flab by the time I arrived. Why do you ask?'

'That fire at St Bernadette's in 1983. He was the lead investigator.'

'Want a tea?' asked Thomas, pouring hot water into his mug, the smell of mint filling the air.

Louise shook her head. 'Mint tea? You feeling poorly, Sergeant?'

'A bit rough. A few of us went out for drinks last night.'

Louise hid her surprise. She'd smelled the alcohol on Tracey, and now Thomas was feeling hung-over. By the sound of it, they'd gone out without her. It was ridiculous – there could have been many reasons for them not inviting her – but she still felt a twinge of jealousy. 'Not sure mint tea is going to help.'

'You're probably right, but the thought of coffee makes me want to retch. So, Farnham, he was the lead investigator you say?'

'Yes. Quite a thorough report, but I'd like to talk to him.'

'I'll track down his number and get him in. He still lives in town so it shouldn't be a problem.'

'Thanks, Thomas.'

Thomas raised his eyebrows in reply and carried his mint tea back to his desk. Each member of her team was either on the phone or glued to their screens. Only Farrell wasn't present, and despite herself, Louise couldn't help wondering if he was also struggling with the after-effects of the night before.

After the morning briefing Louise walked to St Bernadette's. The church website stated there was morning Mass on a Friday and Louise saw it as a potential opportunity to speak to some of the parishioners. She was interested in seeing Father McGuire in action in front of the congregation.

Her paranoid side recalled the newspaper article she'd read that morning. The streets did feel less populated than usual. The few people she passed on the way to church appeared to view her with hostility, as if they knew she was a police officer and was somehow responsible for the trauma the town was enduring.

As she rounded the corner towards St Bernadette's, she was surprised to see lines of children being led into the church by their teachers. They were pupils from the school adjoined to the church. They walked in silence, hand in hand, each wearing identical blue uniforms. What must have been the Reception class was led out by a stern-looking woman wearing a long, flowing dress. They were impossibly young, some of them, moving like toddlers despite being the same age as Emily. It was heartbreaking to think how much things had changed for her niece in the last couple of years. She'd lost her mother, and now she was separated for the time being from her father. Louise tried to see her every weekend, and despite the urgency of the case, promised herself she would go and see her tomorrow.

'Hello.'

Louise was startled, quickly hiding her surprise at the greeting from a smartly dressed man who'd approached her from the side. 'Hi,' she said.

'We haven't met before. I'm Simon Goulding, head teacher here at St Bernadette's.'

Louise nodded and smiled. Goulding was on her list to contact. 'Louise Blackwell. They're very well behaved.'

'Something about going to church makes them this way,' said Goulding, returning her smile. 'They're not always so . . . disciplined.'

'Is morning Mass cancelled?' she asked.

'No, you would be welcome to join us. We are celebrating All Saints' Day.'

'Is that linked to Halloween?' said Louise, knowingly provoking the teacher in order to gauge his response.

'Not exactly,' said Goulding hesitantly. 'I haven't seen you at church before, but you look familiar.'

Louise told him who she was. 'I would like to speak to you at some point,' she said.

His reaction was cordial, but she noted that he shifted his body weight away from her towards the church. 'I have to go with the children now.'

'I'll stay. We can talk afterwards,' said Louise, not leaving any room for the head teacher to object.

He nodded, and she followed Goulding into the church and took a seat at the back. The Mass was not like any she remembered from her childhood. A group of older children sat to the side of the altar, each holding a musical instrument. Once Father McGuire had greeted everyone, wishing peace to his congregation and receiving 'Peace be with you' as a response, the children started to play as everyone stood for the first hymn. Louise hadn't expected such a positive reaction to the Mass. At best, she felt apathetic towards organised religion. She noted the good it could do for the community, but struggled to shrug off the feeling that everyone involved was being deluded and that there was a cultish element to the whole enterprise. Yet she wasn't experiencing that now. The children were having a good time. The hymns were about love and peace, as were Father McGuire's sermons and the passages from the Gospels. It wasn't her place to judge the people here, and by the end of the Mass she had to concede that she felt a little better. An hour of sitting and watching had refreshed her, and she now felt as if she had more energy for the rest of the day.

'Inspector,' said Goulding as he led the children out of the church. 'Would you like to meet me at my office? I'll be five minutes.'

'Thank you, Mr Goulding,' said Louise, catching the eye of one of the Reception girls, who smiled at her.

The head teacher's office was a small room at the front of the school. It was painted a subtle shade of yellow, and a picture of the Crucifixion hung behind Goulding's desk.

'Did you enjoy the Mass, DI Blackwell?'

'Very much so. You have a lovely school here.'

'We are very fortunate. I imagine you're here to discuss the two terrible deaths.'

'Yes. We're trying to reach out to the whole community. Unfortunately, both of the victims have links to St Bernadette's, as you probably know.'

Goulding rubbed his face. 'It's been a terrible few days. Mrs Lloyd used to teach here, and some of the children knew her from church. She was there most days. She was like an unofficial caretaker, I guess. She'll be so sorely missed. And to go in such a way. It's been very difficult sheltering the children from this.'

'They know she has died?'

'Yes. It's been an almost impossible task, discussing it with the children. We've taken advice and consulted with the parents on the issue. Obviously, we didn't provide any more details other than that she has passed away, and the same with Father Mulligan, but we know the older children are already talking about it. They read the newspapers and talk to the younger children. It's a horrendous situation.'

'How are your teachers taking it?'

'We all just get on with it, Inspector. I think the best strategy has been not to think too much about the terrible injuries inflicted on those two souls. We've prayed for them and will continue to do so, and will help the children get through this.'

'Did you personally know Veronica Lloyd?'

'As I said, I saw her on a daily basis. I wouldn't always speak to her, but we would exchange words now and then.'

'And Father Mulligan?'

'I didn't really know him that well. I met him on a handful of occasions but can't say I really knew him.'

'He was the parish priest here in the eighties?'

'So I believe.'

'At the same time as Veronica was one of the school's teachers.'

'I guess so. I've only been here for five years and I'm not originally from Weston.'

'Where are you from originally?'

'Leicester.'

'What brought you to the seaside?'

Goulding's face brightened. 'Love,' he said, smiling. 'Married a Weston girl.'

Louise mirrored his smile, still trying to decipher if he was hiding anything from her. 'Is your wife a member of the parish?'

'She is now. Prior to that she went to church in one of our sister parishes in Worle.'

'So she wouldn't have been around when Veronica was teaching here?'

'No, she didn't go to the school here.' Goulding's smile was now fixed, but Louise could tell the questions about his wife were making him uneasy.

'I have to ask you, Mr Goulding. Can you think of any reason why someone would want to harm Veronica Lloyd or Father Mulligan?'

'Of course not. The very thought is preposterous.'

Louise remained sitting but didn't speak, assessing Goulding's reaction. A few moments passed before the head teacher spoke again. 'Is there anything else I can help you with, Inspector?'

'There was a fire here during the period when Veronica Lloyd was a teacher at the school and Father Mulligan was the priest.'

'I believe so, but as I said, I've only been here a few years. I don't really know anything about it.'

'It was an accident,' said Louise, as a statement rather than a question.

'Yes,' said Goulding, puzzled.

'But there have been rumours?'

Goulding sat straighter in his chair. 'Rumours? I'm afraid you've lost me now, Inspector.'

'Rumours of arson.'

Goulding snorted. 'I've never heard of such a thing. But as I said—'

'You've only been here a few years,' interrupted Louise. 'Who would you suggest I talk to about the fire, Mr Goulding? Your current priest wasn't too talkative about the subject either.'

'I wouldn't know. You can talk to my predecessors, I suppose.'

'Your predecessors?'

'Yes. Well, my direct predecessor was Mr Nathan Forester, but the school was run as a bit of a team effort, and his wife, Janet, was the school secretary. They were here for twenty-odd years until they retired. I believe they were here when the fire happened. Yes, I'm sure they were. We discussed the impact it had on the school when I first arrived.' Goulding hit some keys on his computer keyboard. 'I guess it's not against GDPR guidelines if I give you their information?'

'No, that's very helpful of you,' said Louise, writing the details down in her notebook.

A message from Thomas was waiting on her mobile as she walked back to the station. 'I spoke to Farnham. He's in Turkey at the moment. Back next week. Says he'll pop in to see you first thing.'

Louise placed the phone back in her pocket. The grey sky was pregnant with rain and she upped her pace back to the office. She would have driven over to see the Foresters, who lived in Worlebury, were it not for the upcoming meeting with Assistant Chief Constable Morley at the station. She needed to prepare, to get everything straight, before having to face the indignity of pleading to remain on her own investigation. She couldn't go to Morley with a half-arsed argument about a cold-case fire at the church, even if it was the only solid thing linking Veronica Lloyd and Father Mulligan.

As soon as she entered the station she could tell something new had happened. The uniformed workers were more focused, displaying an intensity to their work which to Louise appeared to be forced. 'What's going on?' she asked the duty sergeant.

'Royal visit.'

Louise checked her phone. 'Morley?' she asked. The assistant chief constable wasn't due to arrive for another hour.

'The very same. He's up in your department, chatting to Robbo.'

'Perfect.' She steeled herself and carried on to her department.

It seemed the new work ethic had spread there. Everyone was either on the phone or studying their computer screen as if their lives depended on it.

'I was just about to call you,' said Tracey, moving over from her desk. She looked a bit fresher than earlier, the smell of alcohol on her breath no longer evident.

'How long has he been here?'

'Ten minutes.'

'Did he come alone?'

'His assistant's with him.'

'Who's that? Superintendent Rouse?

'Yeah, Dan Rouse. You can see his brown nose a mile off,' said Tracey.

The relief that Finch hadn't accompanied Morley was offset by his decision to turn up an hour early. Had Robertson known, or had it been a surprise for him as well?

It was typical of Morley. Arrive early and catch everyone off guard. It was all a distraction, and not what they needed when all their focus should be on catching the killer. The blinds in Robertson's office were open and she could see the back of the grey-haired Morley and his would-be successor, Rouse, sitting opposite.

'You going in?' asked Tracey.

'I'll wait to be summoned.'

In her office, she called the Forester residence and was put through to their answerphone, Mr Forester asking her to leave a message. His voice had a slight lilt to it; South African, if she wasn't mistaken. 'Mr and Mrs Forester, this is Detective Inspector Louise Blackwell from Weston CID. I would be grateful if you could contact me at your earliest convenience,' she said, leaving her number before hanging up.

'They'll see you now,' said Simone, appearing at Louise's desk like an apparition.

Louise logged into her laptop before moving to Robertson's office, giving herself a couple of minutes before having to face Morley. Minutes from now, the case could be taken away from her. Morley had ultimately been responsible for her transfer to Weston. He'd been close with Finch for years and she'd felt his enjoyment when he'd told her the news eighteen months ago. He'd been disappointed when she'd taken the decision with good grace. She was sure he'd have loved an outburst so he could have basked in his power, but she'd refused to demean herself. What he'd really been after was her resignation, but she'd be damned if she was going to let men like Morley dictate to her.

'Ah, Louise, take a seat,' said Robertson as she knocked on the door.

'Sir, sir,' said Louise, turning to Morley and Rouse, both of whom barely registered her.

'You know why I'm here,' said Morley, before she'd even taken a seat.

Not to give support to my investigation, thought Louise. 'Sir,' she said.

'DCI Robertson has kindly updated me on the current investigation. I can't see much progress, if I'm totally honest.'

It had been less than a week and they had a serial killer on their hands. What the hell did he expect? 'It's a very complex case, sir.'

Morley scowled, his face lined with displeasure. 'It is a complex case, DI Blackwell. It is also a very high-profile one. You've read the tabloids this morning, I take it?'

'Sir.'

'What are they calling him again?' asked Morley, turning to Rouse.

'The Pensioner Killer,' said Rouse, half frowning, half smirking.

'Yes, the Pensioner Killer,' said Morley.

'Catchy, isn't it?' said Louise.

'It's no laughing matter, Inspector. Aside from the negative press this is giving us, can you begin to imagine the effect something like this has on your town? I'm sure I don't have to tell you that Weston only survives because of its tourist trade, and much of that, especially in winter, is the retirement brigade. Who in their right mind would want to come here at the moment?'

Louise had been on this side of an argument many times before. No doubt Morley was under his own type of pressure. *Shit flows downstream*, she thought. She glanced at Robertson for support and was pleased when the DCI spoke up.

'We fully appreciate the situation, sir. We are working tirelessly to find the person responsible. We just need some time.'

'I don't believe the killer is targeting pensioners per se,' said Louise.

'Really?' said Morley, sharing his incredulity with a sideways look at Rouse.

'Yes, the two victims were around seventy, and I believe they were specifically targeted. Just not for their age.' Louise proceeded to explain her investigation into St Bernadette's Church and the fire, including her meeting with Monsignor Ashley.

Morley was unimpressed. 'There is nothing concrete here,' he said, stroking his face. He sighed, blowing air through his fingers. 'And no good will come of religious mysticism. If I had my way, I'd take you off this case now. However, I think it would reflect poorly on the department, so I am willing to give you a stay of execution. I will give you until the end of Monday to come up with something concrete or this will be passed over to MIT. Do we have an understanding?' he said, getting to his feet.

Everyone else in the office stood. 'Yes, sir,' said Louise.

Morley nodded as Robertson moved from behind his desk. 'I'll see you both out,' he said, catching Louise's eye as he left. She couldn't tell if he was relieved, triumphant, or a bit of both.

Chapter Twenty-Four

Geoff had felt like a pervert, sitting inside his van watching Mrs Forester enter her house. He knew her address, so had driven ahead of the bus she was on and waited for her to arrive, his van parked on the opposite side of the road – as usual, far enough away so she wouldn't think anything of it, but close enough that he could still scope the house.

He'd been disappointed when he'd seen all the lights were switched off at the front of the building. The Foresters' house was a semi-detached property in Worlebury Hill, the most affluent area of the town. An alley ran behind the house, leading to the adjoining street, and Geoff had checked the area before Mrs Forester returned. The back lights were also off, so he could only presume Mr Forester was still out.

Back in the van, he'd smacked his hand against the steering wheel. He hadn't taken into account the possibility of the Foresters being apart. Like Mrs Forester, Mr Forester volunteered on an occasional basis, but aside from that, they were always together. He'd been here five times this month, planning how he would make his move, and each time both of them had been at home. He didn't want to panic, but he couldn't start without Mr Forester.

They had to be together.

In the end, he'd waited until 10.30 p.m. before leaving the area. He'd already received some funny looks from a lone dog walker and a young couple holding hands, and he couldn't risk being reported.

Where the hell was Mr Forester, and why had he chosen tonight to be absent?

The clouds that had been hanging over the town all day had emptied themselves as he headed back to the centre. The downpour was relentless, and such was the poor visibility, he'd been forced to pull over. Rain darted off the windscreen and battered his van, the drops so fierce they sounded like tiny stones ricocheting against the metalwork. The long day had taken its toll and all he had wanted to do was to go to his mother's and rest. But he'd left the man alone for too long and was forced to make another crossing to Steep Holm.

Even though he'd got another soaking on the way back, it was so tranquil on the island that he hadn't wanted to leave. After checking on the prisoner, he'd spent the night in the warmth of the visitor centre, not minding the long, dark walk across the island when the reward of a hot shower waited for him.

He'd slept the sleep of the just and woken to beams of bright sunshine filtering through the blinds of the small room where he'd spent the night. He was truly the king of all he surveyed. Making coffee and toast in the kitchenette area, he decided to return to his prisoner. His feet squelched in the mud as he crossed the island, but the sun was high and there was no sea breeze to chill him.

The night's rest had filled him with renewed optimism, which was dashed when he saw the prisoner. It seemed as if the man had aged a decade during the night. In the darkness, Geoff hadn't seen the grey pallor of his skin or the yellow of his eyes. A sickness had overtaken him, and the man reminded him of Father Mulligan seconds before he'd died.

'Here's some water,' said Geoff, lifting the man's head and tilting a bottle towards his dry lips. 'How do you feel?'

The man allowed water to seep into his mouth but didn't reply.

Geoff swore and lay his prisoner back down on the floor. What was he to do? In truth, he'd had enough of the mainland. He hadn't said goodbye to Mum but didn't feel it was necessary. She wouldn't understand what he was doing, and saying goodbye to her would only make her fret and cause trouble.

But what about the Foresters? When he'd made his plan, it had seemed so simple. But now, to finish what he'd started would take an almighty effort that he wasn't sure he was prepared for. He would have to return to Weston again, scope the Foresters' house once more and hope they were in, before returning to Steep Holm. Each trip was a risk, another chance he would get caught.

Had he done enough?

He'd punished Mrs Lloyd and the disbelieving priest. Would it be such a crime if the headmaster and his wife lived?

Geoff began shaking his head. 'No, no, no,' he repeated to himself. No, he couldn't let them survive. They were as much to blame as Lloyd and Mulligan. Maybe not as much as the man at his feet, but they'd had an opportunity. If they'd listened to him, none of this would have happened.

He pictured his father in a weightless Purgatory. He didn't have the imagination to visualise anything beyond a man floating in the clouds for eternity, but he knew he had the ability to stop this happening. But for his dad to be saved from this eternal punishment, those who had wronged him needed to be punished.

The Lord had suffered the five holy wounds, and so would they.

He spent the afternoon packing everything up, making three treks across the island. He'd found a trolley in the shed at the visitor centre and the man didn't object as Geoff hoisted him on to the contraption, his arms and legs secure beneath his grotty sleeping bag, his body as light as air. 'We'll get you cleaned up,' said Geoff. 'Then some hot food. I've got a stew on the go. How does that sound?'

His prisoner didn't respond, his death stare focused on the sky above him. He fell off three times on the journey back to the visitor centre, the wheels of the trolley getting caught in the mud, and his sleeping bag was caked in the stuff as Geoff lifted him into the wooden hut.

He should have used the centre from the start, he now realised. At the beginning, he hadn't wanted to risk someone paying the centre a surprise visit, but his fears had been unfounded. The island was a ghost isle during the winter months and, save for the scare with the canoeists, there'd been no one here except him and his prisoner.

The man shivered as Geoff peeled off the sleeping bag. The smell was unbearable, the man's clothes soaked and covered in his waste. Geoff didn't want to touch him, but he refused to move so Geoff dragged him to the bathroom area, where the shower was running. The man crawled beneath the jets, sitting with his back to the tiled wall. Gradually, life returned to him: the filth draining from his body, colour returning to his sagging skin.

'This is like Jesus washing his disciples' feet,' said Geoff, switching off the shower and handing a towel to the man.

'You're comparing yourself to Our Lord now?' The man's voice was hoarse, some of his words lost as he struggled to speak.

'Of course not.'

'Good, because there is nothing holy about this situation.'

'It's more holy than you think,' said Geoff, thinking about what he had planned.

The fresh clothes he gave him were a few sizes too big, and his prisoner looked like a clown as he stumbled through to the main room of the shelter. Despite the man's age and lack of strength, Geoff was still wary. He couldn't run away but wasn't beyond staging some form of attack. He pointed to the long wooden table. 'Sit.'

'What's this? A last supper?' said the man as Geoff poured hot stew into his bowl.

Not quite, thought Geoff as the man devoured the meal, slurping at the red-brown liquid and tearing at the bread as if his life depended on it, barely taking a breath between each mouthful. 'Slow down, you'll make yourself sick.'

The man laughed, stew spilling from his mouth and across the table towards Geoff. 'How come my welfare is such a concern all of a sudden? You've left me to rot in that hole, and now you're being nice to me.'

'Father Mulligan is dead,' said Geoff, changing the subject.

'What?'

'You heard.'

'What, how?' said the man, his hand trembling as the realisation dawned on him. 'You killed him? Why?'

Sharing the information hadn't made him feel as triumphant as he'd expected, and Geoff couldn't immediately answer the question.

'Why are you doing this? I can help you, Geoffrey. You just need to tell me what is going on.'

Geoff's confusion disappeared in an instant. '*You* help *me*?' he said, getting to his feet and moving towards the man. He tied his skeletal hands behind him just as he was reaching for another piece of bread. 'You never helped me before. None of you did.'

'Let me help you now,' said the man. 'This is about your dad?'

Geoff shook his head, warning the man not to continue as heat flushed his skin. The effect was similar to the feeling he experienced in church. It rushed through him, lighting every sinew of his body, but this wasn't a welcome experience. After the incident – they always called it 'the incident', refusing to name out loud what had

173

happened – his dad stopped going to church, had all but stopped believing. Geoff had continued attending, both from the desire to do so, and from the need to protect his dad. If his dad wasn't going to church, then Geoff needed to go in his place. If he'd stopped believing, then Geoff had to believe twice as hard.

He'd hated seeing the change in his dad, his docility, the way he'd surrendered to the destruction of his faith, and this in part fuelled Geoff's own rage. In secondary school he'd found himself in countless fights. To begin with, he'd become involved as a means of self-defence – his pariah status a red flag to the bullies – but soon he was instigating fights of his own. He would convince himself he was trying to right wrongs, but in truth he began to enjoy the sensation of bone on yielding flesh. He would confess his sins to whatever priest would listen, and though he would promise to God that he wouldn't repeat his actions, soon the rage would return and he would start all over again.

But that was then. He could control himself now. He was precise and he was just, and the man before him would receive his punishment when the time was right.

'It's way too late for that,' said Geoff, shoving a gag into the man's mouth and leading him away to the cabin.

Chapter Twenty-Five

Mr Thornton glared at Louise as she left the house on Saturday morning. He was organising his recycling as if fitting a jigsaw picture together, snapping cardboard boxes and arranging them in the small black receptacle.

'Morning,' said Louise, by her car.

'That it is,' said Thornton, shutting his front door behind him.

'Charming,' said Louise.

In the car, she waited for the heater to defrost the windscreen. She'd only managed five hours' sleep last night, having not left the office until 11 p.m. The old head teacher from St Bernadette's, Nathan Forester, had finally returned her call and agreed to meet her that afternoon, which was the only positive thing she had taken from yesterday. The meeting with the assistant chief constable and his sidekick Rouse had been a disaster, and now she had a deadline looming. The thought of losing the case to MIT was unbearable. She could already picture the smug look on Finch's face as the case was handed over to him. It was as if Morley wanted her to fail. She knew the man had an issue with her following the Walton case, but the extent of his animosity baffled her.

The Foresters' house was a pretty semi-detached property in the hills of Worlebury. Louise had looked at a few properties in this area before settling on the bungalow. Although only a couple of miles from the motorway, the area had felt a little too remote at the time.

A slim woman with a mop of silver-blonde hair answered the door. 'Janet Forester,' said the woman after Louise introduced herself, her smile triggering a spider's web of wrinkles on her heavily made-up face.

She was led through to the back of the house, where shelves were filled with framed photos. 'Yours?' asked Louise, pointing to photos of two smiling boys dressed in a dark blue school uniform.

'They are, though they're much older now, I'm afraid.'

'What do they do?'

'Arthur is a doctor, Monty an engineer.'

The pride in the woman's face was obvious, as was the smugness. 'Nathan, DI Blackwell is here to see you.'

A rotund man in a sweatshirt stood up from his kitchen chair. Louise noted that his shorts were pulled high above his waist, tight against the girth of his stomach. 'Nathan Forester,' he said with an air of suspicion. 'Please take a seat.'

Louise accepted the offer of tea and asked Mrs Forester to join them. She wanted to keep things light, needing the Foresters on her side for the time being. 'If you don't mind me asking, where are your accents from? I can't seem to place them.'

'No one usually notices,' said Nathan. 'I guess that's why you're the detective. We're both originally from South Africa. Been here since the early eighties.'

'When you took over at St Bernadette's?'

'That's correct. Is that what you want to speak to us about?' said Janet. The woman was smiling, but Louise had seen her type of smile before. She only had to look into her eyes to see it was devoid of warmth. 'As I said on the phone, I'm investigating the deaths of Veronica Lloyd and Father Mulligan. I believe you knew both of them.'

'Tragic, absolutely tragic,' said Nathan, shaking his head. 'What a thing to happen to the community. Yes, we knew both Veronica and Father Mulligan.'

'In what capacity did you know them?'

'Veronica was one of my teachers. She was there when I became head teacher and retired a year before I did.'

'Before we did,' added Janet, as if annoyed at being left out.

'And Father Mulligan?' asked Louise.

'He was the main parish priest at the time. A wonderful man. I . . . we . . . saw him on a daily basis. He used to come into school and give such interesting assemblies. Quite a talent, being able to hold the attention of four-year-olds through to eleven-year-olds. He was held in such respect, you see. The children doted on him.'

'And Veronica?'

Louise caught the exchange of looks between the married couple.

'She was a great teacher. Quite old-fashioned, you could say.'

'Old-fashioned?'

'She was a bit of a disciplinarian. Ran a strict ship. But she was very well respected. Former pupils used to visit the school all the time to see her.'

'Were there ever any issues you can remember? Any disgruntled pupils or parents?'

Nathan shook his head, his eyes darting towards his wife again then back to Louise. 'Nothing specific that I can recall. There are always issues with parents, as you can imagine. Some tend to interfere too much, some don't get involved at all. Part of my job was to manage parents' expectations, which, particularly in the latter years, were often unrealistic.'

'Unrealistic in what way?'

'Every child is important, that goes without saying, but there are often up to thirty-two in a class and not every child can get the individual attention parents seek. When I first took over St Bernadette's we didn't really have teaching assistants, or if we did, they worked on a part-time, occasional basis, so the teachers would be solely in charge of their class.'

'And teachers think they have it hard nowadays,' said Janet.

'So some of the parents resented Veronica for not paying their children enough attention?'

'We would have the occasional meeting with parents, but as I said, this was mainly a latter phenomenon. I'm afraid I think people feel they have become more entitled in recent years.'

Louise wasn't sure if wanting the best for your child meant that a parent could be described as 'entitled', but she didn't press the point. 'These meetings, were many related to Veronica Lloyd?'

'No, no. This was a general thing. In fact, I don't remember many parent meetings regarding Veronica.'

'They were probably too scared,' said Janet, receiving a look of rebuke from her husband.

'Scared?'

Janet frowned, as if defensive at having said something she shouldn't. 'As my husband said, Veronica could be quite a formidable woman.'

'How did she get on with Father Mulligan?'

Nathan shrugged. 'This was some time ago, you understand. As far as I'm aware, they had a normal working relationship. Veronica was a very devout Catholic and would attend Mass at least once a week.'

'So no animosity between the pair?'

'No, of course not.'

Louise sighed, sensing a dead end to the conversation. 'I believe there was a fire at the church when you were head teacher, Mr Forester?'

The pair exchanged looks again and Louise couldn't tell if it was merely a husband and wife thing or if they were hiding something from her. 'Yes, there was a fire. A terrible tragedy,' said Nathan.

'What does this have to do with your investigation?' asked Janet, with a sour look at Louise.

'Unfortunately, the fire is no longer the only tragedy at St Bernadette's. Veronica Lloyd and Father Mulligan were at the school and the church at the time.'

'Yes, but I don't see how—'

'It's okay,' said Nathan, interrupting his wife and placing a hand on her knee. 'I can see why you would ask the question, but there is no connection between these three tragic events. The fire was an accident. An awful, tragic accident.'

Louise thought about the accelerant mentioned by the newspaper editor, Garrett. 'You sure it was an accident?'

'What a bizarre question,' said Janet. 'This was over thirty-five years ago. Of course it was an accident. Why are you asking these questions?'

'I realise it was a long time ago, but you must see the potential connection. Veronica Lloyd was a teacher at your school and Father Mulligan was the parish priest, and here they are, thirty-five or so years later, murdered.'

Janet sat back in her chair, shaking her head as she looked at her husband for support.

'It was an accident,' said Nathan, without conviction.

'It wasn't thought to be suspicious at the time,' said Louise. 'Can you think of anyone who would have wanted to set fire to the church?'

'Why would anyone want to burn down a church?' he said.

Louise could think of many reasons but didn't push the point. The atmosphere in the room was becoming strained and she wasn't going to get anything further from the Foresters at the moment.

She thanked them both and got to her feet. She would question them again, give them time to consider the implications of their answers.

Nathan showed her to the door, his wife remaining on the sofa.

'Thank you, I'll be in touch,' said Louise, handing him a card. 'Please call me if you can think of anything that might help.'

'Yes, of course.'

'One thing before I go. You mentioned that Father Mulligan was the main parish priest at the time of the fire.'

'Yes,' said Nathan, his eyes narrowing.

'So you had more than one parish priest at the time?'

'Yes. The parish of St Bernadette's was much larger back then. Things changed after the fire.'

'Who was the other priest?'

She noticed that Nathan paused before answering. 'A man by the name of Father Lanegan. He was a very popular priest who everyone loved.'

Like everything else the pair had told her, the information felt incomplete. She was convinced the Foresters were keeping something from her. It could be innocuous, a fact personal to them that they didn't want to become public knowledge, but she was determined to find out what they were hiding from her. Louise often found people to be more amenable once they'd had a chance to sleep on it and for the worry to set in.

Louise kept her gaze on Nathan as he looked away from her. 'Is he still local?'

'No. He left the priesthood in the late eighties. I believe he has retired somewhere by the sea.'

Chapter Twenty-Six

Eileen couldn't remember the last time she'd received so much attention. On her first visit to the station she'd been dismissed out of hand. The grumpy-looking officer behind the desk had taken her details, but she could tell he was just going through the formalities. So she'd been surprised when the young, good-looking officer had called this morning and invited her back to the station. Until the call, her plans for the day had revolved around light housework and an afternoon in front of the television. Her son had bought her some sort of contraption for her television one Christmas years ago. Supposedly, it had hundreds of extra channels, but she couldn't understand how it worked and made do with the four terrestrial channels – even Channel Five was a stretch too far for her.

The walk into town had been wondrous. Outside, it was a beautiful late-autumn day, the sun illuminating the clear blue sky reflected in perfect clarity by the sea. On days like these, she couldn't understand how anyone could live away from the coast. She pitied those inlanders, entrapped by borders of their own making. So many of the young folk chose such a path nowadays. They were desperate to leave the area, seduced by the lure of the big cities. She even saw it in the eyes of the young officer who at that very moment was placing a cup of tea in front of her – there was a restlessness to him, as if he wanted to be anywhere else but here.

Unlike him, the woman dressed in jeans and a thick pullover who introduced herself as Sergeant Joslyn Merrick had a faint Cornish accent and a face well worn by years of sea and sun.

'Thank you for coming, Mrs Boswell. May I call you Eileen?' she asked.

Eileen acknowledged her politeness with a nod. 'You may,' she said.

'Thank you ever so much for coming in to see us today, especially on the weekend.'

Eileen noticed the woman's glance at the young policeman, as if she were rebuking him. 'It was my pleasure. What a glorious day.'

'Wonderful, isn't it? Lovely to have a respite from the recent weather.'

'That it is. How can I help you, Sergeant?'

The policewoman smiled, and Eileen saw she was pleased that there didn't need to be any more chitchat.

'First of all, I'd like to thank you for notifying us about Mr Lanegan. We went to his house yesterday and noticed the broken latch on his door. We have gone through his address book, but we're having trouble locating him at the moment. I know we have asked you already, but I was wondering if you have a mobile phone number for Mr Lanegan?'

'No. I don't do all that modern technology thing. I have a landline, though no one ever calls me on it.'

A weariness crept over the policewoman's eyes at her response and Eileen wished she could help more.

'How long have you worked for Mr Lanegan?'

'Over twenty years now. He is my last surviving client.'

'Wow, that is a long time. How did you first meet him?'

Eileen was about to answer when something held her back, a memory she'd misplaced. All of a sudden, she felt trapped in the windowless room. 'May I have some water?' she asked.

'Of course. James?' said the sergeant. 'Is everything okay, Eileen? You know we are just trying to locate Mr Lanegan.'

The male police officer handed her a paper cup. The water was warm and Eileen felt droplets trickle down her chin as the hand holding the cup shook a little. They looked at her with pity, as if being old was something that should make her feel ashamed. Well, she felt her age now, but she was proud, not ashamed, and she didn't welcome their sympathy.

But why had she forgotten how she had met Mr Lanegan, and why was she reluctant to tell them about it now? She was sure there was nothing shameful about it, though she did recall now that Mr Lanegan had shared a secret with her and she didn't want to betray his confidence. The memories came at her, each clouded like a dream, and she wasn't sure she could trust the images in her head. But she had to help the officers find Mr Lanegan, so she told them what she could.

'I met him in church. I'm not a believer, you understand. It was a summer fete over in Hayle. I used to catch the coastal train in the summer, for the scenery, and the church by the station was holding a fete so I took a walk through the stalls and I saw Mr Lanegan. He was such a handsome man. Still is,' she said, with a smile. 'We got talking and he told me he'd just moved to the area and when I told him what I did he decided to hire me as a cleaner there on the spot.'

The elderly lady had a lyrical voice, her Cornish accent so strong that even Joslyn struggled at times to decipher it. She was clearly in love with this Mr Lanegan, had been since the day she'd met him at the church fete. She was frail in body, but there was a strength to her eyes that Joslyn had rarely encountered. Joslyn was sure the woman was on the verge of sharing something important but was holding back.

'James, please could you make Mrs Boswell a cup of tea. And a coffee for myself.'

James looked at her dumbfounded, and for one unbelievable moment she thought he was about to refuse, but she narrowed her eyes and he soon stood up.

'He's not bad to look at either,' said Eileen, once James had left the interview room.

'I can't comment on that,' said Joslyn with a conspiratorial smile. 'Is there anything you'd like to share with me before Constable Lewis comes back, Eileen?'

The inner debate was visible on the old lady's face. 'It's really nothing, I suppose. Mr Lanegan told me a secret and, stupid as I am, I'd only remembered it just now when you asked me about how I met him.'

Joslyn's mother had suffered from dementia. The disease had slowly eaten away at her until she no longer recognised Joslyn or any of her family, and it was almost a relief when she died. Joslyn understood the vagaries of memory better than she wished to, so she accepted without question what Eileen, who was in her late eighties, had just told her. 'You can tell me, Eileen. We're here to help find Mr Lanegan, nothing else.'

'I guess it couldn't hurt. It was on the first day I worked for him when he told me. It was another glorious summer day and he'd opened some wine for me to drink after I'd finished my cleaning. I had a feeling it wasn't his first bottle of the day. He had such a way about him then. He still does, of course, but there was this extra spark to him back then.' She looked away, some colour in her cheeks. 'Listen to me, I sound . . . anyway, we were drinking and I asked about his past and that twinkle in his eyes disappeared, and I have to say I didn't care for its replacement.'

'And then?' said Joslyn.

Eileen frowned, the full extent of her age showing in the patchwork of lines in her face. 'That was when he told me what he was running from.'

Chapter Twenty-Seven

The sky was getting light by the time Geoff got out of bed, his ancient alarm clock having failed him. He dressed in a hurry, forcing water and bread down the throat of his prisoner before sprinting to the boat.

The air was still, and although the tide was forceful, he pushed out into the body of water with little trouble. It was still dark enough that the chances of him being detected were minimal, and as he finally approached the abandoned jetty of the old pier on the mainland, his was the sole vessel in sight.

He struggled back on to land, managing to stay dry as he hauled the boat into its hiding place, and as he edged along the pier he was still covered by the last vestiges of night.

Back in the van, he let out a long sigh, as if he'd been holding his breath since he'd left Steep Holm. If he'd slept half an hour longer, he wouldn't have been able to return that day, and that would have risked messing everything up. This would have to be the last time he returned to Weston. His prisoner had been cleaned and fed, and although chained and gagged, was now somewhere warm, so he could be left for a day or two.

He would finish what he started, and then he would return to the island for the final time.

◆ ◆ ◆

Mum was up when he got back to the house. She was cooking a fried breakfast, a stripy apron over her dressing gown.

'Hello, love,' she said, in that cautious way in which she always spoke to him. He could tell she wanted to ask him where he'd been but knew better than to ask. 'Would you like some breakfast? I made you some. I thought you were sleeping.'

Geoff's stomach growled. 'Okay, thanks,' he said, sitting down and pouring orange juice into a plastic cup. His mum looked so happy at his response that he almost wanted to forgive her.

'There you go, love,' she said, placing a plate brimming with bacon, sausage and eggs in front of him. 'I'll get the toast. I feel I've hardly seen you in the last few weeks,' she added, sitting opposite him.

'Yeah,' grunted Geoff as he shuffled the food into his mouth, the grease from the fried meat washed down with more orange juice.

'How's work?'

Geoff wiped his mouth with the back of his hand. 'Fine.'

His mum smiled, and for a second Geoff relived a memory from his childhood. He recalled sitting in this very room with both of his parents. He'd been unable to express it then, and struggled now, but he'd been content seeing the happiness on his parents' faces as they talked about adult things while he dipped his toast into his boiled egg.

No, it was more than that.

He'd felt safe.

And he guessed that was why the events that followed – he couldn't say if it was weeks, months, or even a couple of years after that conjured memory – had such an effect on him.

His mother glanced at his gloved hand and he moved it from the kitchen table as she went to touch it. 'I love you, Geoffrey,' she said, her eyes brimming with tears.

Despite everything, he felt his own eyes watering. She'd been saying the same thing to him ever since that day all those years ago, but he'd never said it back to her. Not that he hadn't come close to saying it. He'd been nine at the time, big for his age but still a little boy. He'd needed her then, but his stubbornness had got him through that difficult time. Years after the incident, his father forgave her and, although grateful for his son's loyalty, he had instructed Geoff to be kinder to his mother. But Geoff could never forgive her for what had happened, and now it was too late: the words were impossible to say.

He closed his eyes as her hand reached for his and she began to sob. He thought about what he'd done – the two people he'd killed, the man he'd imprisoned – and his resolution momentarily faded. He was a child again, and he let his mother comfort him. Maybe he owed her this, a last chance to hold her son.

'I love you, son,' she said.

Geoff nodded, breaking away and running upstairs to his room.

An hour later, he retrieved his tool holdall from the shed and left the house. Mrs Forester volunteered in the morning at the charity shop, but her and her husband's movements were more erratic at the weekends. The Boulevard was packed so he was forced to park in Grove Park. Apart from the chill, it was like a summer's day. The perfect blue sky was unburdened with clouds as he walked past the Playhouse, where he'd seen a pantomime one Christmas with his parents, to the flea market, where his granddad had once had a stall. Geoff had sometimes been allowed to help Granddad out on weekends and had felt like a millionaire when he'd returned with his £2 wages. He used to walk home through the high street, stopping in the computer shops to work out how much money he would need to save to get his own personal computer. He smiled as he remembered how his parents had bought him a Commodore VIC-20 on his ninth birthday.

Had he really been that old?

That meant it must have happened the following summer.

It's funny the tricks time plays on you, he thought as he turned on to the Boulevard towards the shop where Mrs Forester helped out. He watched the store from across the road until he saw the thin silhouette of her body within. Happy she was in place, he continued walking along the Boulevard until he reached the library. He'd spent much of his time here as a child, braving the long walk along Winterstoke Road all alone. After the incident, he'd spent nearly every day there, to avoid the fallout from his parents arguing. He couldn't count how many books he'd devoured during that period, and as he entered the now automatic doors the smell of the old books took him back to that time. Few of the books from his childhood were there now, but that didn't matter. The place had hardly changed and, moving upstairs to the reference room, he found a seat and closed his eyes.

What would he tell that nine-year-old version of himself, should he encounter him? Would he tell him to let the bad feelings go or to embrace the pain and to make those responsible pay? He didn't know, but it was too late to go back. As sleep took him, a distant voice told him he was experiencing last-minute nerves and that it would all be okay in the end.

He let out a short gasp as a hand touched his shoulder sometime later, summoning him back from his sleep. A tall man wearing immaculately ironed trousers looked down at him with a frown. 'I'm sorry, sir, you were snoring,' he said.

Geoff shook himself awake and apologised.

'You're not the first and you won't be the last,' said the librarian, walking away.

It took Geoff a few seconds to register what he meant.

Eventually, in his teenage years, he'd managed to control his rage. He discovered woodwork at school and channelled his energy into his creations. He had a natural affinity with the material, finding he could shape it almost to his will. His mother told him he could have made a success of it if he hadn't stuck to the same design over and over again. Geoff didn't care. He loved his creations. Whatever his mother's misgivings, each design was different. Yes, the variances were subtle, but Geoff could account for each difference in design. He'd even proved his mother wrong at one point, selling some of the objects before deciding they were not to be shared by the wider world.

Now he understood that woodwork was a type of therapy. It had helped him keep his mind from what had happened and his reaction to it. He'd hated what had happened to his dad, the way his life was irrevocably changed, but the combination of his carpentry and his almost daily visits to the church had kept his mind occupied.

And then his dad had died.

He forced himself to eat lunch in the fish and chip shop on the Boulevard. He didn't know what the night would entail and didn't want to be hungry as he waited for opportunity to present itself. He had the place almost to himself, only the shuffling of the waitress to and fro from the kitchen reminding him that he wasn't alone. A sense of melancholy had come over him since leaving the library. He understood why – he was saying goodbye to the town that was the only home he'd ever known – but he couldn't shake off the feeling.

After paying up, leaving the waitress a big tip, he left the place, surprised to see Janet Forester leave the charity shop thirty minutes before her shift ended. As if he'd voiced his surprise, she looked across the road towards him, and for the shortest period they were staring at each other, until she broke the spell by turning away towards the bus stop.

It's nothing to fret about, thought Geoff as he hurried back to the van. He tore the parking fine from the windscreen – he'd been too distracted to remember to buy a ticket – and manoeuvred out of the car park.

Mrs Forester wasn't at the bus stop so he continued driving towards Worlebury, as he had so many times before. There had been moments in the last few weeks when he could have finished the head teacher and his wife, but he'd hesitated and now it could spoil everything.

He caught up with the bus in Milton, catching a glimpse of the Our Lady's Church next to Baytree Park, where he'd once, for one unsuccessful season, played football for a local boys' team. His hand itched as he sat in the traffic. There was no real reason to follow the woman this way – he knew her final destination – but he didn't want to leave anything to chance. His tools were ready in the back of the van and, if the chance presented itself, he would act. If he had to wait until tomorrow, then he could do that too. The Foresters went to church every Sunday at a small chapel in Worlebury, had lunch at the Old Pier Tavern pub, and were at home from 3 p.m. onwards. If it meant waiting one more day, then so be it.

He overtook the bus and parked in a spot where he could see Mrs Forester approaching the house. Her appearance hadn't changed much over the years. She had the same figure, the type of body that could only be achieved by chronic undereating, and from the back she looked much younger than she was. Such illusions were destroyed when he saw her aged, ravaged face, her gaunt features and saggy skin.

Her fat husband answered the door, barely acknowledging her as she walked into the house. There had been rumours about the pair at the school, that Janet was having an affair with the caretaker and the head teacher didn't mind. Geoff hadn't understood what the other children meant at the time. It was just playground gossip, which he would acknowledge with a wise nod, but he'd once seen her alone with the caretaker in the office and, in retrospect, he thought their behaviour had been odd, as if they were scared of being caught out.

Maybe that was why she hadn't believed Geoff, why her husband told him he was telling stories. They'd been too wrapped up in their own deceptions to bother with the deceit that was tearing Geoff's family apart.

The thought put everything into perspective and Geoff welcomed the surge of anger and the focus that came with it. Such was his concentration that, at first, he ignored the car reversing into the space opposite the house. He left the van, ready to finish this stage, his attention returning only as a woman got out of the car and walked up the pathway to the Forester house.

Geoff started to tremble. He'd seen the woman before, at the beach after he'd killed Veronica Lloyd. He didn't know her name but knew she was in charge of the police investigation that was hunting him.

Chapter Twenty-Eight

The office was full when Louise returned from talking to the Foresters, the investigation uniting everyone and dispelling any concerns about working through the weekend. She'd decided not to make it public knowledge that the department risked losing control over the investigation to MIT if they'd not come up with at least a credible suspect by Monday. They couldn't work any harder. It would only put undue pressure on the team, and that could lead to mistakes.

Tracey looked tired again, and Louise wondered if she had been out drinking with colleagues from the department.

'Let me get you a coffee later, Lou, I need to get your advice,' she said, stopping by her desk.

Louise nodded, not in the mood to engage her friend in any further conversation outside work. She searched for mentions of Father Lanegan online, but the only thing she could find was a photograph taken from St Bernadette's Church of a plaque listing all the parish priests in the last fifty years.

Mr Forester had said that Lanegan had retired and was no longer with the priesthood. She hadn't paid his remark much attention at the time, but after doing some research, Louise's interest was piqued. Priests did retire, but they often effectively remained as priests, some occasionally doing work as locum priests, such was the worldwide shortage in the clergy. If the Foresters were correct, and Lanegan had left the priesthood, then Louise needed to know why, and decided to call Monsignor Ashley. She retrieved the card the charismatic priest had given her and rang his personal number.

'Inspector Blackwell, this is a pleasure. How may I be of service?'

Louise smiled at the warmth and rich cadence of the priest's voice. 'I appreciate it is the weekend, but I was hoping that we could perhaps meet. I have a few questions you may be able to help me with.'

'Certainly. I happen to be in the area. I'd rather not meet in the police station, if that's all the same to you, but I could be persuaded to share an early dinner with you?'

Louise agreed to meet him in an hour at a small seafood restaurant on the front near Marine Parade. Before leaving, she invited Tracey, who was in a deep conversation with Farrell, across the road to the Kalimera.

The place was empty, so they took a seat by the window. 'Thanks,' said Tracey as Louise handed her the large cup of hot chocolate she'd ordered.

'Another late one?'

'You could say that,' said Tracey, a line of cream sticking to her upper lip as she sipped the drink.

'You're settling in well. Maybe you should join us permanently,' said Louise with a smile.

'A little too well,' said Tracey.

'What does that mean?'

Tracey looked sheepish as she took another drink of the hot chocolate. 'I may have done something I shouldn't have.'

Louise closed her eyes, for a brief second lost in her own world. 'Am I going to want to hear this?'

'Possibly not. But I think you should know.'

'Well, I need to know now, Trace.'

'I guess so. I'm telling you this as a friend, though, not as my boss.'

'Reassure me, why don't you?'

'Jesus, Lou, you're going to kill me.' Tracey looked genuinely mortified, and even a little scared.

'Oh, come on, it can't be that bad.'

'Okay. Here goes. We went out drinking again last night. When I say "we", I mean just me and one other person.'

Realisation dawned on Louise. 'I see.'

'One thing led to another and I ended up staying the night with him.'

Louise rolled her eyes. 'Who was it?'

Tracey sucked in her cheeks, her hand over her mouth. 'Thomas,' she said, glancing at Louise, as if for reassurance.

White noise seemed to fill Louise's head. She liked Thomas, could just about admit to herself that she had some feelings for him, but this didn't explain the visceral reaction she was experiencing now. Her anger was palpable. Tracey didn't know the way she felt about Thomas, and she certainly didn't have any hold on him, but still Louise felt the heat rising within her.

'You know he's married?' she said, regretting using Thomas's marriage as a means to cover up her jealousy.

'I know. They're going through some difficulties. He's been staying at a hotel for the last few nights. Look, Lou, I know I crossed a boundary here. I've spoken to Thomas and we're going to keep it professional from here on in. It was just one of those things. Too many drinks, both of us feeling a bit vulnerable.'

'Why were you feeling vulnerable, Tracey?' asked Louise, her tone harsher than she'd intended.

Tracey looked visibly shaken by the question. 'Come on, Lou. First couple of days in a new department, in a new town, I thought you'd understand.'

Louise thought about her one-night stand with Dempsey when she'd first arrived, and how even now the seaside town didn't feel like home to her. She was pissed with Tracey because it was Thomas, and that wasn't fair on her friend.

'Sorry, Tracey, that was unfair. What about your man in Bristol?'

'Yeah, I feel a bit guilty about that. I'm going to see him tonight.'

'Are you going to tell him?'

Tracey sighed. 'Probably not,' she said.

Louise walked back with Tracey, stopping at the entrance to the station. 'We'll keep this between ourselves,' she said.

'Thank you, Louise.'

'What about Thomas? Do you think I should speak to him to check he's okay?'

'He didn't really share much about his family situation, but he was putting them back last night. He seems like a nice guy. I feel like I may have engineered the situation a bit. He was a bit devastated this morning.'

Louise nodded. It was a weird request, but she needed someone to keep an eye on Thomas, and Tracey was still the only person at the station she felt she could trust. 'Let me know if you have any concerns.'

'Of course.'

'But, Tracey, take my advice, no more nights out with the staff.'

'Understood, boss.'

The monsignor was sitting outside in the beer garden of the restaurant that overlooked the seafront. The sky had darkened and the fiery tip of the thin cigar he held to his lips glowed like a firefly. 'Inspector, excuse me,' he said, getting to his feet.

'Are you not cold?' asked Louise, shaking hands with the priest, the palm of his skin smooth and warm to the touch.

'I like this weather. Invigorating. Are you hungry, Inspector?'

Louise nodded. 'You can call me Louise.'

'I know. I just like saying "Inspector" – it sounds so dramatic.'

Louise waited as he finished his cigar. The tide was in, the water illuminated by a line of streetlights. Louise usually loved the sea but had never been tempted to take a dip at Weston. She guessed it was the colour, the impenetrable brown of the seabed discolouring the water. It was an unfortunate handicap that Weston suffered. Louise wondered how the town's fortunes would fare if the seabed were golden sand, the water a crisp blue, like its neighbours further down the coast towards Devon and Cornwall.

'It was a pleasant surprise to receive your call, Inspector,' said Ashley, once they were sitting inside the restaurant. A wood fire burned away in the corner of the room, the smokiness invisible in the air.

'You were already in the vicinity, you say?'

'Parish matters over in south Bristol. Nothing very exciting, I'm afraid.'

'Well, thank you for coming at such short notice.'

'*Salute*,' said the monsignor, holding aloft his glass of red wine. 'Cheers.'

Ashley was a charming companion and a great listener. Before Louise knew it, she'd told him all about her family and her day trips to Weston as a child, revealing more to him in a few minutes than she had to some of her friends. They were halfway through their dinner before Louise asked him about Father Lanegan.

'Mr Lanegan as is,' said Ashley, ordering a second glass of wine. 'It's okay, I'm using public transport,' he added, noting Louise's quizzical look.

'Yes, I wanted to ask about that. Isn't that a bit unusual?'

'That he is no longer a priest?'

'Yes.'

'Yes and no. Unfortunately, we lose many priests, and for various reasons.'

'Such as?'

Ashley sighed, a sadness in his eyes that she hadn't seen before. 'The priesthood is a vocation, Louise, a calling. It is a formidable commitment, a life devoted to God at the expense of everything else. Quite an undertaking, I'm sure you'll agree.'

'I imagine not everyone is up to it?'

'Sadly not.'

'And Father Lanegan? Why did he choose to leave?'

Ashley drank his wine, giving himself time to think. 'Mr Lanegan was a fine priest in many respects, but I believe, ultimately, the priesthood wasn't for him.'

'That doesn't really clarify things, Monsignor.'

'No, I suppose it doesn't,' said Ashley with a grin. 'Let's just say, he was unable to fully commit to God.'

Louise studied the elderly priest. Two diagonal lines snaked down his forehead towards his eyes, which fluctuated between humour and melancholy. 'You mean he wanted to have relationships?'

'Wanted to, and did. Of course . . .'

'I haven't heard that from you. What sort of relationships?' said Louise, uneasy asking the question.

'It is a sin for a priest to engage in any sort of congress. Lanegan was a very engaging person and had a weakness for sins of the flesh.

There were a couple of incidents early on in his career, which he atoned for with periods of reflection.'

'Misdemeanours?'

Ashley shrugged. 'Indiscretions.'

'Relationships? With parishioners?'

'I have to be very careful what I say, Inspector. I wish to give you as much assistance as I can but cannot risk . . . a scandal.'

'One of your parishioners and one of your priests is dead, Monsignor. Isn't it a bit late for that?'

'I can neither confirm nor deny your speculation, Inspector.'

'I have to ask. These indiscretions, they were with . . .'

'Women,' said Ashley, rescuing Louise from an awkward question. 'Consenting women,' he added, making Louise wonder why he felt the qualifier necessary.

'Married women?' asked Louise.

'As I said, Inspector, I can't comment.'

The conversation was stilted as they finished their meals. Ashley was more reflective, as if he regretted sharing the information.

'Do you know where Mr Lanegan is now?' she asked, once she'd paid the bill.

'He left the priesthood in the eighties, so I don't have that information for you.'

'Was it his choice?'

'He asked to leave. It is quite a procedure, but yes, ultimately, it was his choice.'

The priest accepted Louise's offer of a lift to the train station. In the close confines of the car, she could smell the wine on his breath and the slightly dank odour coming from his skin. She parked up and walked him to the platform, where the train to Bristol Temple Meads was due in five minutes. 'Thank you for your time,' she said, taking his hand once again.

The tiredness in the priest's eyes disappeared in an instant, the sparkle returning as he smiled back at her.

'I have to ask one more thing before you go,' said Louise.

'I would have been disappointed if you didn't,' said Ashley, his smile full of mischief.

'One of Father Lanegan's indiscretions. Would that have been with Veronica Lloyd?'

'That is something I cannot confirm, Inspector.'

'Did Father Lanegan have a confessor? Is that the right term?'

'Yes, even priests have to take confession. We are prone to sinful activity as much as the next man.'

'You took Father Lanegan's confession?'

'At times.'

'And is this why you can't tell me about Veronica Lloyd?'

The train pulled up, the sound of metal scraping on metal echoing in the stone walls of the railway station. The priest looked back at her, his expression revealing nothing. 'As I said, Inspector, that is something I cannot confirm.'

Chapter Twenty-Nine

Geoff didn't place his hand over his nose as he sneezed, sputum hitting the interior of his windscreen. The engine of his van ticked over as he sat in the car park of Weston's train station, waiting for the policewoman to return.

After watching her enter the Forester house, he'd remained in the van in a sort of trance. He tried, and failed, to understand why she'd want to interview the Foresters. It had to be more than routine. The Foresters didn't even belong to St Bernadette's any more. So why would she go to all the trouble of visiting their house?

Every way he looked at it, he came back to one thing. She'd made the connection.

After she'd left the house, he was torn between two options: to stay and pay the Foresters their last visit, as he'd planned, or to follow the policewoman.

He'd chosen the latter, mainly because he didn't know what she'd told them. It could have all been a trap. If she'd warned them they were in danger, they would panic as soon as they saw him. One of them would be poised to call the police, and even if he managed to take their lives, it wouldn't be in the way he intended, and he would never get back to Steep Holm.

Things became worse after he followed the policewoman, first to the police station and then to the seafront, where she'd met another priest. Geoff had no idea who the tall, gangly man was, but the sight of him only served to create more confusion in his mind.

Did they know Father Lanegan was missing?

He felt helpless, was disgusted to find himself on the verge of tears as the windscreen wipers cleared the water in an eternal battle in front of him. What was the policewoman doing with the priest? Were they getting the train together, or were they collecting someone? He'd felt so positive earlier on, his wavering motivation returning, only for it all to be thrown into chaos.

His heart thumped against his chest as the policewoman emerged from the train station. The woman was a bit younger than him, perhaps late thirties. She was pretty, with tied-back dark-brown hair. The rain was soaking her overcoat, but she didn't rush back to her car, as if oblivious to the weather. Geoff thought about the young women he'd seen in the bar on the night he'd met Malcolm Harris from his old school. The policewoman was older, but there was something about the way she carried herself that made her stand out in comparison to them. Fascinated, he watched her rub her hand through her damp hair before opening the car door, a sense of peace coming over him.

Wanting to see where she went next, he pulled out into the traffic once she'd set off. He had to be careful, as he imagined she would be mindful of being followed. He kept his distance, making sure three or four cars remained between them as she turned down Locking Road towards Worle, the rain now so fierce he could hardly see the car in front of him.

A couple of miles later she indicated left into Tavistock Road on the way to the Mead Vale estate in Worle. Geoff continued driving along the main road, deciding he would be too conspicuous if he followed her.

He filled up with petrol at Sainsbury's before returning to Tavistock Road. It didn't take him long to find her car. It was parked on the same road, in a small driveway next to a semi-detached bungalow.

So this was the type of place where policewomen lived? This small building didn't feel like the right sort of place. The street itself was fine, but the bungalow would be more suited to a retired person who struggled with staircases than a young, active police officer. Was this part of some elaborate trap? Geoff parked further down the road so he could view the house from the safety of the van. No lights shone from inside the bungalow and he wondered if she'd already gone to sleep. He felt guilty for being there. The woman had no part to play in his plan and he had no right to be here. Yet, he couldn't deny the illicit thrill of watching her house without her knowledge.

What next? Everything outside of his plan was a risk. With her out of the way, he would have a clear passage to finish the Foresters. But a murdered policewoman would only bring unwanted attention. Geoff wanted to know what she knew, but there was an easier way to find out. Mr and Mrs Forester would know, and he would make them tell him before he hammered the final nails through their bones.

But not tonight. Although the policewoman was home now, it would be too dangerous to go to the Foresters' again. The policewoman's arrival had unnerved him, and he had to be more careful. He would wait. The old man could survive another night or two alone in the cabin. He had shelter and provisions so there was no need to rush back.

As Geoff was about to leave, the policewoman's neighbour left his house. He was carrying a black bin liner, the bag held in front of him like a weapon. At the end of the street he stopped and looked up and down, as if he were disposing of something illegal. Placing the bag in a dark wheelie bin, he glared directly at Geoff. He was some distance away and Geoff was parked in the darkness so he doubted the man could see him, but still the man stared at the van, ignoring the rain lashing down on him.

Geoff waited until he'd gone back inside before pulling away.

Chapter Thirty

The church in Uphill offered standing room only. Although Louise had arrived earlier with Tracey, they stood at the rear as Father Riley headed a procession around the pews of St Michael's, flanked by a procession of altar boys. Smokey incense flowed from the gold chalice which the priest swung as he walked, the scent filling the interior of the building where only a few days earlier Father Mulligan had been brutally murdered.

Earlier that Sunday morning, Louise had summoned the team and informed them of her meetings with Janet and Nathan Forester and Monsignor Ashley. The immediate focus was both locating Richard Lanegan, and questioning everyone they'd already spoken to about Lanegan's relationship with Veronica Lloyd. It was too early to make Lanegan a suspect, but Louise was desperate to have something concrete for Assistant Chief Constable Morley for Monday's deadline.

The journey from the station to St Michael's with Tracey had been fraught. An awkwardness had grown between them following Tracey's revelation about Thomas, and Louise was worried their relationship wouldn't survive it. It was sad to think that their years of friendship could be destroyed so easily. In part, she blamed herself and her own feelings for Thomas. Would it have bothered her as much had it been anyone but him? Tracey had acted unprofessionally, but so had Thomas. The matter had passed now and she shouldn't still be dwelling on it, yet it remained an issue between them.

'It can't always be this busy,' whispered Tracey as Father Riley reached the pulpit.

The incense was making Louise feel dizzy and she wished she'd taken a seat. 'I doubt it very much,' she replied.

Although the Mass was scheduled, it had also been unofficially allocated as a tribute to the departed Father Mulligan, whose funeral was still on hold, pending their investigations. The range of people in the congregation surprised Louise. The elderly ladies they had interviewed were there, but so were much younger people, families and individuals coming together to mourn the loss of the old priest. Many of the congregation openly grieved as Father Riley read his eulogy on his lost colleague. Louise felt like an interloper as the community mourned together. She noticed the odd glance directed their way, the congregation not scared to show their displeasure at two police officers gatecrashing their Mass.

The ceremony was different to the one Louise had experienced earlier in the week at St Bernadette's. She sensed no joy here, and it wasn't just because they were mourning Father Mulligan. The Mass reminded her of the few Sundays she'd attended church as a child. The readings from the Gospel were overly long, and there was a lot of kneeling. A hushed sense of anticipation hung over the church as Riley blessed the sacraments, one of the older altar boys ringing a golden bell after each blessing.

Then, one by one, the crowd filtered towards the altar as Father Riley offered Communion. It was something Louise had once taken part in as a child. She hadn't understood the significance then, and now her brittle faith was so lapsed she felt the congregation was actively fooling itself into believing they were somehow receiving the body of their Saviour into their souls.

Her legs ached by the time the Mass ended. She ignored the glares coming their way as the congregation exited to exchange handshakes and condolences with Father Riley. In the courtyard of the church, Louise was pleased to see Monsignor Ashley. The senior priest approached them and introduced himself to Tracey with a wry smile.

'Magnificent turnout,' said Tracey.

'Ah, yes. Father Mulligan was a much-loved member of the clergy. It is a terrible loss. I am surprised to see you here, Inspector Blackwell. You hadn't mentioned you would be attending.'

She'd only seen the priest the previous evening, when she'd helped him on to the train, his legs rather unsteady after the wine he'd drunk at their meal. 'I didn't know you would be attending either, Monsignor Ashley. If I'd known, I could have collected you from the station.'

Ashley's face hardened slightly, the first time she'd seen this side to the priest. 'I trust you're here solely out of respect for Father Mulligan. It would be unfortunate, and ill befitting, if you were to conduct any official business on such a solemn day,' he said.

Louise considered reminding him that they had two murder victims to consider, as well as a depraved killer on the loose, but saw no need to antagonise the man. 'As you say, we are just here to pay our respects.'

'Splendid,' said Ashley, the twinkle returning to his eyes. 'I'll bid you a good day for the time being.'

'What's his deal?' asked Tracey after the priest had left them.

'I'm not entirely sure. At times I think he wants to help, and then he comes across all obstructive.'

'He told you about these five holy wounds, and this other priest, Lanegan?' said Tracey.

'He mentioned the wounds, but I found out about Lanegan from the Foresters. Why, are you thinking he's trying to distract us?'

Tracey looked uncertain. 'I'm not questioning you, Louise.'

'I know that.'

They stood facing each other until it became uncomfortable. 'You know, I came to you about Thomas because I trust you,' said Tracey.

'I appreciate that, Tracey.'

'Can we get past it, then? I feel shitty enough as it is, without my best friend in the police force getting on my case.'

Louise sighed. Tracey was right. She was being selfish, making it all about her. 'I'm sorry, Trace. It's this bloody case. I'm afraid I'm going to lose it if we don't have something in place by tomorrow, and I'm not sure I can stand Finch taking things over.'

'Well, let's get something that makes it impossible for them to take it from us.'

Louise nodded. 'Wait until the monsignor has left and talk to Riley. Try to find out what the relationship between Mulligan and Lanegan was. Mulligan was effectively Lanegan's boss at the time of the fire. See if there was any animosity between the two. I'll take the car, if you're okay making your own way back?'

'Sure.'

'Oh, and Tracey?'

'Yes?'

'I'm glad to know you consider me your best friend,' said Louise with a wink.

Tracey grinned, and all the tension between them evaporated with that simple exchange.

The journalist, Tania Elliot, stopped Louise at her car. 'I didn't know you went to church,' said the woman, who was wrapped up against the cold in a full-length woollen coat.

The *Mercury* had run a story on the two murders in its weekly edition on Friday. The article hadn't gone into much detail about the killings, but Tania had included a number of follow-up articles interviewing members of the public. There was talk of low hotel bookings, and fears that the summer trade, which was still months away, would be affected. Tania didn't attack the police outright, but Louise had seen an underlying tension between the lines in her articles and it was clear to her that the young journalist saw an opportunity to further her career. 'Hello, Tania. What brings you here?'

'Just paying my respects.'

Louise nodded. 'That's thoughtful of you.'

'What developments can you give me, Inspector?'

'Nothing more to say, Tania. I promised I'd keep you informed, and I will.'

'Can you give us a quote to reassure our readership?'

'You really need to go through our press office. You know that, Tania.'

'People are locking themselves indoors, Inspector. Hotel bookings are down for this time of the year. Would you care to comment on that?'

Louise had experienced winter in Weston before. The town was never busy with tourists in the winter months unless there was a specific event in the town, such as the beach motocross event which was scheduled for the following weekend. She suspected Tania was trying to invent a story that wasn't there, though she conceded that the town had felt emptier in the last few days. 'No comment, Tania. Now, if you'll excuse me, I must be going.'

Tania was silent as Louise got in her car. As Louise drove away, she saw the journalist pull her coat tight against her as if the wind had just picked up.

Robertson wasn't at the station. Louise had hardly spoken to him since the meeting with Morley on Friday. 'Robertson been in today?' she called over to Thomas, who'd just finished a call.

'He was in for thirty minutes then left. He was wearing his coat, if that helps,' said Thomas.

Louise watched him work for a few moments. Did he know that she knew about him and Tracey? As long as it didn't interfere with the investigation, then it wasn't really her business. Tracey was effectively Thomas's superior, but the difference between their ranks was minimal and it wouldn't be the first relationship of its kind to occur between colleagues. The DS still bore the signs of a prolonged hangover, and she wondered if he'd returned to his home yet or if he was still living in that wretched hotel. She was about to ask if he wanted a coffee when Greg Farrell approached her.

'Guv, I spoke to one of the parishioners from St Bernadette's this morning after Mass. Widower in his sixties, says he remembers our Father Lanegan. Apparently, Lanegan didn't have much time for him. This guy said he was a bit of a ladies' man, would you believe?'

'Ladies' man?' said Louise, recalling the 'indiscretions' that Ashley had referred to.

'That's what he said.' Farrell opened his notebook, the hint of a smirk already on his face, and began to read. '"He was good-looking, if you like that sort of thing. All the women were crazy for him and he was keen on them."'

Louise could understand the attraction of something being out of reach. Bizarrely, her thoughts turned to a television series she'd caught glimpses of as a child. *The Thorn Birds* had starred a dashing

Richard Chamberlain as a priest torn between his relationship and his career in the Catholic Church. 'You asked about Veronica?'

'Yes, there were rumours he was having an affair with her, though this guy was heavily biased. I think his wife may have had the hots for the young Father Lanegan. He gave me a few names to chase up, though. Women he thinks Lanegan may have tangled with.'

Could Lanegan really have been so open? Priests were subject to a vow of celibacy, and if he'd broken his vow, she would have expected some discretion. As Farrell said, it could well have been sour grapes on the part of the widower, but if he was right about the priest having an affair with Veronica Lloyd, it could blow the case wide open. 'Good work, Farrell. Chase those leads up and let me know as soon as you get any more information.'

'Guv.'

Farrell's discovery made it even more urgent that they locate Lanegan. The team had been searching for Richard Lanegan throughout the morning, but they'd yet to find a definite address for the former priest. Louise stared at her computer screen, desperate for some inspiration. She doubted the possible link between Veronica and Lanegan would be enough to stall Morley so she now had less than twenty-four hours to locate the man.

Recalling what Monsignor Ashley had told her about Lanegan retiring to the seaside, and with no hit on the PND, she decided to check the databases of constabularies based near the coast. Louise started with the most local, the Devon and Cornwall force, and within minutes had a result. She couldn't believe the stroke of luck she'd been given.

A man by the name of Richard Lanegan had just been reported as a low-risk missing person by Sergeant Joslyn Merrick, although, according to the report, it was possible that Lanegan had been missing, or at least unaccounted for, for nearly a week.

A PC James Lewis answered her call to the St Ives office where Merrick worked. 'May I speak to Sergeant Merrick?' asked Louise.

'It's her day off. Can I help?'

Louise explained the situation and asked the constable if he could provide her with Merrick's personal mobile.

'I'm afraid I can't do that, ma'am, but I was with Sergeant Merrick when she visited Mr Lanegan's residence.'

Louise hid her impatience. 'What can you tell me?'

'There was a possible break-in. The back door was busted, but we were unable to confirm if it had been forced or not.'

'Was there anything religious in the house?'

'Why do you ask?'

'I ask, James . . . it is James, isn't it?'

'Yes, ma'am.'

'Okay, James. I ask because I'm investigating a multiple-murder case which has close links to a Catholic church where a priest by the name of Father Lanegan worked. Father Richard Lanegan. It's been all over the tabloids. Are you catching my drift now, Constable?'

'There were a couple of crucifixes. And some Bibles.'

'There we go, we got there in the end.' Louise punched up St Ives on Google Maps. It was a good three hours' drive. 'James, I want you to tell Sergeant Merrick that I am leaving for St Ives now and will be there in the next three hours. Can you do that for me?'

'I can't do that, ma'am, it's her day off.'

Louise couldn't believe what she was hearing. She gave the constable her number. 'James, I'd better receive a call from Sergeant Merrick in the next hour. I don't care if you have to go to her house, or track her down, but I will speak to her in the next hour. Are we clear?'

She heard the constable mumble something but had hung up before he had a chance to properly reply.

Tracey returned as Louise left the office. 'Father Riley claims not to have known Father Lanegan very well. I pushed him as hard as I could, but I still think he's withholding something.'

Louise told her about her possible missing person.

'You want some company?'

'No, best you head things up here. Speak to Farrell. He has some information on Lanegan which is worth following up on.'

The southbound M5 was quieter than she'd anticipated and she reached Exeter in just over an hour. She'd yet to hear back from the young constable so she called him on the speakerphone as she entered the A30. 'James, DI Blackwell again. Any luck on tracking down Sergeant Merrick?'

The officer hesitated before speaking, confusion in his voice. 'I've left her a couple of messages but haven't heard back from her.'

Louise breathed deeply. 'I don't think you appreciate how important this is, Constable Lewis. I didn't ask you to leave a couple of messages. I wanted you to track your sergeant down. You have an address for her?'

'Yes, but—'

'James, listen to me. I will be in St Ives in less than two hours. Why don't you make things easier for yourself?'

'I can't just give out her address.'

'Call Weston nick and get verification. Then text me her address. I expect her not to be surprised when I turn up so I suggest you find her before I do. I'm giving you a second chance here, James. Do you understand me?'

'Yes, ma'am.'

Louise sighed. 'I feel we're treading old ground here, James. I am serious. Career serious,' she said, the coldness to her words genuine.

'I understand, ma'am,' said the constable, his voice unsteady.

Five minutes later a verified home address for Sergeant Joslyn Merrick was sent to her phone.

While Weston-super-Mare had been reserved for day trips as a child, Louise had spent a number of summer holidays visiting Cornwall. As a family, they'd spent nearly every waking day at the beach, whatever the weather. Her memories were mainly positive. Days of jumping in waves with Paul, learning to boogie board – lying flat on polystyrene surfing boards as the white water carried them to shore – or exploring the rock pools at the various beaches. They'd played well together, then, before Paul reached his teens and his attention turned to other pursuits. Although she would never have admitted it at the time, Paul was the closest thing she'd had to a best friend. She'd been close to a couple of girls at school, but she played with Paul every day and it had probably hurt more than she'd appreciated when he'd finally outgrown her as a child.

She wiped her eyes at the memory as she overtook a campervan struggling up the steep incline towards Bodmin. Louise felt a pang of loneliness as the road cut through the barren landscape of endless windswept fields. Was this some fool's errand, a desperate attempt to find a potential suspect with the threat of Finch taking over her case hanging over her like the sword of Damocles? She had no idea if the missing Lanegan in St Ives was the old priest from St Bernadette's. Robertson would have told her she was desperate, unfocused even, but she was less than an hour away now.

The sergeant lived in a town called Hayle, a few miles away from St Ives. A large sign greeted her as she left the A30 fifty minutes later, proclaiming that the small seaside town had 'Three Miles of Golden Sand'.

Joslyn Merrick lived in a terraced house off the main street in Hayle. Louise manoeuvred through a number of side streets before finding the house. She felt bad for calling unannounced and hoped that the less than efficient PC had warned her she was coming.

The sound of screaming came from behind Merrick's front door. Louise couldn't tell if the noise from the children was joyous or not. She knocked and the sound stopped abruptly. Ten seconds later she saw a silhouetted figure approach through the glass-panelled door. A man, still in his dressing gown, stood in the opening and regarded her. His eyes were creased, his face pitted with stubble.

'Hello,' he said.

'Hello. My name is Detective Inspector Louise Blackwell.' Louise showed her ID. 'I'm here to see Joslyn. Is she in?'

The man didn't reply immediately. He looked uncertain, as if assessing Louise's request, then out of nowhere, he shouted, 'Joss!' before returning back down the hallway.

The man was replaced by a young boy, close to Emily's age, who looked at her with puzzlement. 'I'm Zach, who are you?' he asked.

'I'm Louise, pleased to meet you.'

'Yes,' agreed the boy, as a woman ran down the stairs, her hair wrapped in a towel.

'Hi, sorry about that. I'm Joslyn Merrick. Can I help?'

'Hi Joslyn, DI Louise Blackwell. I called your station earlier. I'd like to talk about Richard Lanegan, your missing person.'

'Oh. Sorry, I haven't heard anything from the station. Who did you speak to?'

'PC James Lewis.'

'Yeah, that figures. And he gave you my address?'

'I did push him,' said Louise, showing the woman her warrant card.

'Okay, you'd better come in, then. You'll have to excuse the mess. We were at a rugby dinner last night so we're not fully functioning at the moment.'

'Not to worry. I'm really sorry to have bothered you at home, but I'm up against it at the moment.'

Joslyn led them through the chaotic but welcoming house. She pointed to a young girl hiding behind the kitchen counter. 'That's Matilda. You've met Zach.'

'Hi, Matilda,' said Louise, poking her head behind the counter and receiving an excited squeal from the girl. 'Looks like you've got your hands full here.'

'Tell me about it. You've met my husband,' said Joslyn, with a chuckle. 'Coffee?'

'That would be perfect.'

Once they were seated, Louise explained the situation at Weston.

'I've read about the case. Sounds horrendous. You think this Lanegan guy could be a suspect?' said Joslyn, sounding doubtful.

'I was told he'd retired to the seaside, and there aren't that many Richard Lanegans out there, so when I saw your missing-person's report I thought it could be a promising lead.'

'Well, I think they're probably the same person,' said Joslyn. 'He was reported missing by his cleaner, and so far we haven't been able to come up with a contact number for him. The lock on the back door was busted, but no firm sign that it was deliberately broken. Chances are high that he's popped off on holiday somewhere and just forgot to tell the cleaner, although we haven't been able to establish this from any of the people listed in Lanegan's address book. The only reason I registered him as a missing person is because of the lock, and the period he's been away. Plus, the poor woman who cleans his house is beside herself.'

'So why do you think he's the Richard Lanegan I'm looking for?'

'The cleaner told me he used to be a priest.'

Louise contained her excitement at this revelation. 'Sorry to do this to you, but could you show me the house?'

Joslyn shrugged. 'Why not? Get him to do some parenting for once,' she said, giving Louise a knowing smile.

Lanegan's house was in a local estate at the top of the hill near the centre of St Ives. The buildings were identical in size and shape, their exteriors a weather-beaten grey.

'The cleaner gave us a key,' said Joslyn, opening the front door.

Inside, the house had the feeling of a place someone had just moved into – or just left. Saying the interior was minimalist would be an understatement, Louise felt. There was little beyond the functional: sofa and armchair in the living room; dining table with two wooden seats; cooker, kettle and toaster in the kitchen. No pictures were hung on the plain white walls, and only a small bookcase in the master bedroom – resplendent with various religious texts – suggested that the owner hadn't any personal belongings.

'I guess the decor makes sense if he used to be a priest,' said Joslyn, once they were back in the kitchen. 'Lack of possessions, devotion to God, et cetera.'

Louise showed her a picture of Lanegan that she'd printed from the old copy of the Weston *Mercury*. 'Did your cleaner have a photo of him?'

'No, but I imagine she could describe him well enough for a sketch artist. I think she's been nursing a crush on the man for twenty years. She'd certainly be able to confirm if this was him or not.'

'What did she tell you about him?'

'He arrived in Cornwall over thirty years ago. She met him at a church fete, in Hayle, actually, just up the road. When she started telling me I thought it was going to be this wonderful love story, but it was just quite a sad story, really. Lanegan moved to Cornwall after being defrocked, or whatever they call it when they sack a priest. Gutter mind that I have, my first thought was some sort of abuse scandal, but it wasn't that. He was made to leave because he fell in love.'

Louise's first thought was of Veronica Lloyd, but she didn't want to mention her name unprompted. 'Who was he in love with?'

'She was a married woman, by all accounts. According to Mrs Boswell, he had an affair with this woman. They'd been in love, but she'd been unable to leave her family, and he the clergy. So they split up, but Lanegan couldn't get her out of his mind and a few years later he left Weston to escape her memory. Mrs Boswell thought he still pined for her.'

Louise couldn't help but be disappointed. Veronica Lloyd had never been married. 'Did Mrs Boswell give you a name for this mysterious woman?'

'No, Lanegan never told her that.'

Chapter Thirty-One

After locking up Lanegan's house, Louise followed Joslyn out of town. The sea was visible at the top of the hill, the sun peering through the clouds and shining a glow on the rippling waves.

Eileen Boswell was a force of nature. In her eighties, she lived alone in an old farmhouse on the long road out of St Ives. 'I'm not used to visitors,' said the woman, leading them through an old-fashioned kitchen where an Aga cooker gave heat to the low-ceilinged room. She insisted on making them tea, which she served with stale biscuits. The gleam in her eye when she spoke about Lanegan was obvious. She'd lost her own husband ten years before meeting him, and though she didn't come right out and say it, Louise could see that Lanegan had become her unrequited replacement.

There was a tear in the old woman's eye as she held the black-and-white picture of Lanegan from the *Mercury*. 'That's him,' she confirmed.

Louise quizzed her about Lanegan's story, but the old woman couldn't give her anything more than what she'd already told Joslyn. 'We never spoke about it after that night. I think he'd drunk a bit too much wine that day and maybe he regretted it. But I know it still pains him. I see it in him every time I go round to clean.'

There was no point in asking Eileen if she thought Lanegan was capable of killing Veronica Lloyd and Father Mulligan. Her judgement was clouded, and Louise saw no need to taint her vision of the man. Louise gave her the names of the victims, but she hadn't heard of them. Eileen offered them more tea, clearly enjoying the company.

'I'm sorry, Eileen, I have to get back to Weston-super-Mare.'

'Do you think you will find him?' asked Eileen, with genuine concern.

'I will do my very best, and we'll let you know as soon as we do. Is that okay, Eileen?'

'I guess that's all I can ask.'

'You live here alone?' asked Louise.

'I'm not about to have any boarders now, dear, am I?'

'No family?'

'I have a son,' said Eileen, with a mixture of pride and sadness. Pushing herself up from her armchair, she retrieved a slim photo album from the sideboard. 'He lives in Australia. I have two grandchildren. Sweet things. It's too far for them to visit, though, I fear.'

Louise took the album from her. Two smiling blonde girls in their early teens grinned back at her from the last picture. The photographs were date-stamped. The latest was taken fifteen years ago.

'They're beautiful,' said Louise, handing the album back.

Louise couldn't get the photographs out of her mind as she drove to Weston. Eileen's grandchildren were adults now, and either the old lady didn't realise, or she was purposely ignoring the fact. And what about her son? How could he abandon his mother to such isolation? The thought prompted her to call her own mother on the car's phone system.

'Hi, Mum,' she said, a feeling of remoteness coming over her as she drove up the deserted A30.

'Hi, Lou, everything okay?'

'Yes, busy day today. Just checking to see how things went with Paul yesterday.'

Emily was still staying with her grandparents, while Paul tried to get his life together. Louise wanted to speak to him face to face, to remind him what he risked losing, but she hadn't had the time.

'Oh, it was okay. There were a few tears from Emily when he left in the evening, but she was fine today.'

'What did Paul say?'

'Not much. I could tell he was hung-over, but he didn't ask if Emily could go back home with him. I'm worried he prefers it this way. It gives him more freedom to go out and get drunk.'

'I'm sure that's not the case, Mum. He adores Emily.'

'I don't doubt that, but he's an addict, Lou. You understand what they can be like.'

Louise knew only too well. She'd seen it all in her time in the police. Wrecks of human beings who'd sacrificed everything for another drink or hit. Paul wasn't quite there yet, but she was worried that her mother's assessment was correct and that separating him from Emily might have a detrimental effect. 'Did you talk to him again about getting some help?'

'Not this time. I hope he's going to come to his senses and volunteer himself. He was sweet with Emily. I know he misses her so much. We'll see how this week goes.'

Louise glanced at the satnav. Two hundred miles to go, followed by paperwork and meetings. 'Okay, Mum, whatever you say. I have no idea when I'll be able to get over to Paul's.'

'What about you, darling? We didn't have time to talk properly yesterday. I know you have this big case at the moment. How are things going with that?'

Fine, thought Louise. *The only suspect I have, if you can call him a suspect, is missing, and chances are the case will be ripped from me tomorrow. Apart from that, things couldn't be better.* She stared at the road ahead of her. 'It's going as well as can be expected.'

'I'm so proud of you, Louise. We both are. You know that?'

'Thanks, Mum, I know. I'll give you a call later in the week. Let me know if you need me to come over and help with Emily.'

'You just concentrate on your work. We've got everything covered here.'

'Okay, Mum. Love you.'

'Love you.'

She reached Weston just before ten. It was too late to go to the station, but she couldn't face returning to the solitude of her bungalow. She chuckled to herself as she headed off the M5, fearing she was on a path similar to Eileen Boswell's. Would she still be living in the bungalow in forty years, retired and alone? She parked up outside her home and took the short walk along the unlit pathway to the pub situated next to the supermarket. With only thirty minutes of drinking time left, the dimly lit bar was full of revellers enjoying the final minutes of the weekend.

The noise level dropped as Louise walked into the bar, everyone taking a quick look at her before returning to their conversations. She'd only been here once, for lunch with her parents, shortly after she'd moved in. The barman greeted her with suspicion, as if he knew she was police. 'What can I do for you?' he said.

'Large gin and tonic, thanks.'

The barman frowned before pouring her drink.

'Don't mind him, he's always this good with strangers.'

Louise turned to see the source of the voice, a thin, wiry man, probably in his late thirties, standing at the end of the bar. Louise offered him a small smile, noting the scruffy tracksuit he was wearing.

She took the drink and found a seat in the corner of the bar, praying that tracksuit man wouldn't join her. It was as if she'd reached a new low, alone in a grotty estate pub in Worle on a Sunday night, all because she couldn't face going home to the silence and her home-made murder wall. She tried to think about the case but couldn't focus with the noise of the music and drunken chatter. As the barman rung for last orders, she ordered a second drink, wondering as she did if this was how Paul had started. The occasional drink alone in the local bar leading to full-blown alcoholism.

She finished the drink in three savage gulps, not wanting to be the last person to leave the pub. Tracksuit man was still at the bar when she left, but she decided to take the longer route home through the better-lit housing estate in case he decided to follow. She slowed her pace as she rounded the corner to her road, refusing to be spooked by thoughts of being followed. The night was still and a thick layer of cloud covered the stars and the moon.

Back in her kitchen, she poured herself a final drink. Drinking alone was not ideal either, but she couldn't face sleep just yet. In the living room, she switched on the television but was unable to focus on the flickering images, the photographs and names on her murder board vying for her attention. She glared at the images of Veronica Lloyd and Father Mulligan, as if they could communicate with her. 'Was it Lanegan?' she whispered to them. 'Why did he do this to you?'

The buzz of her phone made her jump, and she emptied the rest of her drink down the sink before reading the message:

Time's running out, Louise.

She found Finch's number in her contacts, her finger hovering over the call button as the adrenalin and alcohol in her body urged her to ring him. She was tired of all this shit, and wanted to tell Finch and some of her other colleagues exactly what she thought of them. 'Fuck,' she screamed, throwing her phone at the sofa and heading for her bedroom.

She was asleep before she even had time to undress.

Chapter Thirty-Two

Louise was the first person in the office on Monday morning. She'd been dismayed to find she'd fallen asleep in her clothes, yesterday's journeys, two gin and tonics and one vodka proving to be a perfect cure for insomnia. She had wanted to undress and crawl back into bed, but her mind was busy from the second she woke up. She brewed coffee and took a cup into the shower room with her before grabbing a stale croissant from the cupboard and heading into town.

Alone in the office, the sound of her fingers hitting her keyboard was accompanied by the steady hum of the air conditioning she'd never noticed before. It was probably her tiredness, but the place felt foreign to her as if it were her first time there. While she waited for DCI Robertson to arrive, she updated HOLMES, detailing her visit to St Ives and her meetings with Sergeant Joslyn Merrick and Eileen Boswell. Already, her brief time in Cornwall felt like a lifetime ago. She described Lanegan's house, confirming, as well as she was able, that he'd been the other parish priest at St Bernadette's in the early eighties.

On a separate piece of paper, she jotted down some thoughts as to why Lanegan would have killed Veronica Lloyd and Father Mulligan. Eileen had said the priest had been running from an affair, and although Eileen claimed the woman was married, it was conceivable that Veronica Lloyd was the priest's old lover. He wouldn't be the first man to take the life of a woman who'd spurned him, so she had potential motive there. But why kill Mulligan?

Maybe the priest knew too much, or had been instrumental in Veronica ending the affair. Louise dropped her pencil. If Robertson didn't laugh her out of the office, then Morley and Finch certainly would. Everything was beyond circumstantial. Lanegan was little more than a potential suspect. He was only borderline as a missing person, and if he was the killer, what was the link with the five holy wounds theory postulated by Monsignor Ashley? Who was Lanegan going to kill next, and why?

DS Farrell was the second to arrive. He was whistling as he entered the office. Dressed in a well-fitted dark suit, as if he were going to a funeral, his familiar smirk formed as he saw Louise. She shouldn't be so antagonised by the man, but she couldn't help it.

'Morning, Guv, you're here early.'

'Morning, Greg. There's coffee on, if you want it.'

'Thanks. I'm glad you're here. I managed to speak with another of Lanegan's old parishioners yesterday. He didn't want to speak to me on the phone but has agreed to meet this morning.'

Louise told him to add it to the HOLMES file, and with no one else to tell, she updated him on her journey to Cornwall.

Farrell looked genuinely excited by the news. 'Looks like we have an official suspect, then,' he said.

Louise didn't share his enthusiasm. 'We have a missing person of sorts. Not sure if it's much more than that at the moment.'

'Come on, Guv. It would be one hell of a coincidence that Lanegan goes missing at the exact time as two people with close links to him are murdered.'

'We'll see,' said Louise, as Farrell headed towards the kitchen for his coffee.

Farrell returned with a coffee for her. 'I've been thinking, Guv. Have you considered that Lanegan is a potential victim rather than a suspect?'

Louise nodded, annoyed by Farrell's insinuation. Of course she'd considered it, especially after seeing the busted lock in his kitchen. 'It can't be ruled out, but if he has been killed, then why hasn't the killer displayed his body? The two other killings suggest he is proud of his handiwork.'

'Maybe Lanegan was a test run, and it's not as if we've actively looked for his body.'

She nodded again, knowing the DS was right. Although Joslyn had arranged interviews with Lanegan's neighbours, none of the properties had been searched. For all they knew, Lanegan's body was waiting to be discovered somewhere in the Cornish estate where he lived. 'I guess it's something we should work out before proceeding, whether Lanegan is a potential victim or a suspect,' she said as Greg returned to his desk.

Louise assessed every angle as she waited for DCI Robertson to arrive, grinning to herself as she imagined Eileen Boswell holding Lanegan somewhere in her house.

Tracey and Thomas arrived together and Farrell smirked again as he caught Louise glancing over at them. She hoped their arrival was another coincidence. Tracey had promised it was a one-night thing and, her fading jealousy aside, their potential affair was something Louise could do without in her department. As if reading her thoughts, Tracey gave her a minuscule shake of her head as she said good morning.

Tiring of waiting, Louise called a meeting and updated the team on her trip to St Ives. Echoing Farrell's words, she told them Lanegan was now a potential suspect and a potential victim. She didn't know how Robertson was going to react, and she didn't want the team to know this was possibly their last day on the case, at least under her leadership. She could only stress the urgency and ask them to update her as soon as they had anything relevant to report.

She rang Joslyn in St Ives, and asked her to conduct searches of the houses in Lanegan's area. The sergeant sounded doubtful and complained about lack of resources, but agreed to help.

When Robertson arrived half an hour later, Louise presented him with all the information. To his credit, he listened patiently to what she had to say. 'I've read your updates over the weekend,' he said. 'I agree it is possibly fertile ground.'

'But?'

'But I fear it might not be enough for Morley.'

Louise took a deep breath. 'What does he think will happen if he brings in Finch, Iain?'

'I understand where you're coming from, Louise, but you need to have something more substantial to offer him. From what I can see, chances are high that this Lanegan character will simply return from his holiday in the next few days, if that's where he is, and then where will we be?'

'Lanegan used to work with Father Mulligan. He was the local priest at St Bernadette's when Veronica Lloyd worked at the school. Now he's gone AWOL. I don't really know what Morley wants me to do.'

'Come on, Louise. You could start by finding Lanegan.'

'We are in the process of doing that, Iain. I only bloody found out about him on Saturday.'

'I'm just saying what Morley is going to say. If I were you, I would accept the offer of assistance with good grace. That way, you stay on the case. You could even keep your name as the SIO.'

Louise leaned forward. 'You know what happened to me in Bristol, don't you, Iain?' she said.

Robertson closed his eyes as he reclined in his chair, as if recoiling from her words. They'd never fully discussed the Walton case before. They'd always talked around it, but he'd never asked for details of that night and she'd never offered. He would have read the reports, would know the official statements and her side of the story, but he didn't really know what had happened.

'He lied,' she said.

'Now's not the time for this, Louise.'

'No, you're going to fucking listen to me, Iain,' said Louise, fury spreading through every part of her body. 'DCI Finch lied under oath. He told me the man I shot was holding a gun. Now, he may have been mistaken or he may have lied about it for his own twisted reasons, but he told me the victim had a gun and I reacted as I'd been trained. Under oath, he denied ever saying that. He said I panicked and shot the unarmed man because of that.'

'I know what happened,' said Robertson, his voice deep, warning.

'But you don't, Iain. You know what Finch said in court, but he was lying.'

'Louise, you're going to get yourself into so much trouble if you go round saying this. You know what you're suggesting?'

'Yes, I'm suggesting the man you want to take over my case told me to shoot an unarmed man. I don't know if he thought he was armed at the time and changed his story to protect himself,' she said, realising she was repeating herself but unable to stop, 'but if I'm being honest, I think he lied to me on purpose. He saw an opportunity and he took it. I was favourite for that DCI position and, after that, I was lucky to still be in a job.'

Robertson stood up. 'I have no idea what you expect me to do about this.'

'Do you believe me?' said Louise, still sitting.

'That's irrelevant, Inspector. I won't be reporting this discussion, but I suggest you keep your accusations to yourself.'

'That's it?'

'Christ, Louise, learn to help yourself. Morley will be here this afternoon. Get something for him or be ready to accept the consequences.'

Louise felt as if Robertson had punched her in the gut. She got to her feet, unable to meet his eyes as she left the office.

Chapter Thirty-Three

Geoff had worked while the man slept. On returning to the island he'd had to strip him clean once again, sitting him beneath the shower, the prisoner's eyes lowered to the ground like a dog being caught doing something it shouldn't, as the water washed away the piss and excrement from his clothes.

This is the last time, Geoff promised himself as he sanded the wood. The next time he returned there would be to end it. He smiled as he pictured the scene. He prayed the man would have the strength to do what was required.

Once he'd finished with the sanding, he hauled the object out of the visitor centre. It was quite a sight, the join almost invisible.

He daydreamed about it now as he waited at his mother's house for darkness to come. She was off work this morning and he could hear her pottering around as he lay on his bed. He'd thought the last time he'd left the house it would be the last time he saw her. Back in the house once more, an empty feeling had crept over him and he closed his eyes to fight the weakness within him. He wanted to tell her, to explain why he'd done the things he'd done. She would find out eventually, and no doubt the police would call him a psychopath, or something similar. She would receive the blame and there was a chance she would be ostracised in the community. Like his father, she'd stopped attending church years ago, but she still had friends at work and in the various organisations she belonged to. How would they treat her once they knew her son was a multiple murderer?

Leaving a note explaining his reasons would only make things worse. She would blame herself, and although she would be right to do so, Geoff didn't want to inflict any more pain on her. She'd been duped, failed and let down as much as he'd been. She'd had a weakness, but it had been exploited and she'd been punished enough. If he could, he would keep her out of it, but her involvement was inevitable, a final part of her penance.

'Geoff, are you up?' she called, from outside his door.

'Not really.'

'I've washed your clothes. Can I bring them in?'

'I guess so.'

She smiled as she eased the door open, a large bundle of neatly folded clothes under her arm. 'Here, let me put these away for you,' she said, as she began opening his drawers.

As his mother put his clothes away, Geoff was transported to his childhood; to a time when he hadn't had to glove his hands. Things had been much simpler then. He could smell his mum's perfume, which she no longer wore, and for a second he was back to that time of security and happiness. He was on the bed, reading his computer magazines, anticipating his father returning later that afternoon.

'Is everything okay, love?' asked his mum, forcing him back to the present.

He went to speak, his words catching in his throat. If he could only tell her, maybe she could help. She could tell him he'd made a very bad mistake but there was a way out of it, that he could stop now, that he didn't have to return to the island.

He wished he could tell her he loved her one last time, but he didn't have the words, so he said, 'Everything's fine, Mum.'

'That's good, love,' she said. 'That's good.'

He waited until the front door shut before leaving his room. His mum had left his lunch in the fridge and he ate it at the kitchen table, washing it down with a glass of milk. The killing didn't bother him. He'd been studying for years, and although there'd been an initial hesitation when he'd first captured Mrs Lloyd, it had soon become second nature.

He was righteous, that he did know. Mrs Lloyd had deserved to die, as had Father Mulligan, and so did the Foresters. They'd taken from him, destroyed his life, but Geoff could end that now; he could redeem his dad.

Yet he couldn't fight the empty feeling in his gut and chest.

He'd known at the beginning that he would experience such moments of self-doubt. It had occurred when he'd taken Mrs Lloyd, and he had to fight now as he'd fought it then.

It's not an ending but a beginning, he told himself as, for the final time, he left the house.

He felt a sense of serenity as he drove the van to Worlebury. He moved through the traffic as if in slow motion, the sole sound he was aware of his own high-pitched whistling. He found himself parked outside the Foresters' house, not remembering the last mile or so of his journey.

He only had a three-hour window to get the job completed and return to the old pier before he lost the tide. From the rear of the van he retrieved his tool bag and walked towards the Foresters' front door before he had a chance to change his mind.

It was Mrs Forester who answered. In retrospect, she'd always acted as if she was above everyone else, and he should have known that time he came to speak to Mr Forester about what he'd seen that she would dismiss him. Well, she wouldn't dismiss him now. She smiled in that false way, her lips moving but no warmth showing on the rest of her face as she tried to recall where she'd seen Geoff before.

'Hello, Mrs Forester,' he said, noting the split second of recognition and fear as she realised who he was, before he brought the metal down on the side of her face.

Pushing her inside, he closed the door. From further down the hallway, he heard the sound of the woman's husband, his old head teacher, and he let Mrs Forester slip to the floor as he prepared himself for the attack.

Only it didn't come. Instead of trying to help his wife, the cowardly man was trying to escape through the back garden. Mrs Forester was out cold and Geoff placed her on to her side before moving down the hallway.

Mr Forester was scrabbling at the conservatory door, his hands shaking so badly he couldn't turn the key in the lock. 'What do you want?' he asked as he struggled with it.

'It's over now, Mr Forester,' said Geoff, placing his hand on the man's shoulder.

Chapter Thirty-Four

'You okay, Lou?' said Tracey, placing a coffee on her desk.

'You heard?'

'Your disagreement with Robertson? I think the whole station, if not the town, heard it.'

'I don't know what to do, Tracey. I think they're going to give the case over to the MIT.'

Tracey knew the history, and how divisive the decision against her by the Major Investigation Team had been. Since Louise's departure, Finch had managed to transfer a further three team members who'd spoken up for her to other departments. 'We've still got this Father Lanegan character. We keep doing our job, try to find him, we've still got a chance.'

'Thanks, Tracey.'

Tracey paused at the door. 'I'll give you some time.'

Louise wasn't a quitter, but it was hard to motivate herself to keep working when the case was likely to be taken from her in the next few hours. *It's bad enough working in this fucking town*, she thought, *but if every decent case was going to end up with MIT, then what was the point?*

All eyes were on her as she departed the office. Downstairs, the uniformed officers, and even the handful of civilians in the area, seemed to be staring at her as if they knew what was happening. She welcomed the rush of cold air outside, the distant smell of the sea, and the cacophony of the gulls circling the sky above her.

It would be easy to give up, to leave the town for good, but she wouldn't let them beat her again. She would continue working on the case until she was told to stop; and for the time being, that meant finding Lanegan.

Her first stop was a return to the Forester house. Mr Forester had mentioned Lanegan's name when she'd quizzed them about the fire. She'd had the feeling then that they'd been withholding something, and now she wanted to question them without notice.

It was dark when she'd left her bungalow that morning and it was dark now. It was the way of winter in the seaside town, a season of unrelenting darkness and shadow. 'Cheery thought,' she muttered to herself as she slowed the car to a stop. In her rear-view mirror, the flashing lights of an ambulance blinked at her, followed by the wail of a police car siren. She called in to find out there was a road-traffic accident half a mile down the road.

As the car in front of her edged forwards, she did a three-point turn and headed back the way she had come until she found a turn that would lead to a back route to Worlebury. Her stomach rumbled as she passed a local fish and chip shop. She'd had nothing to eat since her croissant that morning, but there was no time now. The call from Morley could come at any second, and the thought of Finch taking over banished all concerns of hunger.

A number of other drivers had taken the same decision, so she was stuck for another twenty minutes at the top of Worlebury Hill before the traffic began to relent as she turned towards the Foresters'.

With no free parking spaces along the Foresters' road, she was forced to park two streets away and left her car at the precise second that the clouds opened. A freezing wind rushed around her body, her umbrella all but useless against the battering rain, and she was drenched by the time she reached the house.

Shaking out her umbrella, she knocked on the front door, only to find it was already open.

Chapter Thirty-Five

Geoff watched the policewoman approach the house in the rain. The attack had extinguished his strength and he'd spent the last few minutes in the van, the images of Mr and Mrs Forester fresh in his mind, his skin and clothes still slick with their blood.

After Geoff had touched his shoulder, Mr Forester struggled. At first he'd put up quite a fight, and the ensuing conflict had made Geoff careless. Once he'd subdued Mr Forester, a red mist had descended over him, and even now the memory of the next few minutes were clouded. He'd worked on the pair with a zeal he'd never experienced before, but his work was shoddy and unprofessional. The incisions into the ankles had been rushed and lacked precision. He could still hear the snap of Mrs Forester's bone as the nail crushed her ankle, her screams still finding voice through the gag in her mouth.

In the end, he'd just wanted to get it over with. But he couldn't drag himself away just yet. The policewoman was on her phone and it would be a matter of minutes before her colleagues joined her and they found out what he'd left for them. So why didn't he move?

He cowered in his seat as she scanned the street, her vision all but obliterated by the lashing rain, before moving into the house.

How easy it would be to follow her in, he thought. Would one extra body matter? She didn't deserve to die, but she was on to him, that much he was sure about.

His thoughts turned to Dad, and what he had to do for him. The prisoner still waited for him in Steep Holm and Geoff didn't want to jeopardise his chances of returning.

Yet the woman would be unarmed, and he had strength and surprise on his side. Yes, he'd be taking a chance, but could he take the risk of not doing it?

The smell hit her as she edged through the door: blood and excrement, sweat and the dying embers of fear. This time she didn't have a gun, only her pepper spray and extendable baton. It took a few seconds for her eyes to adjust to the haze of red as she stepped into the front room. The living-room lights illuminated the blood-splattered corpses of Janet and Nathan Forester as if they had their own spotlights. Ropes bound the pair together, their bloated and lifeless eyes staring at Louise as if still in shock.

Louise didn't encroach any further into the crime scene. She examined the room, trying not to dwell on the mangled mess of the couple's legs. Off to the right of the living room was the kitchen, and she shuffled along the walls, the pepper spray in front of her, as she secured the area.

Chances were the killer was long gone, but she edged slowly back to the hallway and decided to ascend the staircase, all the time convincing herself that this wasn't the Walton farmhouse.

A sweet, sickly smell, a mixture of potpourri and disinfectant, hit her as she opened the bathroom door. Louise hung back, the white porcelain of the washbasin and the bath speckled with puddles of blood. Had the killer been so calm that they'd had the composure and time to wash away the blood before leaving the house?

She secured the other upper-floor rooms, pausing on the landing as she heard the front door creak open.

Geoff pulled away seconds before the wailing sirens hit the street. What the hell had he been thinking? It was as if he'd wanted to be caught. The policewoman was not part of the plan, wasn't one of the five, yet he'd had an urge to repeat his actions on her. Some part of him wanted to enjoy the sensation of metal through flesh and bone again, and he didn't fully understand what that meant as he drove to the old pier.

In the car park, he climbed into the back of the van and changed, savouring the coppery smell of the clothes he peeled from his skin. It didn't matter now if he left them in the van. By the time they located the vehicle and checked what was inside, it would be all over. Still, there was no point in taking chances, so he wrapped the clothes in a black bin liner, stuffed them into his backpack and headed towards the pier.

Rain was still falling, the little shop at the foot of the pier long shut. No one in their right mind would be out in this weather, and that was all to Geoff's advantage. A metal gate, the top lined with springs of barbed wire, blocked the entrance to the pier, but there was an easy route around the sea wall. As long as he kept his footing steady and his grip firm on the metal railings, he wouldn't have a problem. He was so close now that it didn't seem fair to fail at this point.

But the weather had a different opinion. The wind had grown into a gale, and his raincoat billowed off his flesh as his hands slipped on the railing. 'Not now!' he screamed, his words lost in the storm as his left leg gave way.

Farrell was the first through the door, his baton extended in front of him as he announced his presence. Louise moved from her position at the top of the landing. 'Don't go any further, Greg,' she said, causing the DS to jump.

'Jesus, Guv, you scared the hell out of me. Everything okay?'

'Two bodies through there,' she said, pointing to the living-room door. 'Secure the front door. I don't want anyone else in here until the SOCOs arrive.'

Within minutes the area was closed down, emergency services lining the street. Louise didn't care that it was raining, her clothes were already soaked; she was just glad to leave the house and be outside in the cold fresh air.

The enormity of the situation hit her as she saw DCI Robertson pull up. She'd met the Foresters on Saturday and now, forty-eight hours later, they were victims of the killer. How far away had she been from catching their killer? If it hadn't been for the road traffic accident in Milton, she would have arrived thirty minutes earlier. Then what? Would she have been able to successfully contain the killer, or would she have become another victim?

'How are you, Louise?' asked Robertson, handing her the umbrella he was carrying.

'Thanks. I'm fine. I'm gutted I didn't get here earlier.'

'You don't need to worry about that.' He paused before continuing. 'Why were you here in the first place?'

'I was about to question the Foresters further about Lanegan,' she said, studying his reaction as best she could in the gloom of the driving rain. 'The Foresters' deaths suggest my working theory is correct. From what I've seen in the living room, the Foresters have suffered the third and fourth wounds to their ankles, so the next few hours will be pivotal in catching the killer.'

Robertson nodded, but said nothing more before strolling inside to study the crime scene.

An hour later, Assistant Chief Constable Morley arrived, accompanied by DCI Finch.

Time seemed to slow down as Geoff grabbed the railing, his fingers struggling to grip the metal before he found purchase and hauled himself back up. Clear of the wall, he hunched over, the sound of the rain battering his raincoat matching the thump of his heartbeat. He laughed at how close he'd come to falling into the fast-moving waves, before hoisting himself over the final barrier and on to the rotten wooden boards of the old pier.

The storm was now so strong that it pushed him backwards like an invisible hand, his feet slipping on the grimy wood. Below him, waves crashed against the rusted metal pillars, giving the impression that the pier was no longer fixed and was being pushed along on the rising tide. Every part of him was sodden, and although the shelter at the end of the pier was welcome, it didn't provide any warmth.

Shivering, he pushed beyond the doors of the old lifeboat station to the concrete platform where he'd chained the boat.

Only, the boat was no longer there.

Chapter Thirty-Six

Louise had never seen the station so busy. The main reception was jammed with civilians and officers, both uniformed and plain-clothed, some local to the station, some familiar to Louise from the MIT. The sheer number of people, combined with an overactive heating system, made the room hot and languid. She could taste the sweat in the air; it clung to her skin like the smell of blood and bodily fluids from the Forester house. Like Louise, the majority of people were soaked through. All she wanted to do was strip off and take a long, hot shower.

The incident room was as active. All eyes turned to her as she arrived, reminding her of the aftermath of the Walton affair, when she'd been regarded with a mixture of awe, pity and disgust, depending on the perspective of the viewer. Ignoring everyone but Tracey, who nodded at her in support, Louise closed the shutters in her office and changed into dry clothes, her pale skin prickling from the change in temperature.

She'd remained at the Forester house until the photographs and videos were taken and the SOCOs had finished, after which she'd studied the corpses, along with Dempsey. This attack seemed more frenzied. The couple lay together in a seeping pool of blood that seemed to spread to every part of the room. Janet Forester had a blunt trauma to her head, which Dempsey believed was the cause of her death, after the hideous brutalisation of her legs and ankles. Nathan also appeared to have been conscious when his legs were hacked. Dempsey pointed to the ruin of tissue and muscle where Nathan's anterior tibial artery had been severed. He measured the puncture wounds on what remained of the Foresters' ankles and concluded that the shape and size were consistent with the wounds found on Veronica Lloyd's and Father Mulligan's wrists.

Louise had tried to ignore the presence of Morley and Finch. They'd certainly reached the crime scene in a hurry, and although both men kept their distance from her, they were busy speaking to the SOCOs and the other officers on the investigation, as if they'd been part of the team all along. And now they were waiting for her in Robertson's office.

The DCI had disappeared not long after arriving with Morley and Finch. She'd spoken to him briefly when they'd returned to the station, and he'd sounded exasperated, as if, somehow, this latest development was her fault.

After changing, she sat at her desk preparing herself for what she was about to face. In the past, she would have thought they wouldn't dare take her off the case, but bitter experience had made her more of a realist. The police force was a strict hierarchy and they didn't have to give her a reason, whatever her objections. All she could do was present her case and try not to lose her temper. She regretted her earlier falling-out with Robertson. He'd always backed her, and her outburst about Finch, however justified, had made their relationship fragile at a time when she needed his support more than ever.

Robertson returned and knocked on her door. 'Ready,' he said. 'Sir.'

He stopped, hesitating, as if playing the words out in his head. 'Louise. Listen to what they have to say,' he said, the warning clear.

Louise nodded and followed him to his office.

'DI Blackwell,' said Morley as she followed Robertson in. 'Quite a night.'

'Yes, sir.' Louise sat in the seat next to Finch. She could smell the familiar tang of his aftershave and felt nauseous as she recalled how intimate they'd once been.

The focus turned to Robertson. She'd never seen her superior look as uncomfortable as he did at that moment, especially in his own office, and she wondered what Morley had said to him earlier.

'Louise, I've explained as best as I can what you told me earlier about the investigation and your reason for going to see the Foresters today. Can you give us your version?'

There was no hiding the accusatory tone to the question, and Robertson lowered his eyes after he'd finished, as if signalling that he was under duress.

Louise paused before answering. Morley and Finch wanted her off the case, and showing any anger or insubordination would only hasten her demise. Slowly, she told them about her investigation from beginning to end, as if lecturing a class of trainees. Morley stopped her when she told him about her trip to Cornwall.

'You went all the way to St Ives?' he asked, begrudgingly impressed.

'I couldn't get any firm answers from their station so I took matters into my own hands.' She explained about Lanegan, and the Foresters' link to him.

'But you'd already spoken to the Foresters?' said Finch, tilting his head, as if surprised by his own revelation.

'Yes.'

'So why see them again so soon?'

Louise held Finch's gaze, wondering how it was possible to hate a person as much as she did him at that moment. 'The Foresters effectively led me to Lanegan. I thought at the time they'd been hiding something, and after speaking to Eileen Boswell, I wanted to challenge them.'

'If only you'd been an hour earlier,' said Morley.

'Sir,' said Louise, unable to hide her contempt for the assistant chief constable's statement.

They went to and fro, discussing the issues and the way she'd handled the case. 'It would appear Monsignor Ashley's assertion about the five wounds is correct,' argued Louise. 'That means there will be one more victim.'

'We need to speak to this Ashley,' said Finch, as if he were now in charge.

Louise ignored him. 'I will speak to him again, but for the time being, Lanegan remains our priority. If we find him, we either find the killer or the fifth victim.'

There was a natural pause as Morley gestured that he was about to speak. 'I have discussed the matter with DCI Robertson, and I believe it's prudent for you to remain as SIO on the case, DI Blackwell.'

Louise didn't react, as she noticed the tiniest smile forming on Robertson's face. It would have been criminal to have taken the case from her, but she feared that the assistant chief constable was paying her lip service.

'However,' continued Morley, 'I have no option but to involve DCI Finch and the Major Investigation Team. The case is too high profile not to use all our experience. The two teams will work together with immediate effect,' he said, as if that weren't already happening.

'Are you sure you're able to continue, Louise?' said Finch.

He wanted to antagonise her, and she almost let him. 'What do you mean?'

'It was a terrible scene, and as you conceded, if you'd only got there an hour or so earlier—'

'Let me stop you there, Tim,' said Robertson.

Louise appreciated her boss's interjection. Finch was a fine manipulator. Under the pretence of concern, he was suggesting she was weak and ill equipped to deal with the case and was all but blaming her for the deaths of Nathan and Janet Forester. She felt sure he would have mentioned Walton, and his own distorted view of the events, had he not feared her reaction. It was absurd that Morley would let them work together and it would do neither of them any good to mention Walton now. 'That's fine, Iain. I'm sure Tim isn't suggesting I'm to blame for the deaths of Mr and Mrs Forester. Are you, Tim?'

'Of course not,' said Finch, mustering every centimetre of disdain in his response.

'Good. Then, with all due respect, I think your question is redundant. Like you, I'm a police officer. I'm accustomed to such crime scenes and my priority now is finding the killer. So if there is nothing else, gentlemen?'

'Thank you, Inspector,' said Morley as Louise left the office.

It was 2 a.m. before she managed to get home. After Morley and Finch had left, Robertson produced a bottle of single malt by way of an apology. The slug of fiery liquid hit her bloodstream as if it had been injected straight into her veins, and she left soon after, before sleep overcame her.

No text message was waiting for her as she poured a shot of vodka from the freezer, downing it in one as if it were a bitter medicine. Finch wouldn't risk contacting her now. Why would he, when he could openly provoke her in the office?

She updated her murder board before sleeping, adding the pictures of the Foresters and placing a question mark next to the grainy picture she had of Lanegan.

If Lanegan was the killer, what was his motive? If he was to be the last victim, then where was he? The questions vexed her, circled in her head, accompanying her memories of the scene at the Forester house, as the whistle of cold air escaping through the small cracks in her bedroom windows finally lulled her to sleep.

Chapter Thirty-Seven

Geoff stared out at the frothing waves in disbelief. He'd chained the boat to the steel girders high above the tide level, so the sea couldn't have taken it. He swayed in the onslaught of the swirling rain, his clothes already soaked through, as he thought about what he could do next. The last thing he wanted was to crawl back along the pier, but staying here for another day wasn't an option either. Even if hypothermia didn't get him, the problem would remain when night next fell.

He was too self-aware, even *in extremis*, to conclude that this was some sort of test. *The problem I'm facing is down to sheer bad luck*, he thought, just as the light hit his eyes.

'I thought it would be some kids. You should be ashamed of yourself,' said the bearer of the light, a heavy-set man holding his torch in front of him like a gun.

'What do you mean?' said Geoff, stunned by the surreal apparition.

'I've been watching you,' said the stranger, his torch pointed centimetres below Geoff's eyes.

'Watching me?' said Geoff, fearing the worst.

'Treating this place like your own bloody mooring post. You should be ashamed of yourself.'

Did the man know where he'd been, and why? 'Where's the harm?'

'Where's the harm? Can you not read? "No trespassing" signs are up everywhere. How did you get over here in the first place?'

'I climbed over.'

'Exactly. What if something happened to you? We put the signs up for a reason. For your protection. We had a gang of teenagers caught here by the tide a couple of months back. Emergency services had to risk their lives getting them to safety.'

It sounded as if the man had no idea what he'd been doing. He was just a busybody whose main interest was the health and safety issues of the decrepit structure. 'Where's my boat?' said Geoff.

The man lifted the torch higher, momentarily blinding Geoff as he took something from his coat pocket. 'Don't you concern yourself with that,' he said, lifting the phone to his ear.

'What are you doing?'

'What do you think? I'm calling the police.'

Geoff shivered, the adrenalin fading, the coldness of his damp clothes seeping into his bones. He hadn't been prepared for such an eventuality and didn't know how to react. 'Please don't. I'm sure we can sort this out by ourselves.'

The man shook his head, disgusted by the very idea. 'That time has long passed.'

Geoff couldn't let him make that call. It would be the end. The reason for everything, every action, awaited him on the island. Lanegan had to be sacrificed; there had to be five wounds.

At first, he told himself he hadn't wanted to hurt the man, but the ferocity of his attack made him realise that somewhere deep down he enjoyed what he was doing, what he'd done. He ran full on, snatching the phone away as he crashed into the stranger's chest. The torch spiralled in the air, illuminating the confusion on the man's face as his head hit the jagged concrete beneath him. The noise reminded Geoff of John Maynard's teeth smashing against metal. The torch landed next to him, giving Geoff the opportunity to see the change in the man's eyes as he repeatedly struck the back of his skull on a loose rock – the rhythm and intensity more and more frenzied – way beyond the point where it was necessary to continue. He stopped the movement some time later, his hand wet with blood and matter, as if waking from a dream, and crumpled back against the interior wall of the pier.

What had he done? With Mrs Lloyd, Father Mulligan and the Foresters, everything had been planned. Every killing had been necessary, but this man – *Dear God, I don't even know the poor man's name* – was an innocent. Yes, he'd killed him out of self-preservation, out of his need to finish what he'd started, but he acknowledged that part of him, the part fully detached from the act, had enjoyed what he'd done. It was a different joy to the one he'd experienced before. It was raw and savage and, even now, his body shook at the power he'd held over the man.

But there was a comedown he'd not experienced with the others. Looking at the lifeless body next to him, the man's face now unrecognisable, a sense of regret washed over him, which he tried to dispel with a scream that was muffled by the raging water beneath him.

The boat had been hauled into the old lifeboat station and was hiding under a sheet of plastic. Thankfully, it was perched on a small trolley, but he had to wonder if the man had moved the boat himself. If he'd had help, then someone would be expecting him back.

Geoff's fingers were rigid with the cold as he pulled the boat to the head of the jetty. His window to leave was down to its last thirty minutes, but he was sidetracked by the sight of the corpse.

He couldn't leave it here to be discovered. Heaving the boat off its trolley, he set it down on top of the runway. It would take all his strength just to get the boat launched, but he had to take the body with him.

He blew into his cupped hands, desperate for some heat on his flesh, his tired lungs ineffectual. Geoff gagged as he hoisted the corpse on to his shoulders, something wet oozing down his chest. Staggering as he carried the remains of the man across the concrete, he fell, the corpse crashing into the boat. His victim's neck caught the metallic side of the vessel and made a cracking noise as the rest of his body slipped inside it.

Geoff cleaned up as best as he could, using the puddles of rainwater to dilute the blood. If he was in luck, it would be days, maybe weeks, before the area was checked.

The corpse had taken up nearly all the space inside the boat, and for a second Geoff stood, laughing at the absurdity of it all. He had no way of knowing if he would be able to shift the boat down the jetty. He risked ripping the hull away, then everything would have been in vain.

Gripping the side of the boat, the metal rim as cold as ice, he levered it down the slip before jumping in. The boat loitered near the top of the ramp and slid into the water. The landing in the sea knocked Geoff backwards until he was face to face with his victim. He screamed into the mess of a face, dirty seawater pouring over them as the boat veered wildly on the carpet of sea. Using the corpse as leverage, Geoff pushed himself upright until he found his balance.

The waves rolled the boat towards the jetty and the surrounding rocks. Dropping the outboard motor, Geoff was amazed when it started first time.

The corpse seemed to smile at him. With the flesh loosened from its jaw, it resembled a clown from a horror movie. Geoff pictured himself on the boat for all eternity, his only companion this smiling doll, as he bid farewell to Weston for the final time, the garish lights on the seafront blunted by the haze of black clouds covering the peninsula like a shroud.

The crossing was the fiercest it had ever been, the waves metres high as he approached Steep Holm. Geoff screamed into the night air, receiving a mouthful of water as his reward. The salt stung his eyes and his throat was red raw as he fought against the stiff current, the boat's engine groaning in displeasure. Revving the throttle for all it was worth, he finally steered the boat to the side of the jetty at Steep Holm before killing the engine, grabbing the mooring and securing the boat.

He couldn't spend a second longer on board. He jumped from the gangway and slipped on the jetty, landing on his right elbow. He lay that way for an indeterminable time as rain and seawater fell on him, too exhausted to move.

How easy it would be to slip into the sea, he thought, closing his eyes.

Chapter Thirty-Eight

The whistle of the wind through the cracked windows stirred Louise from her sleep. She doubted the windows in her bungalow had been replaced since it had been built sometime in the eighties, and she made a mental note to contact the landlord about them. She could see her breath clouding in front of her, and the thought of leaving the warmth of her bed was unappealing. She retreated beneath her duvet, ignoring her bladder, and replayed her dreams – abstract imaginings of the Forester killings mixed with lucid recollections of the night she'd killed Walton – her mind already overstimulated.

Still wrapped in her duvet, she shuffled to the bathroom and relieved herself. In the living room, she switched on the gas fire and sat zombie-like as the coffee pot filled. The murder board loomed over her, the names and photographs overbearing. She'd yet to fully process what had happened to the Foresters, but she was reminded of Finch's words as the coffee pot beeped and she poured her first cup of the day.

If you'd only got there an hour or so earlier.

Logic told her his inference was nonsense – she couldn't be held responsible for the Foresters' deaths because she hadn't arrived thirty minutes earlier – but it was difficult to respond logically. In his deluded way, Finch was right. If she'd reached the house earlier, not only could she have saved the Foresters, she could have apprehended the killer.

'If ifs and buts were candy and nuts,' she heard her dad say. She laughed at the memory, the release of emotion almost causing her to spit coffee on to the living-room floor.

Mr Thornton was outside when she left the house thirty minutes later. 'Morning, you're up early,' she said to the man, who appeared to have a never-ending supply of recycling to do.

'Good morning. Early bird catches the worm,' he said, with something approaching a smile.

'Have a good day,' said Louise, getting into her car. Thornton's wife had died five years ago and she guessed that loneliness could explain his surly manner. She thought of Eileen Boswell in Cornwall, her isolated existence without her son and grandchildren. From the small period of time Louise had spent with her, it seemed that Lanegan had become her life. The woman lived for her weekly visits to the man's house, and she wondered what would happen to Eileen if they never found the old priest.

With no time to stop at the Kalimera, and her body already overflowing with coffee, she drove straight to the station. She took an inward sigh as she saw Finch standing in Robertson's office, his pinstriped suit tight against his broad shoulders. His aftershave lingered in the air, as if he'd sprayed it across the room like air freshener, marking his territory.

Ignoring him, she went straight to her box-room office. The morning's briefing was in thirty minutes and she wanted to read up once more on the five holy wounds before it started. The monsignor's prediction had been correct. Four of the five wounds suffered by Jesus on the cross had been inflicted on the murder victims: Veronica Lloyd, the right wrist; Father Mulligan, the left; the Foresters through the ankles: Janet the left, Nathan the right. That left only the spear through the side. Was Lanegan lying somewhere, dead from a dagger wound? Or was he holding the dagger, approaching his final victim?

In the briefing she repeated her research, ignoring the incredulous looks from Finch and the handful of officers he'd brought with him from head office.

'I want to meet this Ashley,' said Finch, interrupting Louise.

She ignored him, catching Tracey's eye, her friend nodding in support, and continued. 'Everything has to be focused on Lanegan and his link with the four victims. If he is the killer, why did he want them all dead? If he is the next victim, why? There is a link between the victims, St Bernadette's for one, but there is something else we're missing.' Everyone knew about the fire, but she didn't push the point, fearing she would sound obsessed. She could explore that avenue of the investigation herself.

Ten minutes after the briefing, Finch was outside her office. 'A word, Louise,' he said, closing the door and sitting opposite her.

A sense of claustrophobia came over her. He'd trapped her in her own office. His presence filled the air, and for a second she was back at the Walton residence and he was telling her to pull the trigger. 'What is it, Finch?' she said, clearing her mind.

'This Monsignor Ashley.'

'What about him?'

'As I said earlier, I'd like to meet him.'

Louise almost snickered. She had to hand it to Finch. Here he was, sitting in her office, acting like nothing had happened. As if he hadn't destroyed her career, as if he didn't send her anonymous text messages nearly every night. It took a special type of psychopath to behave that way, and yet here he was, effectively in charge of this multiple-murder case, when he had no right to be in the force in the first place.

'He's my contact, Timothy,' she said, using his full name, which she knew he hated.

He could only partially hide his displeasure. She saw it in his eyes, the slight twitch in his lips, and was pleased that she could still get to him. 'He's a potential witness, Louise. It would make sense for someone else to speak to him.'

He was right, but that didn't make it any easier when she gave him the monsignor's details.

'Now, that wasn't so hard,' said Finch, smirking as he left her office.

How had this happened? Just over a week ago her most pressing concern with Finch had been his intrusive texts and her constant dreams of the Walton house. And now here he was. Not content with pestering her from afar, he'd somehow managed to worm his way into her new life.

Trying to shut him out, she checked her diary, noting that the retired police officer Benjamin Farnham had returned from holiday last night. Maybe Farnham had the missing answers to this case, could explain what exactly had happened during the fire at St Bernadette's.

Leaving the cloying confines of her office – the walls of which felt narrower, the ceiling lower, since Finch's arrival – she walked over to Thomas and waited for him to finish a call. He looked tired and unkempt. She should speak to him about his wife and his current living arrangements, but there was no time. A distant part of her wondered if he was still seeing Tracey, but she banished the thought, worried again that her concern was more personal than professional.

'Louise,' said Thomas, hanging up.

'Morning, Thomas. That retired officer, Farnham, he's back off his holiday.'

'Sure, I have it in the diary. Shall I give him a bell now? I'm about to leave with Tracey to speak to some of the St Bernadette parishioners again.'

Louise understood the weariness evident in the way he said 'again', but that was the reality of modern police work. 'Call him now and I can see him.'

He called, and she heard him leave a message. 'He got in late last night. Probably having a lie-in,' said Thomas.

'You got an address for him?'

Thomas pressed a few buttons on his keyboard and the printer next to him whirred into life. 'There you go.'

'Is everything okay, Thomas?'

'Of course, why do you ask?'

'It's none of my business, and let me know if I'm out of line, but you look . . .'

'I'll stop you there,' said Thomas with a forced smile. 'I'm not sure I want to hear the rest of that sentence. I am feeling a bit rough, as it goes. Burning the candle at both ends. It's this bloody case. You know how it is.'

Louise nodded but didn't move. She could warn him not to let it affect his work, but that wouldn't achieve anything other than bad feeling, and his work hadn't slipped since that night she'd seen him at the hotel. 'You know where I am if you need to talk, Tom. I mean it.'

'Thanks, Louise, I appreciate it.'

She returned to her office to get her coat, noting Tracey glancing her way in her peripheral vision. 'Farrell?' she called over, as she was about to leave.

'Guv?'

'I could do with your help,' she said.

Farrell looked surprised at the request but picked up his coat and they left the station together.

Farnham's address was in central Weston, a few streets away from St Bernadette's. They could have walked it in five minutes but the rain was so ferocious that she told Farrell to drive.

'Must be hard, having your old team back on the case?' said the DS as he pulled out of the car park.

There had been no malice in the question. If anything, he looked a bit nervous about having her in his car. 'It is a bit strange,' she said.

Like everyone else, Farrell knew about the Walton house, about the differences between her recollection of events and Finch's. She couldn't work out Farrell's agenda. Sometimes she thought he was actively hostile to her, but recently she'd come to believe that his little smiles were possibly some kind of defence mechanism. In part, that was why she'd asked him to accompany her.

'This is it,' he said, with his huge grin as he parked outside a detached Victorian house near the golf course. 'Nice place.'

The house had its own driveway, a rusting green VW Beetle looking out of place in front of the house. A television was on in the living room and Louise was surprised there was no answer when she knocked on the door. She nodded to Farrell to look through the front window. 'There's some kid on the sofa, bloody ignoring us.'

He knocked on the glass. 'He's coming now.'

A minute later, the door opened. A teenage boy, wrapped in a dressing gown, stood in the opening. 'Can I help you?'

'Why didn't you answer the door?' asked Louise, not bothering with any pleasantries.

'Wasn't expecting anyone.'

They showed their warrant cards. 'DI Blackwell. DS Farrell.'

If the youth was bothered, he hid it well. 'What do you want?'

'We are here to see Benjamin Farnham.'

'Well, you've just missed him.'

'Are you related to him?'

'Kind of.'

'Kind of?' said Louise, her patience at snapping point.

'Stepson. But as I said, you've just missed him.'

'When are you expecting him back?'

'Who knows? He's just left on holiday with my mum. Didn't even say where they're going.'

'On holiday? Hasn't he just got back from holiday?' said Farrell.

The teenager looked surprised. 'Yes, but they're always going on holiday.'

Louise thought the boy was lying. 'Where are they going this time?' she asked.

'I told you, I don't know,' said the boy, his voice rising.

'Can we come in for a second?'

'I suppose so. Do you really have to?'

'Yes,' said Louise, slipping past the teenager.

The interior was no reflection of the dishevelled youth. Polished wooden floorboards lined the hallway, and the walls were sparsely decorated with expensive-looking oil paintings and well-presented family photographs.

'Where shall we sit?' said Louise, brushing the rain from her face.

'You'd better come into the kitchen,' said the boy.

The kitchen was as well appointed as the hallway. A granite island took centre stage in a room bigger than the whole of Louise's bungalow.

'What's your name, sir?' asked Farrell, taking a seat on one of the high bar stools next to a secondary kitchen counter.

'Raymond.'

'Thanks, Raymond,' said Louise. 'As I said, my name is DI Blackwell and this is DS Farrell. We were hoping to speak to your stepfather today about an ongoing investigation. A colleague of ours spoke to him during his holiday and he agreed to call us on his return.'

'I'm not sure what you want me to say,' said Raymond, nonplussed.

'You could tell us exactly where he's gone, for a start,' said Farrell, clearly not believing the boy's tale.

Raymond shrugged. 'I honestly don't know. They got back from Turkey last night. Didn't even bother unpacking.'

'Were you expecting them to go on holiday again so soon after returning?' asked Louise.

'No, but it's not that surprising.'

'They do this often?'

'They're retired. Always off somewhere.'

'And you get the house to yourself?' asked Farrell.

'That's one of the perks.'

Louise exchanged looks with Farrell. She believed the boy was telling the truth, but something was definitely off. 'Would you call him for me?'

'Who? Ben?' said Raymond, not hiding his displeasure.

'Yes. On speakerphone.'

'What's this about?'

'Just do it, Raymond.'

'He's going to think it's weird. I never call him.'

'Could you just try for me, Raymond? It's very important we speak to him.'

'Okay, I'll need to get my phone,' said Raymond, leaving the kitchen.

Farrell frowned. 'You'd think Farnham didn't want to speak to us.'

'Yes, you would,' said Louise, as the boy returned.

'Is he in trouble?' asked Raymond, who'd lost some of his earlier indifference.

'No.'

Raymond frowned but called his stepdad's number, placing the phone on the kitchen table. The phone rang with a UK tone, so Farnham hadn't left the country. He answered after four rings. 'Ray?' came the voice through the crackling static of the speakerphone. 'Everything okay?'

'Yeah, sorry to bother you,' said Raymond, looking at Louise, who nodded back to him to continue.

There was a pause on the other end of the line. 'Someone there with you, Ray?'

Raymond didn't respond so Louise picked up the phone. 'Mr Farnham, this is DI Blackwell from Weston CID.'

'Inspector,' said Farnham. 'What's going on?'

'We've been trying to contact you this morning. You were supposed to speak to us about one of your old cases, the fire at St Bernadette's in 1983.'

'Oh, yes, sorry, I intended to call your colleague DS Ireland later today. Been a bit busy.'

'It would be really helpful if you could pop over to the station today, Mr Farnham.'

The man paused, giving himself time. 'I'm afraid that isn't going to be possible. We're on the road now.'

'Where are you going?' asked Louise.

The hesitation was minimal, but Louise caught it. 'Scotland.'

'Scotland?'

'Yes. We found a little cottage near the lakes. It's school season, so very cheap. Listen, I shouldn't really be talking, as I'm driving. Can I call you back later?'

'I need to talk to you now, Mr Farnham.'

'Sorry, I really must go. I'll call your station later,' said Farnham, hanging up.

Louise redialled the number, but it went straight to answerphone.

'What's going on?' asked Raymond.

'I'm not sure. How was your stepdad when he got back? Did you notice anything – any change of behaviour?'

'No, why?'

'Do they go to Scotland often?' asked Farrell.

'No. My mum doesn't like the cold.'

'Is there anywhere else they could have gone?'

'I don't understand. Why do you want to speak to them?'

'That doesn't matter. Do they have a holiday home anywhere?'

'They have a couple.'

'A couple? Where?' asked Farrell.

'One in Devon, one near here.'

'We'll need the addresses.'

The boy looked defensive and glanced at the fridge, where, Louise immediately noted, there was a flyer for a static caravan park in Brean Down.

Louise took the flyer and gave Raymond her card. She told him to call her as soon as he heard from either parent, wishing she had the ability to tap his phone, as she was sure the boy would call them as soon as they left.

'What the hell is going on?' asked Farrell, once they were outside.

'Something must have spooked Farnham. He was clearly lying.'

'What now?'

Louise waved the flyer she'd taken from the fridge. 'He's not going to Scotland. We can get to Brean in forty minutes. If he's trying to ignore us, then he'll keep his phone switched off for the time being. Who knows? Maybe we can surprise him.'

Chapter Thirty-Nine

The ray of sunlight through the heavy black clouds roused Geoff from his slumber. He was lying on the damp jetty at Steep Holm island, only metres from the pebbled beach. His sodden clothes clung to him, his skin numb, as a coldness he'd never experienced before chilled his blood. Less than fifty metres from him, the boat rocked against the mooring. He couldn't believe he'd slept so long. Flipping on to his side, nausea swarmed through his body as he remembered the cargo in the boat.

Every part of him hurt as he hobbled over to the boat. He dry-heaved as he saw the corpse. The daylight highlighted the severity of Geoff's frenzied attack, his victim's skull all but obliterated.

The man's death had cheapened Geoff's work. He tried to convince himself he'd had no choice, that the man had threatened everything, but he couldn't hold back the tears as he lifted the corpse from the boat. Geoff fell to his knees, dragging the body ashore and placing it beyond the reach of the tide. Exhausted, he collapsed next to his kill. Blood roared behind his closed eyes and he feared he would never awake if he didn't open them.

Turning the man over, his ruined face merging with the semi-frozen mud, Geoff forced himself up the stone steps and across the island to the visitor centre. Last night's storm had eased, but the thick clouds above him suggested it was only a respite.

The smell hit him first. The remains of the stew he'd cooked hung in the air, mingling with the more primal stink of Lanegan, who'd soiled himself again. The old priest was still chained to the radiator in the cabin, the blanket covering his lower half sodden. Geoff touched his cold skin, fearing the worst, and was relieved when the man cowered at the sight of him.

Geoff left Lanegan where he was and stepped fully clothed into the shower. The hot water was painful at first, sending shivers through him as his body thawed. He ignored the red circling beneath his feet as he pulled off his clothes, noticing the numerous cuts and bruises all over his torso. He remained under the jets until his skin was red raw before reluctantly making the short walk across the hut to his store of fresh clothes.

After changing, he put on another pot of stew and warmed a frozen loaf in the oven. Then he went into the workshop and focused on the final touches, locking the pieces together. Standing back, he admired his handiwork – the smooth edges and beautiful symmetry of the object. All he needed now was the spear. He'd left it in the cave where Lanegan had spent his first few days on the island, and they would be back there soon enough.

Back inside, Geoff unchained Lanegan and made him shower before giving him the black robe to wear. 'Come and eat,' he said as Lanegan placed his meatless limbs into the oversized garment Geoff had stolen from Father Mulligan.

Lanegan was a shadow of the person he'd been that night in Cornwall when Geoff had broken into his house and drugged him before carrying him into his van. His face was gaunt, his eyes hollowed and resigned.

'Eat up, you'll need your strength,' said Geoff, tearing off a piece of bread for him.

Lanegan's hands shook as he took the bread and dipped it in his bowl of stew, half of it falling to the floor as he tried to place it in his mouth.

'Try again,' said Geoff.

They sat that way until Lanegan finished his bowl, his empty eyes staring back at Geoff like a lost dog's.

Geoff poured him some water. 'Drink.'

Lanegan drank, the warm water dripping down his chin on to the black frock.

'What is the matter with you?' said Geoff, wiping the man down.

Lanegan seemed to find some amusement in this remark, the dry skin on his face cracking into a half-formed smile.

'You're still with us, then?'

'I'm here,' said Lanegan, the strength of tone in his voice surprising Geoff.

'Good, then we can finish this,' said Geoff, noting the look of relief coming over Lanegan. 'I wanted to ask you, now you're no longer a priest, can you still hear confession?'

'I am still partially ordained, so I can, on occasions, hear confession.'

'Good,' said Geoff. 'Bless me, Father, for I have sinned. It's been thirty-five years since my last confession. Here are my sins.'

Chapter Forty

Finch called as they left Farnham's house. 'Timothy?' said Louise, noting Farrell's smirk.

'Where are you, Louise?' asked Finch, indignant.

'Running my case as SIO. You?'

Louise heard his sharp intake of breath. Finch might be her superior, but she was technically still SIO. It was why she hated these cross-team operations.

'I was hoping you could return to the office. I'm having some issues with this Monsignor Ashley.'

It must have been difficult for Finch to be so conciliatory, and she pictured him wincing in his seat. 'What issues?' she said.

'For one, he's not answering his phone. For two, I've spoken to the head of the diocese and Ashley no longer has an official role within the Church.'

'He works as a consultant, Tim. He was at St Michael's Church for Father Mulligan's memorial. He was talking to the parish priest, Father Riley.'

'That may well be the case, but he's not returning my calls and I don't have a fixed address for him.'

Louise recovered the monsignor's card from her wallet. There was no address on it. 'I'll call him,' she said, hanging up. 'Let's go,' she said to Farrell.

The outsiders from headquarters had made her feel more trapped than ever in the seaside town. Unlike her, when the case was over, they would escape to the city. As Farrell reached the end of Farnham's road, the windswept seafront just out of sight, Louise conceded that she might never leave the place.

The torrent worsened as Farrell left the town and headed towards Brean Down. It was only 1 p.m., yet the sky was darkening, the thick clouds blanketing a sun Louise had hardly seen in the last few days.

'It must be hard working with Finch again,' said Farrell, out of nowhere.

He was smiling as he followed the slow traffic up the meandering incline. Yesterday, she would have read something into that. But she was beginning to read Farrell differently. *Some people just like to smile*, she told herself. 'What do they say, "Never go back"?'

'You don't have much of an option, though, do you?' he said.

That was true. She was still part of the Avon and Somerset Constabulary, so she should have expected this to happen at some point. Still, it was hard to swallow, seeing Finch and his subordinates taking over her station.

Farrell went to say something else and stopped. His hesitation was so obvious it was comical.

'What is it, Greg?'

Farrell mumbled. 'You can tell me if it's none of my business, Guv.'

'Not sure I like where this is going, but continue.'

'DCI Finch.'

'What about him?'

'I heard what happened during the Walton case. The . . . shooting.'

'I imagined news would even have reached Weston,' said Louise sardonically. 'You want to know what really happened?'

267

'As I said, it's none of my business.'

Although inclined to agree with him, it had been over eighteen months now. Time perhaps to destroy some of the myths circulating around the station about her. 'You know as well as I do what Walton did. We saw the bodies when we arrived,' said Louise, rekindling the smell of that night, as if she were back at the farmhouse. 'But whatever his crimes, Greg, I would never have shot him if I didn't think he was armed. We were in a very tight spot, in near-darkness, and Finch told me he was carrying. I knew what Walton was capable of, so I shot him. It's as simple as that.'

Farrell nodded, tapping the steering wheel and refusing to look her in the eye. 'Why do you think . . . ?'

'Why do you think Finch said something different?' she prompted.

For the first time in minutes, Farrell looked her way. He was smiling, but she could see nothing malicious in the look. 'Why did he?'

'Look, Greg, I'm not going to bad-mouth a senior officer to you. I guess you've read my transcript. You'll have to decide for yourself why he did it, but it's no secret that he was made DCI after the case.'

'And you were sent to Weston. Harsh,' said Farrell, with a laugh.

'Harsh, indeed,' said Louise, surprised to be sharing a moment of affinity with the officer.

They drove the rest of the way without speaking, as if an understanding had been reached, the sound of the rain pelting the car their only accompaniment.

Brean Down was an extension of the Mendip Hills that fed into the Bristol Channel. A static caravan park stood on the promontory looking over the water. A small wooden cabin situated by the entrance was unmanned, so Farrell drove on into the park. 'Who would want to stay here in the winter?' he said.

A few cars were parked up next to the caravans, and an elderly couple descended the metal steps of one of the contraptions, the decking of which was draped with plants and vines. Farrell stopped at a crossroads.

'Over there,' said Farrell, pointing to a bright-green caravan with a BMW parked outside.

Louise took down the number plate and told Farrell to drive further down the road, then called the station to check. 'It's Farnham's car,' she said, as the caravan door opened and a man stumbled out carrying a suitcase.

Farrell wasted no time, reversing back towards the caravan. The man was getting into the car as Farrell sped back along the concrete road and broke hard, blocking the BMW.

'What the hell?' said the man, stepping out of the vehicle.

'Benjamin Farnham?' said Louise, showing him her warrant card.

'Yes,' said the man, under his breath.

'DI Blackwell, DS Farrell. I must say, I'm a bit confused,' said Louise, glancing towards Farrell, who was edging towards Farnham. 'I was under the impression you were on your way to Scotland.'

'Change of plan.'

'These things happen, I suppose. I think we need to talk to you, Mr Farnham.'

Farnham turned off the car's engine. He was a short, squat man, with random patches of grey hair on his sunburnt scalp. His face was blemished with patches of red, his nose the ruby colour of a drinker.

Rain continued bouncing off Louise's raincoat on to the slippery ground beneath. 'Shall we go inside, or would you like to discuss this further at the station?'

'Am I under arrest?' said Farnham sarcastically. The man had been retired for fifteen years, but he had the air of someone who thought he knew best.

'No, but those are your only two options, so which is it?' said Louise.

Farnham kept them waiting in the heavy rain while he considered his response. He could dry off and change, whereas they were stuck with their sodden clothes. It was petty, but it was effective. Louise's temper was rising and she was thinking about arresting him for obstruction when he finally spoke up. 'Better come inside, then.'

The interior of the caravan had the damp plastic smell Louise remembered from childhood, when her family had spent their summers in caravan parks in Cornwall. It had always felt like an adventure, though it had been much easier on sunny days, when they could play outside. She agreed with Farrell: how or why anyone would want to stay here during the winter was beyond her.

'You alone today, Mr Farnham?' asked Farrell.

'That I am, son.'

'Where's your wife?' said Louise, noticing the two suitcases outside the bedroom door.

'Shopping.'

Farnham led them to a curved settee at the front of the caravan. Louise sat nearest the door in case Farnham decided he wanted to leave. 'You were in a rush before,' she said.

'I have to go and pick the wife up.'

'Oh, right. It's not that you don't want to talk to us, then? I don't know why, but that was the impression I got when I spoke to you on the phone.'

Farnham didn't respond.

'When you lied to me and told me you were on the way to Scotland.'

'I didn't lie.'

'That's exactly what you did,' said Farrell.

Farnham grimaced. 'What is it you want?'

'We want to speak to you about the fire at St Bernadette's Church in 1983.'

'What about it?'

'Something is going on here, Mr Farnham. You were on the force – put yourself in our position. I've been waiting to speak to you, and today you've actively avoided me. To update you on the case, four people from that period have been found brutally murdered. The schoolteacher, Veronica Lloyd; the parish priest at the time, Father Mulligan; and Mr and Mrs Forester, the school's head teacher and secretary, were found in their home bludgeoned to death. Furthermore, one of the other priests from that time, Father Lanegan, is missing.'

'Whoa, that is a lot of information for me to process,' said Farnham, his already red face flushing with colour.

'I think you already know about the case, Mr Farnham,' said Louise.

'It hadn't dawned on me that this was related to the fire.'

'Talk me through what happened at St Bernadette's.'

'It was some time ago.'

'I've gone through your case notes, if that helps,' said Louise, handing him a copy of his old file.

Farnham glanced at the papers with little curiosity. 'You'll probably know more than me, then.'

'The fire was an accident?'

'Yes, of course it was.'

'Of course?' said Louise.

'Come on, what is this? Do I need a solicitor here?'

'I don't know, Mr Farnham, do you?'

'Listen,' said Farnham, his voice shaking. 'I was a police officer long before you were a glint in your daddy's eye, so don't come to my home and start questioning me about my work.'

Louise saw through the mock-anger. Farnham was defensive. He had something to hide, and she needed to exploit that knowledge while she had time. 'I'm giving you an opportunity here, Mr Farnham. If I take you in, this becomes news. We will go through that old case with every means available to us. You tell me what I need to know now, and we don't have to go through that.'

'What the hell are you talking about?'

'It wasn't an accident, was it?'

'Don't talk nonsense—'

'There was accelerant found at the site, I know that much,' said Louise, interrupting.

Farnham went to speak, his open mouth falling silent.

Farrell looked at Louise, equally confused.

'I don't know what you're talking about,' said Farnham after a period of silence.

'I've spoken to Monsignor Ashley.'

'Monsignor?'

'You would have known him as Father Ashley at the time.'

Farnham was an obvious read. He was weighing up his options, his eyes darting to the window as he recalled the incident and considered his best move. Farrell gave her a questioning look as they waited for Farnham to answer.

'I don't know anything about an accelerant,' said Farnham, finally.

'Okay, let's say I believe you, for the time being.'

'Yes, let's say that,' said Farnham.

Louise paused. She was seconds away from taking Farnham into custody. She had no doubt he was hiding information from her. Something had spooked him since he'd returned from the holiday. The only reason she'd yet to drag him in was the delay she feared it would cause. Investigating an old case could take months, and with no definite solution at the end of it, chances were this line of enquiry would be dismissed by Robertson and Finch. 'Tell me what I should be looking at, Farnham. There's a killer on the loose. You've seen what they've done? It's all tied into the church, that I know. Where should I be looking?'

Farnham rubbed his chin, clearly deciding if what he was covering up was worth it. 'There was a boy. Young lad, nine or ten. Admitted to Weston General with burn wounds to his hands.'

'That wasn't in the report,' said Farrell.

'I can't comment on that.'

'You were told to cover it up?' said Louise.

'The church weren't keen on prosecuting one of their parishioners, especially a young lad.'

'So you turned a blind eye?' said Farrell, incredulous.

Farnham let out a breath but didn't answer.

'What did they pay you?' said Louise.

Farnham scowled but remained silent.

'I hope it was worth it. Who was this boy?'

'He was one of the pupils at the school. Simmons, Geoff Simmons. After the fire, he moved schools.'

'You met him?'

'Briefly. Weird kid. Doted on his dad, from what I remember. Every time I saw him, he was with his dad. His mum was always there, but you could see a distance between them.'

'So that was it. This Simmons kid burnt down the church and he was let off.'

'As I said, the Church wasn't interested in prosecuting and didn't want the publicity. Father Ashley made that particularly clear.'

Louise shook her head. Ashley had guided her to this end, albeit slowly. Had he finally succumbed to guilt from his secrets? 'Do you know if this Simmons guy is still local?'

Farnham nodded. 'Yes. They live on one of the estates.' He took out a notepad and wrote down the address for her.

'Been keeping an eye on him?'

'They never moved,' said Farnham defensively. 'One thing you should know,' he added.

'Go on,' said Louise.

'The boy's father. He died three months ago.'

Chapter Forty-One

Lanegan turned away. 'I'm not listening to any more of your confession, Geoffrey,' he said.

'I thought you'd want to hear it,' said Geoff, lifting the old priest on to a chair, his bones so light Geoff had serious concerns about the next stage.

'I've heard all I can stomach from you. Your mother would be ashamed if she knew what you're doing.'

'Don't you talk about my mother!' screamed Geoff, specks of spittle falling on to the old man's skin.

'Look at yourself, boy, you're a bloody mess. You think she would want this, want you to do whatever it is you are going to do to me?'

It was like being back in church as an altar boy. Like his father, Lanegan could be strict back then – 'Old Testament-style', his fellow altar boys had called it. Geoff had thought the old man was no longer capable of such tirades, yet he'd summoned some final embers of will and Geoff was impressed. But Geoff was no longer that cowering little boy, and he wasn't going to let Lanegan dictate the conversation. 'You think this is all about you? You'll sit there and listen. Listen to everything I have to say.'

Lanegan trembled. 'What have you done?'

His resolve vanished as Geoff told him about Mrs Lloyd, Father Mulligan and the Foresters. Geoff realised he was smiling as he detailed the gruesome acts. There was the sin of pride, but Geoff was proud of what he'd achieved.

'Why?' said Lanegan when Geoff had finished his confession. The old man was full of tears, but his remorse was decades too late.

'My father is dead,' said Geoff.

'I heard, and I am very sorry,' said Lanegan.

'Sorry? You weren't sorry, then, were you?'

'You don't understand, Geoff, your mother and I—'

'Don't!' screamed Geoff, his voice hoarse from all the talking, the sound echoing in his ears as they sat opposite each other.

'I can understand why you want to hurt me, Geoffrey, but why the others?' said Lanegan, after what seemed like an eternity.

The words would be wasted on the old priest. The others were complicit. If they'd only listened to Geoff, then it might never have got to this stage. They'd had to die, in order to save his dad. There had to be five deaths, five wounds. They had to suffer as Jesus had suffered. Jesus had saved their souls; between them, they would save the soul of Geoff's father.

They sat in silence, staring at one another. Geoff saw the slight tremor on Lanegan's lips as he comprehended what had happened and his role in it.

'I saw you, you know?' said Geoff.

'Saw me?'

'I saw you. With my mother.'

Lanegan closed his eyes. Geoff felt his shame and fed upon it. 'She never knew; doesn't even now. She was supposed to be meeting me after school, but when she wasn't there I went next door to the vestry, and I saw you both. You were kissing her, in the church, of all places.'

'You shouldn't have seen that, Geoffrey, I'm sorry,' said Lanegan, lowering his eyes, which were wet and bloodshot.

'Dad knew something was up. That was why they were arguing all the time, why he was going to leave. I couldn't believe you would do that. You betrayed my family, betrayed your God.'

'I am sorry, Geoffrey. Truly, I am.'

'But that wasn't the worst thing. I went to them all. First to Mrs Lloyd, who told me not to tell stories, then to Father Mulligan, who made me do penance, then finally to Mr and Mrs Forester, who promised they would look into it for me.'

Lanegan looked up at him, his eyes wide. 'You were let down, son, but all this?'

'It was me who started the fire, but you knew that,' said Geoff, showing the priest his scarred hands, where the paraffin had ignited.

'I don't know what you want me to say, Geoffrey. You shouldn't have seen what you saw.'

'Dad blamed himself. He blamed himself,' repeated Geoff, elongating each word. 'For Mum having the affair with you, for what happened to our family. He never recovered. He carried that burden for the rest of his life, Lanegan!' Geoff screamed into the priest's face. 'Carried it all his life until he could carry it no more. I burnt the church down to cleanse the place from what I'd seen, from the horrendous sins committed within it. I hoped it would stop my dad from blaming himself, but it didn't make a difference. But it will work this time. Now you'll have the chance to redeem yourself for what you did. Now, you're going to save my dad.' Geoff saw in the way the priest's eyes narrowed that he understood.

'If you are worried about the mortal sin of suicide, Geoffrey, it is not as cut and dried as you may think. I know your father was not buried in a Catholic church, but the church understands that sometimes people are not fully themselves. Even though your father

277

committed this grave act, he may not be morally responsible for his actions.'

Geoff had heard enough. He dragged the priest outside, a sprinkling of rain falling from the twilight of the sky, and pointed to the object he'd been working on. 'You're going to carry that all the way to your resting place.'

Chapter Forty-Two

There was no time to arrest Farnham. Louise warned the retired officer not to leave the county and left with Farrell to find Geoffrey Simmons. Another storm was raging, the static caravans shaking on their foundations as the rain resumed.

'We're not going to arrest him?' asked Farrell, once they were back in the car.

'Farnham? That's a case for Anti-Corruption. I don't care if they were protecting a child. If Farnham had a hand in fudging that fire report, I'll see he's prosecuted.'

Louise ignored her missed calls from Finch, only for Farrell to relay his own voicemail message. 'Finch wants us back at the station. Something about this Monsignor Ashley.'

'He can wait,' said Louise, switching the windscreen wipers to full speed.

Traffic was slow out of Brean, the rainstorm hampering their progress. 'Shall we call it in? About this Geoffrey Simmons?' asked Farrell, once they were back on the main road.

'Let's see if we can locate him first, start with the address Farnham gave us and go from there.'

Neither Finch nor Robertson needed to know about Simmons yet. Louise decided she would inform them after she'd spoken with a member of the Simmons family. Until then, she wanted to know more about the fire and why it was covered up; and more importantly, who else was involved.

The Simmons house was in Holms Road in the Oldmixon estate, Louise cutting through the back of Uphill to reach the address. The road was off the main Winterstoke Road, Simmons's house two doors down from the end of the road. All the lights were switched off and no one answered when Louise pressed the doorbell. 'Let's head back to the station, find out what we can about them and come back later,' she said.

The darkened sky was so low by the time they reached Weston seafront that, through the rain-drenched windscreen, Louise struggled to tell where sea and sky met. One gigantic black cloud stretched along the coast, as if the town had been walled in. She turned the car around and headed back towards the station, ignoring another call from Finch.

Damp heat and the odour of sweat and food filled the reception area of the station, the windows misted with condensation. A silence descended over the incident room as they arrived. Finch was in Robertson's room and Louise prepared herself for one of the men calling her out in front of her team. *I dare you*, she thought. 'See what you can find out about the Simmons family, I'll go and speak to Robertson,' she said to Farrell, deciding to pre-empt the two DCIs.

'Guv.'

'Greg, let's keep this strictly between ourselves for the time being. That okay?'

Farrell grinned at her, and for once the gesture wasn't off-putting. 'Of course, you're the boss, Guv.'

'Boss, Guv, I like it. Thanks, Greg.'

Farrell nodded and moved towards his desk.

'You're alive, then?' said Robertson, as she entered the DCI's office.

The annoyance was palpable on Finch's face. If Robertson hadn't been there, or if they'd been back at headquarters, then he would have ranted at her. But for now, she was protected.

'Care to tell us where you've been?' said Finch.

'Out following leads,' said Louise.

'All day.'

'That's right.' She gave them a version of her meeting with Ben Farnham and how he'd tried to avoid their questioning, stopping short of mentioning Geoff Simmons.

'Well, I've been trying to find this Monsignor Ashley all bloody day,' said Finch. 'He's not responded to any calls. The Church says he's retired but works on an occasional freelance basis. But they didn't ask him to be involved with Veronica Lloyd's or Father Mulligan's deaths.'

Finch was repeating himself for Robertson's benefit, but Louise was unmoved. 'He approached me,' said Louise. 'It's all logged on HOLMES.'

'I've read that, Louise, but under what authority did he contact you?'

'He never claimed to be representing anyone. The first time we met he told me about the five wounds. The second time, we discussed the fire at St Bernadette's.'

'It would be good to speak to him, Lou. He's a potential suspect,' said Finch.

Louise couldn't believe he had the temerity to call her Lou. 'I'll call him now, but I don't think he's a credible suspect . . . Timothy,' she replied.

Robertson closed his eyes, clearly unhappy to be in the middle of two warring factions. 'Could you do that now, Louise? Thank you,' he said.

'Sir,' said Louise, leaving the office.

Tracey stopped her as she left. 'You okay?' she asked. She was carrying a large file of papers, a bead of sweat trickling down her forehead.

'Yeah, it's a bit weird having Finch here. He's trying to take over, which isn't surprising. Let me take some of those,' said Louise. The heat in the office was oppressive, the building's caretaker over-zealous with the thermostat control.

'You have to ignore him, Lou. Get on with what you're doing.'

'I'm trying, believe me.' She wanted to tell her about the late-night texts, the man's continued harassment since the Walton case, but if there was ever going to be a time to share that information, it wasn't now.

Tracey walked her over to a spare desk, out of earshot of everyone else in the office. 'Listen, I just wanted to tell you that Thomas is back with his wife. I don't think he's had it easy recently, but he's told me they're going to make a go of it.'

'That's good. He told you all that after . . .'

'I know. I feel very grown-up all of a sudden. It was just a mistake for both of us, and I'm pleased for him.'

'And your guy in Bristol?'

'I feel guilty for saying it, but what he doesn't know won't hurt him, and all that. That's terrible, isn't it?'

Louise didn't feel in the position to offer any relationship advice. 'You've only been seeing him for a few weeks?'

'Yeah, a couple of months. No point messing things up for one stupid night, is there?'

Louise smiled and placed her hand on her friend's arm.

Farrell was waiting for her in her office. She shut the door behind her, noticing Finch glancing their way. 'What have you got for me?'

'From what I can see, Geoff Simmons works as a man with a van,' said Farrell, showing her a print out from the *Mercury* with an advert for the man's removal service.

'You tried the number?'

'Answerphone.' I also found some old stuff for him. Used to be a bit of a carpenter. I managed to track down a former client of his from a review online, said he was quite skilled. A bit of a withdrawn character, by all accounts, and always wore gloves. Haven't managed to track down the mum yet.'

'Okay, keep trying, Greg.'

'One more thing. The dad. Trevor Simmons. He didn't just die. He committed suicide.'

Chapter Forty-Three

They grabbed some sandwiches from the canteen before leaving for the Oldmixon estate. 'I take it you're up for some unpaid overtime, Greg?' said Louise as they set off.

'What else are my evenings for?'

The storm was in full force, Louise inching the car along, her vision restricted to the tail-lights of the vehicle in front. She tried her best not to think about Finch, but doing so was unavoidable. As he'd requested, she'd called Monsignor Ashley, but had received the same answerphone message. She didn't see the man as a potential suspect but at this stage wasn't ruling anything out, especially as he'd gone AWOL.

There were still no lights on at the Simmons house, but Louise tried the front door again, getting drenched in the process. She returned to the car and switched on the heater, surprised at how soaked she'd become in the short journey from car to house and back again.

'Still raining, then?' said Farrell, with his unreadable grin.

'You're going next time.'

The romanticism of the stake-out had died for Louise after her first night spent as a rookie detective outside a suspected drug den. She'd been partnered with an obese detective, Darren Wood, who'd proceeded to eat, smoke and fart his way through the night, only for nothing to happen before the morning shift took over. It was one part of the job she hated. The wasted hours with no result guaranteed.

They had no idea when Geoffrey Simmons or his mother would return. For all they knew, neither person would appear that evening. 'I could go door to door. Find out if anyone knows where they are or when they're due back?' asked Farrell.

They'd only been waiting half an hour, but already the boredom was setting in. The residents of such areas were often close-knit and would either not talk to the police, or worse, warn their neighbours. 'We'll leave it for now,' she said. 'I don't fancy sitting in this car all night, soaked through.'

With nothing else to do except stare through the rain peppering the windscreen, Louise sent a text to her mother to see how things were with Emily.

She's fine. Ready for bed. Watching a bit of TV, came the reply.

Has Paul said anything?

No, not today. Let's chat later?

On a stake-out.

What a life!

What a life, indeed, she thought. Trapped in a car with someone she wasn't sure she could trust, waiting for some people she wasn't sure would even arrive. The short exchange with her mother did little to eliminate her fears over Paul and his drinking, but she couldn't fret about that. Finding the killer was her priority now.

'This is not too far from Veronica Lloyd's house,' said Farrell, breaking the uneasy silence.

'Yeah, just around the corner.'

'Not far from a handful of drug dealers I know as well.'

Louise felt the DS was trying too hard to connect the dots, so she tried to rescue him. 'What was your reading on Farnham?' she asked. 'You heard of him before? Thomas said he knew him.'

'He was before my time,' said Farrell, grinning. 'I heard a few stories about him, though. Old school . . . and not in a good way.'

'How's that?'

'Rumours about backhanders, that sort of thing. Some of the dealers round here claimed he was on their payroll, and they offered me the same deal before they learnt different. They were probably chancing it, but I've heard enough about him to be wary and today confirms it for me. He was running from us, I'm sure. That bollocks about changing his mind about going to Scotland.'

'We need to speak to his wife.'

'Be worth having another go at the stepson. That was a bloody nice house they had as well. Lots of nice stuff. Bit much for a police pension. You notice that?'

Louise had noticed but didn't want to reach any unfounded conclusions. 'Let's leave that to Anti-Corruption, but definitely worth speaking to the wife and son again.' Farnham had all but admitted his illegal role in the fire investigation and she could imagine he'd benefited from keeping his mouth shut. Her worry was that Monsignor Ashley was involved as well, and it was at best disconcerting that he wasn't answering his calls.

It was another two hours before someone approached the house, a woman carrying shopping bags in both hands. They waited for her to start unlocking the front door before leaving the car. They tried their best not to startle the woman, which was difficult, considering the time of night and the poorly lit street.

'Mrs Simmons, sorry to bother you. My name is DI Louise Blackwell, and this is my colleague DS Greg Farrell.'

The woman stared at them, open-mouthed.

'So sorry to approach you like this,' said Louise, showing the woman her warrant card.

'It's eleven o'clock at night,' said Mrs Simmons. 'What on earth do you want?'

'We'd like to speak to you about your son, Geoffrey.'

'What's happened?'

'It's fine. Nothing has happened,' said Louise. 'May we come in and explain?'

Mrs Simmons shrugged and unlocked the door. 'I suppose so.'

The interior of the house reminded Louise of her bungalow. The lurid wallpaper was similar, as was the lush carpet long out of fashion. They accepted the offer of tea and took a seat on the yellowing sofa, which, like the rest of the house, felt out of time.

'So what is this all about? What has Geoff done?' asked Mrs Simmons, taking a seat on a lone armchair.

Where to begin? Louise explained about the killings and how she believed there was a connection to the fire at St Bernadette's, all the time studying Mrs Simmons's reactions, which ranged from shock to a growing indignation.

'This is ludicrous. What has this to do with Geoff?'

'Probably nothing. We'd simply like to speak to him to eliminate him from our investigation. When did you last see him?' asked Farrell.

Mrs Simmons's eyes darted upwards as she recalled a memory. 'Yesterday morning. I made him breakfast.'

'Did you notice anything different about his behaviour? Yesterday, or over the last few months?' asked Louise.

'Last few months? Why, I don't understand.'

'We understand your ex-husband passed away. How did Geoff react to this?' asked Farrell.

'Oh, I see. Yes, they were very close. There's no denying that. He was always a bit of a daddy's boy. Ever since . . .' Mrs Simmons stopped talking, lost in her own thoughts.

'Ever since?' said Louise.

Mrs Simmons shook her head, as if dragging herself back into the present. For a split second she looked surprised to see the two police officers in the room with her. 'Sorry, it's been a long day. Shift work at the supermarket.'

'Of course, I understand,' said Louise.

'Yes, they were close, and his death hit Geoff very hard. He's been very withdrawn over the last few months. I've hardly seen him, actually.'

'Do you know where he is now?'

'No. He stays out sometimes. He's a grown man, I don't keep tracks on him.'

There was an emphasis on 'grown man', as if the woman didn't quite believe what she was saying about her son.

'So you're not expecting him back tonight?' said Farrell.

'I don't know.'

'Mrs Simmons, what can you tell us about the fire at St Bernadette's?'

The woman shifted in her seat, a slight twitch to her lips as she answered. 'What do you mean?'

'We have reason to believe that Geoff was involved with the fire. He was admitted with burn marks at the local hospital on the same day as the fire,' said Louise, deciding to be fluid with her knowledge of the facts.

'He didn't have anything to do with the fire,' said Mrs Simmons, shaking her head, as if trying to convince herself.

'Look, Mrs Simmons, I understand you're trying to protect your son. We're not here to investigate the fire. It's possible that Geoff is in danger.'

Mrs Simmons sat up straighter. 'What do you mean?'

'Do you remember a priest by the name of Father Lanegan?'

Mrs Simmons stared hard at Louise, as if she'd sworn at her.

Before bursting into tears.

Chapter Forty-Four

Louise let Mrs Simmons cry, surprised by the intensity of the woman's emotions.

'I'll get you some water,' said Farrell, returning seconds later with a glass tumbler.

Louise sat on the edge of the sofa as Mrs Simmons sipped from the glass. 'Take your time,' she said.

'It's such a mess,' said the woman, still sobbing.

'What is, Mrs Simmons?' said Louise softly, aware that the next few minutes could be crucial and it was imperative to keep the woman on side.

'Everything. My life, what happened to Geoff, what happened to Trevor.'

'And Father Lanegan?'

'Richard. I knew him as Richard after a time. I haven't seen him in thirty-odd years. Why are you asking after him?'

'We have been trying to contact him for the last few days.'

Mrs Simmons nodded as if this was to be expected, and then her face changed. 'You don't think he's . . .'

'We don't think anything at the moment. We'd simply like to talk to him.'

'Richard wouldn't hurt anyone. He was the gentlest man I've ever known.'

Louise had heard similar pleas countless times before. Usually from loved ones refusing to believe their lover or family member could possibly be capable of anything untoward. 'You and Richard were close?' she said.

'Yes. We were together,' said Mrs Simmons, unashamed, smiling with fondness at the memory.

'What happened?'

Mrs Simmons began sobbing again. 'Geoffrey found out.'

'Take your time, Mrs Simmons.'

'I only found out afterwards. After the fire, when Trevor left me. He's never discussed it with me, not even after Trevor's . . . death, but I know he saw us.'

'What happened?'

'Geoffrey saw us in the church. We must have been kissing. I never wanted him to find out that way. Do you believe me?'

Louise was beginning to understand. 'And the fire? He started that to get back at Father Lanegan?'

Mrs Simmons didn't answer.

'We know about his hands. The burn marks,' said Farrell.

Mrs Simmons shook her head, ignoring the comment. 'I don't understand what is happening.'

Louise told the woman the names of the other victims, noting her recognition at the mention of each name. 'Geoffrey knew all these people?' she asked.

'I don't understand,' repeated Mrs Simmons. 'Veronica was his teacher, Nathan Forester his head teacher, Mrs Forester the school secretary. And Father Mulligan worked with Richard.'

'Would Geoffrey have any reason to hurt them that you can think of?'

'Hurt them?' said the woman, confused. 'You don't think Geoff . . .' Mrs Simmons stopped herself, as if acknowledging some long-ago buried truth. 'During the divorce, after the fire, Trevor told me some things. They were accusations more than anything. You see, Geoff hadn't gone straight to him to tell him what he'd seen. He'd felt ashamed at . . . at what I'd done. I know he spoke to Father Mulligan about it, but the priest hadn't helped him. He gave him penance instead.'

Louise pictured the boy speaking to the priest, his life in tatters, only to be turned away by another authority figure he trusted. Had the same happened with the others? Had he sought help from all the responsible adults in his life only to be ignored, so turned to the fire as a last resort? 'Greg, why don't you make Mrs Simmons another cup of tea? May I use your bathroom, Mrs Simmons?'

'Upstairs, first on the right.'

Louise turned left at the top of the stairs, searching for Geoff's bedroom. It was at the end of the corridor and she prepared herself before entering. At first, she wasn't sure what she was seeing. The room was filled with hundreds of wooden crucifixes of various sizes. Some included the Christ figure, others not. Every centimetre of wall space was taken up by them, many more piled high on a wooden desk and a set of drawers. Louise picked one up off the floor. It was made of mahogany and was about half a metre in length. It was heavier than she'd anticipated, the sides smooth and varnished. Turning it over in her hands, she couldn't make out the joins and wondered how it had been made.

'He used to sell them,' came Mrs Simmons's voice from the hallway. She didn't appear angry that Louise was snooping, more proud.

'They're amazing. He makes them himself?'

'There's a workshop out back. He stopped making and selling them when Trevor died. That's why there are so many here.'

'They must be expensive,' said Louise, placing the mahogany cross down.

'He contributes to the house.'

Whether he was selling the objects or not, there was an obsessiveness to the work that was frightening. 'Do you know where he is, Mrs Simmons?'

The woman looked resigned, as if she finally understood what her son was capable of. 'If I knew, I would tell you.'

'Would you phone him for us? See if you can get him to come back to the house.'

Mrs Simmons didn't answer. She looked drained, her eyes blank.

'Mrs Simmons?'

The woman blinked and looked about her as if surprised to find herself in the room. 'My phone's downstairs.'

Louise followed Mrs Simmons to the living room and told Farrell to take a look at Geoff's bedroom.

'What should I say to Geoff?' asked the woman.

'Just ask him to come home,' said Louise gently. 'Tell him a fuse has gone and you can't fix it. Would he believe that?'

'Possibly.' After dialling, she shook her head. 'Answerphone.'

'Leave a message.'

'Hi, Geoff. Sorry to bother you, but there's something wrong with the electrics. I think a fuse may have gone. Let me know when you're back.' Mrs Simmons paused, and Louise was about to take the phone from her when she said, 'Love you,' before ending the call.

Louise added Geoff's number to her phone as Farrell returned from upstairs. The DS was wide-eyed. 'What the fuck?' he mouthed, out of Mrs Simmons's eye line.

'Where do you think Geoff could be?' asked Louise.

'As I said, I have no idea. He goes driving in his van sometimes.'

'Does he have a partner, or some friends he likes to hang out with?'

'No, he's very solitary. He does like to go to church . . . it's very sad to say, but his only real friend was his dad.'

'His death must really have hit him hard.'

Tears welled up in the woman's eyes again. 'It did. I know he blames me for it, though he would never come out and say it.'

'Why would he blame you?'

'You know Trevor killed himself?'

Louise nodded.

'I don't know. Trevor changed after he found out about Richard . . . Father Lanegan. He was never the same again. He started drinking heavily, gave up church, went from one dead-end job to another. I tried to reconcile with him. I ended it with Richard immediately, even though I wanted to stay with him. He asked me to elope, but I couldn't take Geoff away from his father. So we went our separate ways. I tried to make it work with Trevor, but we only survived a few months. He was a very religious man, you see. Well, until what happened with Richard. Without his faith, he had nothing to hold on to. But I know Geoff blames me to this day for the way things turned out for Trevor. And I can't blame him.'

'That was a long time ago, Mrs Simmons.'

'Not for Geoff.'

'I know this must be painful, but can you tell me what happened with Trevor?'

'How he killed himself?'

Louise nodded.

'I guess he finally gave in.' Mrs Simmons began shaking her head. 'I didn't see him very often, but I know he'd been struggling particularly of late. He was holed up in one of those hostels. Geoff used to go and see him, and his mood always changed when he returned. He wouldn't speak about what happened, but it was my understanding that Trevor's drug habit was getting the better of him. Trevor used to captain the ferry that went from Weston to

Steep Holm. He took Geoff on some of the trips and it became a special place for them. So, naturally, that's where he went to kill himself. Jumped off one of the cliff faces. Bloody fool couldn't even do that properly. Managed to survive the initial fall and died three days later in hospital.'

'Did he speak to Geoff in that time?'

Mrs Simmons shook her head. 'No, he was in a coma.'

'This might be a stupid question, Mrs Simmons, but would Geoff have any means of getting over to Steep Holm himself?'

Mrs Simmons squinted her eyes as if playing out various scenarios in her imagination. 'With the money he got from the crosses, he bought himself a little speedboat.'

That was enough for Louise. She thanked Mrs Simmons and told her to inform them as soon as Geoff contacted her, though she didn't think that would happen.

'There is one more thing,' said Mrs Simmons, from the doorstep.

'What's that?' said Louise.

The woman looked at her watch. 'Tomorrow. It would have been Trevor's birthday.'

Chapter Forty-Five

The boat and the birthday was one coincidence too far for Louise. 'The five holy wounds,' she said to Farrell, once they were back in the car.

'Lanegan is number five?'

'We have motive now, and you saw his room.' Louise had never been prone to making absolute statements, but she struggled to see beyond Geoffrey Simmons.

'Now we just have to find him,' said Farrell.

Louise turned to him. 'After that conversation, where do you think he is?'

'Steep Holm?'

'It would make sense. A place of happiness from his childhood, but also the place where his dad killed himself. He has a boat. What a fitting place to end things. We need to get there.'

'Shall we call it in? If we get it to headquarters, we could arrange for a helicopter.'

Louise had thought of that and was worried it would take too long to get it all signed off. They would have to convince Robertson and Finch, most probably Assistant Chief Constable Morley as well. Even if she could convince them, it would be early morning before they got the go-ahead. It was 11.30 p.m. already.

'In thirty minutes it's his dad's birthday. He's going to kill Lanegan after that,' said Louise.

'I do agree with you, Guv, but how else are we going to get to Steep Holm now? It's at least six miles out to sea.'

'Know anyone who could lend us a boat right now?' asked Louise.

Farrell paused and surprised her by answering her rhetorical question. 'My uncle has a speedboat. Goes waterskiing sometimes over by Knightstone.'

'I was joking, but do you think he'd help us?'

'Start driving,' said Farrell. 'I'll call now. I hope he's still up.'

Louise listened to the negotiation as she drove, the sound of Farrell's uncle's objections tinny in the speaker of the mobile phone. Part of her wanted to call it in, but they could already be too late. In twenty-five minutes it would be Wednesday, and Trevor Simmons's birthday. If Geoff Simmons was planning to kill Richard Lanegan, then he was going to do it tomorrow, and she didn't have the time to convince Robertson, Finch and Morley that her prime suspect was currently holed up in some island off the coast of Weston. Thinking practically, and from their point of view, her theory was in part circumstantial and she wasn't convinced they would assign her the necessary resources. At best, they would wait until light, and she didn't want another death on her conscience.

'He's going to do it, but he's not pleased, especially in this weather. Says he wants promises he isn't going to be prosecuted for using the boat at night. He also said the tide at Steep Holm can be, in his words, a right bugger.'

'Whatever he wants. As long as he can get us there. Are you sure he'll be able to help us?'

'He likes to moan, but he's an ex-marine. He'll be fine.'

The roads were empty and they reached Knightstone Harbour in five minutes. There was a lull in the storm, an eerie silence to the seafront as they left their car, Louise stepping across the road to view Marine Lake Beach, a man-made lagoon on the seafront. She gazed out at the mound of shadow that was Steep Holm towards the horizon, and wondered what was playing out there at that very moment.

Farrell's uncle arrived fifteen minutes later in a large white SUV, the boat pulled behind on a trailer.

'Louise, this is Danny Barnett. Danny, my boss, DI Louise Blackwell.'

They shook hands. 'Thank you, Mr Barnett.'

'You can call me Danny.'

Louise saw a glimpse of Farrell's future in the man. He was about twenty years older, with the same build and upturned grin. The only real difference between the two was Danny's spreading bald patch, and the lines around his eyes and mouth.

'Follow me,' he said. 'Might be best if you switch off the lights.'

Danny reversed the SUV halfway down the slipway. A number of boats, mainly fishing vessels and small dinghies, bobbed on the sea. 'It's going to take me some time to get things ready. Get a life jacket on. It won't be the most pleasant of journeys when we get out into the channel.'

The speedboat was not the size Louise had anticipated. It was little bigger than a rubber dinghy and she was concerned it wouldn't be able to safely carry the three of them across the Bristol Channel, but she said nothing.

Steep Holm lay behind the tilt of the grand pier. Such was the dense cloud, it was close to being invisible from the vantage point of the harbour. Louise had never paid much attention to the island. As a child, her dad had explained the names of Steep Holm and Flat Holm as they'd walked along the beach one day. The differences between the two islands were obvious in their naming and shape. She'd seen them countless times since, but it had never occurred to her to visit either. They were a couple of large rocks in the sea, part of the landscape, but nothing she ever thought about.

Adrenalin rushed through Louise as she stumbled aboard the speedboat, Danny grabbing her arm as the boat swayed on the moving tide. She imagined Farrell would be thinking the same as her. Now they were here it all felt a little foolhardy, and as Danny jumped from the boat to untie the mooring rope, Louise began to regret her impulsiveness. It was strange how quickly her relationship with Farrell had changed in the last few hours, but that alone would not protect her if things went awry. If Simmons or Lanegan were not on the island then, at best, she would be ridiculed. With Morley on the warpath, and Finch out to ruin her career, it might lead to something much worse.

The wind picked up as they moved out of the marina on to the main stretch of the channel. The boat rocked as it bit through the bulging waves, the wind face on, making it uncomfortable to look up. Danny was bent over as he steered from the rear of the vessel. He shouted something, his words lost in the sound of the motor and the waves.

They were saturated by the time Steep Holm loomed in front of them, the shadow of the island appearing to emerge from the water. Louise had little idea what to expect as they got nearer, beyond a brief bit of research on her phone as she'd waited for Danny to arrive. Her presumption at this point was that the island was deserted, at least in the winter months. The island had a small visitor centre, and a passing tourist trade in the summer months, but the place was difficult to access and, from what she could decipher, there was very little in the way of available transport to and from the island.

It was incongruous to think of a deserted island so close to the mainland. She would probably die of boredom within a day or two if it was her home, but there was a certain romanticism to the idea of being totally alone, if only for a short time.

Danny guided the vessel around the first rock face as the clouds above burst open again. Sheets of rain fell on them in seconds, the coldness intensified by the swirling wind. Farrell was not enjoying the experience, leaning over the edge as if he was going to be sick, his hair matted to his scalp.

'Are you going to be able to moor the boat?' shouted Louise, her voice swallowed by the storm.

'There's a jetty on the north side of the island. Whether I can get her in is another matter,' screamed Barnett in return.

The sea raged beneath them as they reached the north face. Rain fell hard into the swelling waves like tiny bullets. *Luckily, it's only the Bristol Channel, not the North Sea*, she thought.

'There.' Danny pointed to a wooden jetty by a rocky shore under attack from the crashing waves.

'Can you get us over there safely?'

'It won't be an easy job in this weather and visibility, plus, there's a bastard of a tide to contend with.' Such was the force of the storm that Danny had to shout each word, wiping the oncoming rain from his face as he spoke.

'If you can just get me there, that would be enough,' Louise shouted back.

'We've come this far, I guess.' Danny revved the engine and swung the boat around so it faced the shoreline. 'And I have to admit, I'm enjoying myself. And Greg said police work was boring.'

Louise looked over to Farrell, who was standing unsteadily towards the rear of the boat. 'You okay?' she called.

'Finding my sea legs,' shouted Farrell.

Even in the darkness, she could see the lack of colour in his face. 'Why don't you wait on the boat?'

'You must be joking,' he shouted back, a gust of wind forcing him to stumble towards her.

'Okay, brace yourselves, we're going in,' announced Danny.

Seawater attacked from all sides as the boat crashed through the waves, the salt stinging Louise's eyes and searing her throat.

'Get that rope ready,' said Danny, turning to face them, the veins in his neck and forehead protruding as a sheet of water crashed over the boat. The engine sounded like it was groaning for its life as Danny turned the craft so that the right side was facing the jetty. 'I can hold her if you can jump over and snag the line on the mooring post,' he shouted, using his last ounce of strength to keep the boat in place.

'Let me,' said Farrell, reaching for the rope.

Louise glared at him, leaving him in no doubt as to what she thought about his gallantry. 'You're about to puke, Farrell. Wait here.'

The distance between the boat and jetty was only a matter of centimetres, but with the underlying movement from the sea, it may as well have been metres.

'Go,' shouted Danny.

Farrell hovered next to her as she placed her foot on the side of the boat. 'Be careful,' he said, redundantly.

Louise grabbed the rope and jumped, slipping on the jetty. A searing pain ran through her knee, and she closed her eyes, still holding firmly on to the rope, as she waited for it to subside. Between the sounds of the howling wind and the waves, she heard Farrell screaming for her.

'I'm fine,' she called, tying the rope to the post.

As Danny secured the boat, she walked inland to the small pebbled beach, almost tripping over another boat. She ran her torch over the vessel, and as the light reached the space beyond the boat she saw that she'd made the right decision in coming to the island.

'Stop,' she said to Farrell, who was running to catch her up.

'Jesus,' he said, staring at the remains of the corpse.

Chapter Forty-Six

Geoff watched with mounting joy as he finished explaining his plans to Lanegan. The man seemed captivated by the crucifix. It was his greatest creation. Years of honing his craft had come down to this, a working model ready for Lanegan to carry across the island.

'What's wrong with you?' said Lanegan, still staring at the object.

Geoff checked his watch. 'It's my dad's birthday today. At least it would have been, if he hadn't died three months ago.'

'I am sorry about your father, Geoffrey, but this is madness.'

'He died here, on this island he loved so much. He died because of you.'

'Because of me?' said Lanegan. 'I haven't seen your father in decades.'

'You killed him a long time ago. Now pick up your cross. You're going to carry it to the place where he died.'

The issue with the design had been making sure the cross was light enough to carry while being substantial enough to hold Lanegan. Fortunately, the disgraced priest now looked about as heavy as a bag of sticks, so the second part wouldn't be an issue. The difficulty would be in forcing him to carry the burden across the island with the storm picking up.

Lanegan bent to his haunches, his eyes pleading with Geoff as he hoisted the cross beam on to his shoulders. Geoff smiled, picturing the second Station of the Cross painting at St Bernadette's, where Jesus accepts his burden.

As if in response to his memory, he felt the deep sting in his hands where his flesh had caught fire. He'd never meant to hurt anyone then. It had been a last resort after everyone had ignored him. He'd snuck into the church late at night, using keys he'd stolen from Father Mulligan, and made sure no one was inside the building first. It was the only way he could get them to listen to him, and to a certain extent it had worked. In hospital, his mother had cried and promised herself to him and the family. She didn't mention Lanegan directly, but she told him all his worries were over and that they would be a happy family forever. She'd probably meant it at the time, but she couldn't have foreseen how his dad would react.

For a time, they were happy. Only later did Geoff come to realise that the fire couldn't cleanse everything. Although Lanegan stopped bothering his mother, eventually leaving the area completely, his father couldn't live with what had happened. He began drinking and lost his job. By the next year he was gone, living alone, sometimes homeless. Meanwhile, the ones who had betrayed him carried on as if nothing had happened. His teacher, his head teacher and his wife, the parish priest and Lanegan himself were all alive while his father was forever cursed. And when his father had finally given in and taken his life, Geoff knew there was only one way to save him.

Suicide was a mortal sin and, as such, Geoff's father faced an eternity without salvation, whatever Lanegan may have claimed about the growing leniency of the church. The only way to save him was to inflict the holy wounds on those persons who had betrayed him. Geoff knew he had it within his powers. He saved that intolerable brat, John Maynard, by smashing his front teeth, and for a time the marriage of his parents, by starting the fire. His dad had taken his life because of Lanegan and those who'd conspired against him. Now he was suffering the perpetuity of Purgatory because of what he'd done, but Geoff had it within him to atone for that sin. Lanegan was the final sacrifice. God would understand, He'd guided Geoff to this point. His son had endured those five holy wounds, and so would Geoff righteously inflict them to save his dad.

Lanegan stumbled for a few metres before collapsing on to the wet ground, the cross heavy on his shoulders.

Geoff pictured the Roman guards whipping Christ as he struggled with his burden. The old priest wouldn't endure such punishment, but one way or another, he would carry the cross to his resting place. 'Get up!' shouted Geoff, as the black sky opened and freezing rain fell on them.

Lanegan lost his footing again and Geoff helped him to his feet. 'Move,' he said, pointing to the darkness at the far end of the island.

The driving rain hampered their progress as the swirling wind billowed in from all directions. Lanegan kept losing his footing in the darkness and Geoff was forced to help him over some stubborn terrain, their way lit only by the dim light from Geoff's torch.

It felt as if their destination was forever out of reach, as if they were walking on a treadmill. For every ten metres or so Lanegan covered with the cross, the island's edge appeared to retreat an equal distance.

Geoff screamed at Lanegan, but his words were lost in the storm. In the end, he was forced to lift the back of the cross and, together, they stumbled their way to the end of the island.

'Lanegan or Simmons?' asked Farrell, bending over the body.

Although she didn't want to disturb the crime scene, Louise checked the deceased's pockets and found a wallet. 'Sydney Creswell,' she said, recovering the man's driving licence.

'Who the hell is Creswell?'

Louise shook her head. This wasn't like the other victims. She shone her torch on the corpse, revealing the gaping wound where the side of the man's head used to be. His clothing was intact and there didn't appear to be any wounds on the rest of his body.

'Could be a boating accident. Maybe he injured himself at sea and washed ashore here,' said Farrell.

The boat was similar to Danny's, the outboard motor resting on the thick pebbles of the beach. 'Looks recent to me,' said Louise. 'Why would he be out here at this time of night? Call it in. We need a helicopter over here and full backup.'

'Do we wait here?' asked Farrell, once he'd reported his position to the incredulous operator at HQ.

Louise glanced at the stone steps. The rain was relentless and her extremities felt numb. 'He must be here,' she said. 'Mr Barnett, are you happy coming with us? I don't want to leave anyone alone.'

'I'm sure I was safely in bed a couple of hours ago,' he said, shivering. 'Sure, whatever. It's not as if I can get any more wet. You guys armed?' he asked, retrieving a torch and a couple of flare guns from the boat.

'We've got batons and pepper spray,' said Farrell apologetically.

'Great, should be fine, then,' said Danny, as Louise and Farrell switched on their torches. With Louise in front, they made their way up the steps, the wind lashing at them from all sides. It was like moving against an unmovable force, as if the island were warning them to stay away.

'Where now?' said Farrell, staring into the empty darkness.

Louise shone her torch, the illumination stretching only metres in front of them. If anything, the rain was harder now. It cascaded down on them, bouncing off the frozen ground. She uploaded the map of the island on her phone. At best, it was a crude representation. If she was correct, there was a building somewhere off to their left. It would be as good a place as any to start.

'Maybe we should wait until the helicopter arrives? Get some light on to this godforsaken place,' said Farrell.

'I don't know about you, Farrell, but I'm freezing. The least we could do is move inland and find some shelter.'

Farrell's uncle was still shivering and Louise was worried she'd made a mistake taking him along. 'Come on, this way,' she said, her feet sliding as she moved forwards, directed by little more than instinct.

If they'd been a second sooner or later, or if they'd moved in a different direction, she would have missed it. It was a spark of light, a torch's ray piercing the darkness at the opposite end of the island. 'Did you see that?' she asked, already changing direction.

'What?' said Farrell.

'That light,' said Louise, just in time to see it for a second time. This time, the light was pointed in their direction, like a beacon, before instantly being extinguished.

Geoff couldn't believe he'd been so stupid. He'd seen their lights, and instead of switching off his torch he'd turned it towards them. Such was the darkness that the tiniest spark of light was enough to penetrate the gloom. He switched off his torch but felt sure the beam had been spotted.

He wanted to believe that it was the canoeists returning to the island to camp. If it was them, they would possibly be too indifferent or too wary to approach him, but he couldn't take any chances. Not now he was so close.

Lanegan was strapped to the cross. His body was so frail and brittle that Geoff feared he wouldn't last the insertion of the nails, which Geoff had retrieved from his other victims. Prone on his back, the old priest faced the heavens unmoving, the rain striking him so hard that Geoff feared he was already dead.

Despite his thick gloves, Geoff's hands were numb as he hoisted the cross into its resting position using the pulley system he'd designed. Thankful for Lanegan's lack of weight, he secured the crucifix in place, for the briefest of time admiring his own handiwork.

Although his eyes were closed, Lanegan now faced the sea. He was perched on the edge of the cliff where Geoff's father had taken his life. It was a fitting place for him to take his last breath. He imagined a Purgatory where Lanegan was stuck in perpetual agony on the cross, looking out at the area where he'd effectively killed Geoff's dad.

As Lanegan opened his eyes, the sky was illuminated by a fierce brightness, as if God himself were forcing Lanegan to consider what he'd done.

Only when Geoff reached for the spear did he realise the light was not God speaking to him but a flare gun fired into the air by the three people running towards him.

Using the flare gun was Farrell's idea, and before Louise had time to object, Danny had shot it into the air.

The flare illuminated the end of the island in a moment of singular clarity. Louise turned to Farrell for confirmation, struggling to accept what she was seeing. A full standing cross was pitched at the top of the cliff. She couldn't see if anyone was attached to it, but a figure brandishing a spear stood at the foot of the structure, staring back at them.

All three stopped in their tracks, gaping at the sight in disbelief. 'That must be Simmons,' said Louise as the flare faded in the night sky and darkness fell again.

The next thing she knew, she was running, baton in hand, her eyes playing tricks on her as the afterglow of the flare remained in her vision, careless of the potential dangers underfoot, only to stop as Farrell crashed into her, his shout muffled by the falling rain and the screeching gale.

She turned back. Farrell held his hand out and Louise grabbed it as his injured foot touched the ground. He couldn't even speak as she asked him if he was okay.

'What's happened?' asked Danny, walking over, his torch sensibly pointed towards the ground.

'My ankle is fucked,' said Farrell, finding his voice.

'You stay here,' said Louise.

'Wait for backup, Guv, you can't go in alone. He's a fucking madman.'

'You saw what he was carrying. He's going to stab whoever is on that cross.'

'What're you going to do? Batter him with that?' said Barnett, looking at the baton in Louise's hand.

Louise ignored him. 'Do you have any more flares left?'

'One,' said Danny.

'Give me two minutes then send it up,' said Louise, heading off before either man had time to object.

307

A superstitious man would have seen it as a sign. On the cross, Lanegan was fighting against his binds. He was shouting as Geoff raised the spear. 'This is for my dad!' screamed Geoff, not sure if the words had even left his mouth as he thrust the spear towards the side of Lanegan, only for a flare to illuminate the air once more and for a woman to appear from the shadows and strike him across the temple.

She continued moving across the island, her only guide the vague outline of the cross. Louise ignored the nagging remembrance of the Walton house, the sight of the unarmed man with his vacant eyes. This wasn't then. Simmons was a real threat and she would take him down whatever way she could, armed or not.

Two minutes after she'd set off, Danny launched another flare. It rocketed into the air like a firework, lighting the sky crimson red, just as she placed her hand on the cross. Baton in hand, she was ready.

She caught Simmons in a moment of confusion and hesitation and swung the baton across his temple, only for him to jab the spear towards her as he fell to the ground.

At first there was no pain, only a steady throb in her right forearm where the spear had penetrated her flesh. If there was any blood, it was washed away by the never-ending rain. Ignoring the wave of nausea flowing through her, Louise shone the torch towards the blurry image of Geoff Simmons, who was now crawling away towards the edge of the cliff.

Tentatively, she touched the area where the spear had struck her. It couldn't be that serious, or she would have collapsed. She hoped Danny was close behind her as she assessed the primitive-looking pulley next to the cross. With Simmons still in her sight, she shone the torch towards the crucified figure she presumed was Richard Lanegan, but couldn't determine if he was breathing or not. 'Try and get him down,' she called, as Farrell's uncle approached. One thing was for sure, she wasn't about to let Simmons take the easy route out.

Even in the rain and the dark, Geoff recognised the policewoman. He should have taken her out when he'd had the chance, and now it was too late. Why had he hesitated? Was it too late? Would his dad still be saved without Lanegan suffering the fifth holy wound? He glanced behind him as he kept going to the cliff edge, dismayed to see the policewoman's colleague working the pulley system. If he was lucky, Lanegan would already be dead, but it still pained him that he would never find out.

Three months ago, his father had fallen from this very spot, and now it was his turn. *We will be together again soon*, he thought as he stepped towards the edge, the policewoman calling out to him.

The wound had taken more out of her than Louise had first thought. She was dizzy, the pain intensifying as the storm began to ease. Simmons was nearly at the edge of the cliff, but she was moving more slowly. 'Stop!' she shouted as he reached it.

Simmons did stop, balancing precariously towards the drop below.

'I saw your mother tonight,' called Louise, now almost within touching distance of the man.

He was difficult to read, his long hair matted to his face like a distorted mask as he turned to face her.

'She wouldn't want this for you, Geoffrey. You are all she has. I know you've faced some hard times, but she loves you very much. She was so worried about you. Come back with me now and we can get you some help. Just don't do this to your mum.'

Simmons smiled at her and jumped.

Chapter Forty-Seven

Time didn't slip slowly by, there was no chance to view the pivotal incidents in his life as Geoff fell like a rock dropped into a river. The ground came up at such tremendous speed that the impact came as a surprise, his left side crashing into the rocky ledge with a sickening crunch that reverberated throughout his body in the split second before he slipped from consciousness.

He would never know if he drifted into unfathomable darkness before the light came. One moment he was out of existence, the next the glow was pushing at his eyelids, calling to him.

Geoff opened his eyes. The rain in front of him was illuminated, swirling in a pattern he'd never experienced, as a monstrous noise assaulted his ears. He tried to return to the impenetrable darkness, but the noise and pain wouldn't allow him to rest. Was this the Purgatory he'd wished upon Lanegan, or was he experiencing the worst nightmare of his life?

Louise had reached out for Simmons, but he was too quick. He'd hovered over the precipice as if defying gravity, before disappearing into the darkness. Seconds later the helicopter arrived, the wide beam of its lights illuminating the area like the flares preceding it, and then Louise saw that Simmons had failed to reach the bottom, his body catching on a small ridge less than twenty metres below. She couldn't be sure, but he appeared to be breathing.

She hoped he was in pain.

Danny had managed to get the cross down, and as Louise stumbled back to him she checked the faint pulse of Richard Lanegan, noting there were no puncture marks on his frail body – no nails hammered into his wrists or ankles, no fifth wound to his side – and wondered if somehow the elderly man would survive the ordeal. 'Try to keep him warm,' she said as she made her way to Farrell, who was lying in the muddy field.

'You get him?' asked Farrell, grimacing through the pain.

Louise checked the swelling on the man's ankle. It didn't look good. 'They're both alive, I think. Simmons tried to kill himself, but he may have failed.'

Farrell was in too much pain to answer immediately. 'Danny okay?' he asked, falling back on to the ground.

'I don't think he'll be lending you his boat any time soon. Aside from that, I think he'll be fine.'

Farrell forced himself up on his elbows so he was facing her. 'You're bleeding,' he said, managing to smile while his eyes were full of concern.

'I think I took the fifth holy wound. Barely scratched the surface.'

The police helicopter was soon joined by the air ambulance, both landing further down the island, on a flatter piece of land. Thankfully, neither helicopter contained Finch, Robertson or Morley, so for now Louise wouldn't have to begin explaining herself.

As the rescue team worked on retrieving Simmons, Louise presided over the paramedics working on Lanegan. 'You go back with your nephew,' she said to Danny, who was shivering beneath a foil blanket supplied by the aircrew. The man was in shock, still wide-eyed as he was led away by a paramedic to the waiting helicopter where, some minutes later, Lanegan too was placed on board.

It was another two hours before Simmons was hoisted to safety from the ledge. In that time, Louise contacted the station and updated Robertson and the rest of the team. She was surprised when Robertson didn't berate her for her actions, but presumed that would come.

An oxygen mask was strapped to Simmons's mouth as he emerged over the lip of the cliff edge. News had come in that Lanegan had survived the journey to the hospital, but Louise still wanted to rip the mask from Simmons's face and send him back towards the sea. At that moment, she couldn't care less about his difficult upbringing or his strained relationships with his parents. All she cared about was the lives that he'd taken and the injustice of him surviving when so many hadn't.

'He's lucky to be alive,' said one of the female paramedics. 'Multiple fractures, but I think he'll make it.'

'Wonderful,' said Louise as they carted Simmons away to the helicopter.

Chapter Forty-Eight

Eileen Boswell was used to sudden changes in her environment. Her little part of Cornwall could change from perfect calm to ensuing storm in a heartbeat, but in her blood she was convinced this wasn't going to be one of those days. Outside her house, the sun was high, the sky clear, and the trees were not stirring. It was the second day of the new year, a day she'd been looking forward to for some time. Her memory wasn't what it once was, but she'd marked the day on the calendar that lovely woman, Joslyn, had given her for Christmas and had been gazing at the mark on it ever since.

A hot cup of lemon tea in hand, Eileen was wrapped in the multiple layers the season dictated. She tried not to stare at her front door, but it was difficult. Joslyn's family had been so kind to her since that time she had visited Eileen with the other policewoman, but she was still sure it wouldn't last, even though Joslyn and her family had visited on numerous occasions since then. The children – Matilda and Zach – were a joy, and it was like having grandchildren. They'd even invited her for Christmas lunch, which she'd obviously refused. 'Christmas is for family,' she'd told them, only for them to turn up on Christmas Day and take her back to their house.

Such times, and here they were now, knocking on the door in the impatient incessant way that only children could. 'Nana

Boswell,' said the little girl, Matilda, wrapping her arms around her as Eileen opened the door.

Although she braced herself, the impact still winded Eileen slightly, but she didn't care. These little kids – Joslyn and her husband no longer had parents, so neither child had ever known a grandparent – gave her a reason to keep going. 'Let me get my coat,' she said, locking the door and following the girl to the waiting car.

She'd read about it in the papers, of course, but to Eileen it was like something she would read in one of the trashy novels she'd sometimes pick up at the charity shops. Supposedly, that madman had put Mr Lanegan on a cross after keeping him prisoner for days. Joslyn had told her that if it hadn't been for her they may never have found him, but Eileen didn't care about all that; she just wanted to see him again.

After the drive, Joslyn held her arm as she led her from the car to the nursing home. 'Remember, his health has suffered after the incident,' she warned.

'Just let me see him, please,' said Eileen.

He was sitting up in bed. He looked older, but there was still that glint to his eyes as he smiled on seeing her. 'Come to clean my room?' he said, his voice ragged and deep.

'I hear you've been getting yourself into all sorts of mischief?' said Eileen, sighing as she sat down on the firm seat next to his bed.

'We'll give you some time,' said Joslyn.

The next hour reminded Eileen of the first time she'd met the man. He'd had too much to drink then, but it was something else that made him open up this time. He told her about the whole ordeal as if they were in confession and she his priest. How his former lover's son had kidnapped him and taken him to the island and tried to kill him. But more than that, he told her about the woman he'd left behind. How, in his own words, he'd stolen her from another man. 'You see, Eileen, I should have died on that cross. I destroyed that family. First their marriage, then their lives. And because of me, all those other people died. I made the first kill.' Wet tears ran down his brittle skin and Eileen leaned over and wiped them away.

'Don't be foolish now. You made a mistake as a young man, like so many before you. You had no way of knowing things would turn out this way. That boy Simmons was out of his mind. He killed those poor, innocent folk. That's on him, not you,' she said, as if that were the last word on the subject.

Sometime later, Joslyn came back. 'I can bring you back tomorrow,' she said, kindly, as Eileen kissed the man on the cheek goodbye. It was the first time she'd ever kissed him.

That night, the old priest passed away in his sleep.

Chapter Forty-Nine

Emily's eyes were full of laughter as Louise bent down and kissed her goodbye. Louise winced as the girl grabbed her arm. The wound had healed in the weeks since Simmons's attack but was still tender to the touch.

Paul was standing in the doorway. He'd been sober for a month now, and although he still had a long way to go, it had been enough to convince her parents that Emily should return home.

'I love you, Aunt Louise,' said Emily.

'I love you, Emily.'

The melancholy that hit Louise as she reached the M5 was tempered by the memory of the last few days. She'd been at her parents' house since Christmas Day, enjoying the lack of responsibility for a few days. With Paul not drinking, the festive period had been one of the happiest in memory, and the thought helped lighten her mood as she drove over the Avonmouth Bridge.

The period up until Christmas had been challenging, with the fallout from the Simmons case. Geoffrey Simmons was currently under psychiatric evaluation, but the CPS were convinced he would eventually stand trial for the murders of Veronica Lloyd, Father Mulligan, Janet and Nathan Forester and Sydney Creswell.

Louise carried those names with her, as she knew she always would. Coming off the motorway at Worle, taking the bypass into the town centre, she played through the whole investigation again in her mind, as she had hundreds of times before, searching for an error, a missing link that would have stopped the subsequent murders after Veronica Lloyd's body was discovered. She'd uncovered the link with the fire, but had she been too tentative in her investigation? Maybe if she'd been more thorough they would have uncovered the link with Lanegan sooner. She'd raised such concerns with Robertson, but he'd dismissed them, in his gruff Glaswegian drawl. According to him, finding Lanegan in time, and keeping Simmons alive, was a result that she should be proud of. Louise wasn't convinced.

Out of habit, she took a lap of the seafront. The third of January, and the sun was high in the sky and the sea – for once at high tide – was still, glass-like in its serenity. On days like this, Louise could almost abide, if not love, the old seaside town.

She'd requested to meet some of the team at the Kalimera, and Thomas, Farrell and Tracey were waiting for her there.

'Hello, Inspector,' said the restaurant owner.

'Hello, Georgina.' Ever since the news of the arrest on Steep Holm had reached the newspapers, the proprietor of the restaurant had treated her with a new-found respect. Their conversations rarely went beyond pleasantries, but Louise no longer had to endure the cold glances from the woman first thing in the morning.

'For you,' said Louise, handing Tracey a bottle of champagne. Today was her friend's last day on secondment to Weston. From tomorrow, she would be back with Finch and the rest of the MIT.

'Oh, you shouldn't have,' said Tracey, smiling. 'Can we open it?'

'Not in here,' said Georgina, placing a cup of coffee in front of Louise.

'Thanks for coming. I just wanted to say a personal thank you to you all before we head over to the bar,' said Louise as she sipped her drink.

Thomas and Tracey exchanged looks, Farrell looking uncomfortable, and for a second Louise worried that the two had rekindled their affair.

'Some bad news, Guv,' said Farrell. 'News came in this morning that Richard Lanegan passed away in his sleep last night.'

'Natural causes,' said Tracey, as if needing to offer an explanation.

Louise ran her hand through her hair. The old priest had been in his early seventies, but she couldn't help but think that the days of imprisonment on the island had accelerated the natural causes.

'Come on, let's get to the bar and toast a drink to him,' said Tracey, taking Louise by the arm, the smell of sweet perfume drifting from her as she helped Louise to her feet.

It felt like the whole of the police station was waiting at the hotel bar. Robertson greeted them with a tray of single-malt whisky shots, Louise excusing herself to the toilet to escape having to drink one.

Finch had returned to HQ a couple of days after Simmons and Lanegan were flown from the island. He'd made a few overtures about Louise's recklessness during the case, but Robertson had all but laughed him out of the station. Louise's respect for her boss had reached a new high.

Anti-Corruption had been called in and were investigating the fire at St Bernadette's. The retired DS, Benjamin Farnham, was under investigation, as was Monsignor Ashley, who'd taken himself to a station in Bristol following Simmons's arrest.

'Here she is,' said Thomas, thrusting a champagne flute into her hand as Louise returned to the bar.

'To Tracey Pugh,' said Robertson, lifting his glass into the air. 'She will be missed, but not forgotten.'

'Tracey,' said Louise, grinning at the cherry-red cheeks of her friend.

Louise waited an hour before making her excuses. 'Thanks for everything,' she said to Tracey, who walked her to her car.

'Thank you. I've had a wonderful time. My God, you'd think we were saying goodbye. We live about twenty minutes apart.'

'I'm sad to see you go. You sure you're not going to hand in a transfer request?'

'You know what they say, it's a lovely place to visit, but to live . . .'

'Tell me about it,' said Louise.

She took the old toll road home via Kewstoke, the moon now full in the cloudless night sky. In the last two months, Weston had been recovering from the fallout of the murders. The killings had brought the town together. Although still reeling from the notion that something so tragic could happen to the quiet seaside town, its inhabitants were resilient, and already the place was showing signs of recovery. Tania Elliot had sold her story to one of the national broadsheets and, perversely, the town had enjoyed a sense of notoriety, leading to increased hotel bookings for the forthcoming summer season.

Shrugging off her sense of melancholy at being back in the bungalow, Louise switched on the gas fire and began dismantling the murder board. Placing the photos of the murder victims into a plastic folder, she thought how easy it was to forget. How the stories of these five people, six now, if you included Lanegan, would be forever intertwined.

She checked her phone – there had been no messages from Finch since he'd left Weston, but she waited for them to resume every evening – before pouring a single shot of vodka from the freezer.

Drink in hand, she gazed at the empty space where the murder board had been, deciding that the faded area needed some fresh paint, as did the rest of the place.

ACKNOWLEDGMENTS

Thanks to everyone who has helped me with this book: my agent, Joanna Swainson, for her support and advice; my editor, Jack Butler, for his excitement about this series; and Russel McLean, for his excellent insights.

Alison, Freya and Hamish, for visiting Weston again with me and for their enduring love and support.

And special thanks to all the wonderful people of Weston-super-Mare and, in particular, to my much-loved nan, Eileen Burnell, who built her life in Weston.

ABOUT THE AUTHOR

Photo © 2019 Lisa Visser

Following his law degree, where he developed an interest in criminal law, Matt Brolly completed his master's in creative writing at Glasgow University.

He is the bestselling author of the DCI Lambert crime novels *Dead Water*, *Dead Eyed*, *Dead Lucky*, *Dead Embers* and *Dead Time*; the acclaimed near-future crime novel *Zero*; and the US-based thriller *The Controller*.

Matt also writes children's books as M. J. Brolly. His first is *The Sleeping Bug*.

Matt lives in London with his wife and their two young children. You can find out more about Matt at www.mattbrolly.co.uk or by following him on Twitter: @MattBrollyUK.

Printed in Great Britain
by Amazon